COUNTDOWN

COUNT

DEBORAH WILES

DOWN

SCHOLASTIC INC.

No part of this publication may be reproduced, stored in a retrieval system, or transmitted in any form or by any means, electronic, mechanical, photocopying, recording, or otherwise, without written permission of the publisher. For information regarding permission, write to Scholastic Inc., Attention: Permissions Department, 557 Broadway, New York, NY 10012.

ISBN 978-0-545-10606-1

12 11 10 9 8 7 6 5   14 15 16 17 18/0

Printed in the U.S.A.   40
First paperback printing, January 2013

The text was set in Futura.
Book design by Phil Falco

for the peacemakers

YOU'LL NEVER WALK ALONE

"We and you
ought not pull
on the ends of
a rope in which
you have tied the
knots of war.

Because the more
the two of us pull,
the tighter the knot
will be tied."

Nikita Khrushchev, First Secretary of the Communist Party of the
Soviet Union, to U.S. President John Fitzgerald Kennedy, October 1962

JOHN F. KENNEDY

"We have enough missiles to blow you up thirty times over."

PRESIDENT OF THE UNITED STATES OF AMERICA

19

62

NIKITA KHRUSHCHEV

"We have enough to blow you up only once, but that will be enough for us."

FIRST SECRETARY OF THE COMMUNIST PARTY OF THE SOVIET UNION

FALLOUT SHE

The Camp Springs Crier January 5, 1962

Civil defense officials have decided to emphasize fall-out shelters over evacuation in all future civil defense planning against nuclear attack. Air raid sirens will be tested on the first Saturday of each month at noon. Local air raid shelters are easily recognized by locating the black and yellow civil defense bullseyes on public shelters. Camp Springs Elementary School has been designated a local fallout shelter.

In May 1961, President Kennedy sends 500 more American advisors to Vietnam, bringing American forces to 1,400 men.

In August 1962, he signs the Foreign Assistance Act, which provides "military assistance to countries which are on the rim of the Communist world and under direct attack."

There was a turtle by the name of Bert,
and Bert the Turtle was very alert.
When danger threatened him he
never got hurt,
he knew just what to do.
He'd duck and cover, duck and cover.
He did what we all must learn to do,
you and you and you and you:

Duck and cover!

The price of a gallon of gas rose to 31 cents today.

ANTI-CASTRO UNITS
LAND IN CUBA
REPORT FIGHTING AT BEACHHEAD
RUSK SAYS U.S. WON'T INTERVENE

New York Times, April 18, 1961

James Meredith became the first Negro to enroll at the University of Mississippi today. Federal marshals escorted Meredith onto the same campus where Governor Ross Barnett declared last week:

"No school in our state will be integrated while I am your governor."

DON'T BE AFRA

"WE CHOOSE TO
GO TO THE MOON."

John F. Kennedy, September 1962

ID OF THE DARK

"Beauty can't amuse you, but brainwork—reading, writing, thinking—can."

Helen Gurley Brown

"The truth is that women are . . . second class citizens."

New York Times Magazine, September 2, 1962

"Koufax set—and the pitch—*FAST BALL*—big bouncer down to Wills—he has it!

NO-HITTER!

Sandy Koufax pitches a no-hitter for the Dodgers!"

Vin Scully

"The threat of nuclear warfare is a threat to all of us. How can we live with this threat? Our best life insurance may be summed up in four words: Be Alert, Stay Alert. This will take some doing on your part. It will take ingenuity, it will take fervor, it will take the desire to survive. And it need not take a lot of money. All you'll need is shelter and common sense."

"What To Do In Case Of Nuclear Attack," by CONELRAD

YOU'LL NEVER

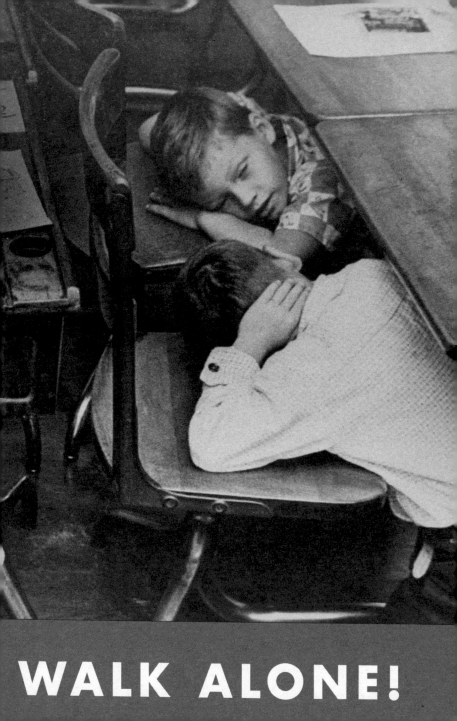

WALK ALONE!

1

I am eleven years old, and I am invisible.

I am sitting at my desk, in my classroom, on a perfect autumn afternoon — Friday, October 19, 1962. My desk is in the farthest row, next to the windows. I squint into the sunshine and watch a brilliant gold leaf fall from a spindly old tree by the sidewalk, and then I open *Makers of America* to page forty-seven because it's social studies time. I love social studies, love everything about it, and most of all I love to read aloud.

Mrs. Rodriguez, my teacher, has skipped me twice this week — twice! — when we read out loud during social studies, going down each row, desk after desk. I am determined not to let that happen again.

Mrs. Rodriguez wears square shoes with thick soles, and glasses on a beaded string around her neck. After conferences last week, I heard Mom describe her to Daddy as *thick-waisted.* Her fingers are the strong, blunt kind that put me in mind of my grandmother, Miss Mattie, who runs a store in Mississippi and is always hauling around boxes of boots or barrels of pickles. Miss Mattie's fingernails are cut straight across, but Mrs. Rodriguez has short, pointed nails that look like little triangles.

I thought she liked me. When we practiced duck-and-cover

under our desks the first week of school, my headband popped off my head and I didn't even try to retrieve it — I just kept my head down and let my hair fall all over my face. Mrs. Rodriguez complimented me right in front of everyone and told me I was a perfect turtle.

"Carol," she says now, "will you begin, please, at the top of page forty-seven?"

Carol's desk is in front of mine, on the front row. She begins reading:

> "Enemy Indians attacked the marching men as they made their way through the wilderness. Fever laid many of them low. But they were not men to turn back. Day after day they pressed on. At last, after three weeks, Balboa's Indian guide told him that, if he would climb to the top of the mountain just ahead, he could look over to that 'other sea.' Only a third of the Spaniards were strong enough to attempt the climb with their leader. But at the break of day, those men set out from the forests toward the bare mountaintop."

We're getting to the good part (I read ahead), and I am so determined not to be skipped again that I dangle myself over my desk as Carol reads, then I incline sideways like the Leaning Tower of Pisa, in an effort to make sure Mrs. Rodriguez sees me. I crook one foot around my chair leg, for ballast.

This is a slow and subtle maneuver (thank you, *Word Wealth Junior*); I don't want the other kids to notice me, while at the same time I imagine Mrs. Rodriguez spotting me and saying,

Heavens to Murgatroyd, Franny, you are the best read-alouder in the entire fifth grade, and somehow I missed calling on you all week! Go ahead, dear, read away. Read twice!

Instead, Mrs. Rodriguez says, "Thank you, Carol. Jimmy, pick it up, please."

I slump against the back of my chair like a lump of biscuit dough. I am thunderstruck. Sick to my stomach. This makes *three times* Mrs. Rodriguez has jumped right over me — she must be doing it on purpose, she must be. Here I am, all set to read the part where Balboa tops the mountain rise and discovers a mighty ocean on the other side, but Jimmy Epps gets to read the heroics! And he's a moron.

All right, he's not a moron. I don't know what he is. I barely know him. But he's not a good reader, I know that. I start to raise my hand, to protest, to stick up for myself, but I can't. Even after two whole years in this school, I still feel too shy to speak up. I just don't have it in me.

Jimmy — who picks his nose at recess — doesn't sound the tiniest bit heroic. He can't pronounce "Isthmus of Panama" — he stumbles all over the entire "Isthmus" and I get to read noth-ing — nothing! — in the entire social studies period. Again.

I stop paying attention. I pull a thread out of my sweater and start knotting it in a half hitch, the way Uncle Otts taught me. Kids drone on, one after another, in order, down the neat, straight rows, but I no longer hear them. Why does Mrs. Rodriguez hate me, why? It makes my heart hurt like it's a washrag and Mrs. Rodriguez has just wrung it out and slapped it against the side of the sink.

I can't stand to think about it anymore, so I focus on adjusting my headband — I'm wearing my best one today, the wide red one with little teeth on the bottom that comb my hair when I push it onto my head. Then I look out the window to find something else to think about.

The sun is blindingly beautiful this time of year. I cup my hands at my eyebrows to shield my eyes. There's my brother, Drew — Mr. Perfect — and all the other third graders lining up on the playground to come inside. He doesn't look the least bit like astronaut material. He's all angles and bones and too short. He looks like a little-bitty Uncle Otts. I'm going to tell him so on the way home from school.

The bell rings — we never had school bells in Hawaii — and Franny-hater Mrs. Rodriguez proclaims, "Time for second recess, class." The third grade marches in to school, the fifth grade marches out. We don't pass one another — we're on opposite sides of the school — so Mr. Perfect and I don't see each other. That's fine with me. It's hard to be in the presence of saintliness all the time.

I file past Mrs. Rodriguez, who is waiting to close the classroom door. She smiles at me as if nothing has happened, but I won't look at her — I look at the checkered floor and keep walking. *You have skipped me three times,* I telegraph her, as the pit of my stomach burps my lunch into my throat. *You probably don't even remember my name.*

The darkness of the hallway blinds me — I am still surprised by the hallways with no windows and the closed-in way people go to school in Maryland. At Pearl Harbor Elementary School, the hallways had no walls. The classrooms had windows on both sides. Sunshine drenched everything. Camp Springs Elementary School feels like a cave.

I trudge down the steps, past the new black and yellow signs that look like bumblebee bull's-eyes, and step into the sunlight and the noise of kids who have been set free-free-free! But I feel deflated, which is almost worse than invisible.

I've forgotten my book — *The Clue in the Diary*, my newest Nancy Drew — and without a book I don't want to be alone at recess — it looks bad and people think there's something wrong with you.

Already there's a kickball game going on. Do I want to play kickball? No. I'm a terrible kicker. Do I want to play jacks with Carol and Marcy? No. They don't like me all that much. Do I want to jump rope? I'm a great jump-roper, and there's my best friend, Margie, in the jump rope line, waiting her turn. She's deep in conversation with Gale Hoffman, a girl who lives in the neighborhood behind ours and whose mother lets her wear lipstick already and do whatever she wants.

When Gale went trick-or-treating last year, she knocked on our door at eight o'clock, when everybody else was already long home. I was upstairs trading candy with Drew, but I heard everything. Mom answered the door, gave Gale a Tootsie Roll, and told her to go home, it was too late to be out trick-or-treating. Even my toes were embarrassed. Gale's mother is divorced, and Mom doesn't want me associating with Gale, but Margie likes her, and Margie's mother doesn't seem to mind.

I hold my head high and make for the jump rope line. "Hey, Pixie!" I yell at Margie, waving. Eight girls look my way — I hate that — and Margie lifts a hand in return.

"Hey, Dixie," she says, but she doesn't sound as enthusiastic as I do. She brightens when she says, "Gale has the *best* idea for a Halloween costume!"

"Oh, yeah?" I risk a big smile for Gale and hope she'll smile back. "What is it?"

But before Gale can smile, before anyone can answer, the sky cracks wide open with an earsplitting, shrieking *wail*.

It's the air-raid siren, screaming its horrible scream in the play-ground, high over our heads on a thousand-foot telephone pole — and we are outside. *Outside.* No desk, no turtle, no cover.

We are all about to die.

We hope it never comes, but we must get ready.

It looks something like this:

There is a bright flash, brighter than the sun,

brighter than anything you've ever seen!

It could knock you down hard, or throw you

against a tree or a wall. It's such a big explosion, it can

smash in buildings and knock signboards over and

break windows all over town.

But if you duck and cover, like Bert,
you will be much safer.

2

PANIC!

There is no order, because there's no order at recess anyway, and all the fifth-grade classes are mixed up and all over the place, and I have no idea what to do, even though I was told what to do a million times, and I think we're supposed to go inside — they've changed the rules for being outside — but no one can remember and nobody cares about that anyway. We're all completely scared out of our minds — the siren has never gone off at school before. Suddenly I don't know where I am or what day it is or how I got here, and I don't know which way to go.

Kids are running into me, spinning me around like a top — *Where is Margie?* — so I run, too, and I trip over my own feet. As my right knee kisses the pavement, I stretch out my hands to break the fall and my palms scrape across the asphalt. My headband pops off my head.

Everyone is screaming.

"Over here!" shouts Mrs. Rodriguez. "My class! Over here, against the wall!"

"No! No! Inside!" shouts Mr. Adler. "We're a fallout shelter!" He points to the black and yellow signs.

I'm sitting on the pavement, just sitting there. My palms are scraped and red. My knee wants to bleed — I can see the blood coming to the surface, crowding into the white, scraped places. Someone trips over my headband and breaks it. I snatch up the pieces.

Mr. Adler is standing by the double doors, shouting and waving his arms. The kids in his class are lining up. Gale Hoffman is in that line.

Maybe this is the real thing, an actual atomic attack, and we're so disorganized we're all going to get creamed. Bert the Turtle would not give us good marks. Drew must be under his desk in his classroom, clutching that ratty book he takes everywhere, *Our Friend the Atom*.

I lurch to my feet and drop the pieces of my headband. Mrs. Rodriguez is running — running! — and gathering kids like she's herding sheep. She grabs me by the dress and shouts into my face, "Over there!"

She points to the brick school wall, where kids are crouching in that familiar pose, heads down, hands clasped together behind their necks, so they can save themselves from nuclear destruction. The siren keeps on *wailing* in that world-ending, earsplitting arc.

I do as I'm told. I run for the wall, squat, and scrape my knuckles on the brick as I bring my hands up to clasp them behind my neck. My body is having a hard day. The grass by the wall is tall, thick, and weedy. It stabs my legs and shoves up under my dress as I settle next to Denise Dubose and lower my head. I stare through my hair at the weedy space between my black Buster Brown shoes and realize it's crawling — leaping! — with tiny grasshoppers.

"Eeeeeee!" I scream, and as soon as I do, Denise sees what I see and she screams, too, and then ten girls are screaming and

leaping and Mrs. Rodriguez magically appears in front of us like General MacArthur in the Pacific and commands us to *"Squat down and be quiet!"* And you know what? We do.

The air-raid siren is still blasting — my ears are going to ring right off. I gather the bottom of my dress around me tightly and do a sit-squat on it, but I don't clasp my hands behind my neck again. I need to be on the defensive here. What's worse: nuclear annihilation or becoming an insect lunch? At this moment, I can't decide.

My heart, which has been pounding like a conga drum, is about to burst through my chest and run itself home. I telegraph it, *Be calm!*, but all it says back is *I want to go home! I want to go home! Home to Mom and Dad and mysterious Jo Ellen and Saint Drew and of course Jack and even crazy Uncle Otts. I-want-to-go-home.*

I don't live far away. I could get home in four minutes — I've timed it, running through the neighborhood.

In the event of an emergency, STAY IN SCHOOL. That's what our teachers tell us. That's what Uncle Otts's civil defense pamphlets say, too: *Your parents will come to your school and pick you up when it's safe to do so.*

I'm not buying that for a red-hot minute. What if it's *never* "safe to do so"?

I shove my hair out of my face, lick my lips, and search the horizon for . . . something. Russian airplanes dropping bombs? My dad is a pilot and he would never drop bombs on a school. I hope the Russian pilots are like Daddy.

I see Margie against the cafeteria wall with her teacher, Mrs. Scharr (The Nightmare), and Mr. Mitchell, the principal, who has appeared out of nowhere. There's a sidewalk outside the cafeteria, so Margie doesn't have to worry about grasshoppers or a garter snake slithering up her dress.

We're supposed to keep our heads down, but I can't breathe like that so I stare at the playground. A kickball has drifted into the backstop. Jump ropes lie abandoned on the pavement. The jungle gym is empty. And we are, every one of us, as still as stones.

After an eternity, the siren begins to wind down, and a frazzled Mrs. Rodriguez says, "Merciful heavens!"

"It's just a drill, everybody," says Mr. Mitchell, now that we can hear him. "Just a drill. You know that signal." He's standing with his big hands on his hips like he's John Wayne in a cowboy movie, saying, *Don't worry, ma'am, it's just a possum.*

I take a slow breath so my heart will calm itself. Denise Dubose starts to cry. I don't know whether to touch her or say something or just be quiet, so I close my eyes and pretend I don't hear her. The bell rings, signaling the end of recess. Really.

And then —

I hear snuffling and jingling, and I am being licked in the ear. Not by Denise, but by my dog, Jack, who has run all the way from home to school to find me. That's just the way he is, Jack. Every so often he sneaks away from home when Mom isn't looking and comes to school to find me and Drew. Of course, he never finds us, because we're inside and he's outside, and someone in the office always calls Mom to come get him, and she does. Then we hear all about it at dinner, how Mom drives to school in our station wagon, puts Jack in the car, sighs heavily, and drives home.

"The last thing we need right now is a dog." That's how Mom always ends the story. Then she lights a cigarette and blows smoke from her lips in a thin stream, like a long punctuation mark.

But I know better. Jack is the best part of the day, every day. I hug him hard now — he's just what I need. I bury my face in his brown, shaggy body. Then all the other kids are all over Jack — and he's all over them — as the all-clear signal sounds and kids come to life again. Even Denise is better. Some kids are laughing, and Jimmy Epps shoves Tom West and says, "You run like a gooney bird!" and Tom slugs Jimmy in the arm. "Weirdo!"

"All right, class, all right," says Mrs. Rodriguez. "Jimmy and Tom, gather the playground equipment. Everyone else, line up so we can go in. Your homework assignment is on the chalkboard."

And then . . . . Mrs. Rodriguez is standing next to me, patting Jack, who has brought her a softball. He tries to give it to her, his head bopping up and down, happy-happy-happy.

Mrs. Rodriguez actually laughs. I don't think I've ever heard her laugh. I take the slobbery ball from Jack and say, "He does that." Because he does.

Mrs. Rodriguez smiles at me, a Miss Mattie sort of smile. She's surely as old as Miss Mattie. This time I can't help it; I smile back. But my stomach gives a furious little flop and says, *I'm not going to forget you skipped me.*

"Why don't you bring your dog inside while you get your things, Franny?" she says, "I'll dismiss you early so you can walk him home and your mother doesn't have to come get him."

"Yes, ma'am!" She *does* remember my name.

Yellow school buses chug one by one into the front parking lot as kids and teachers and one fine dog make their way inside the fallout shelter that is also Camp Springs Elementary School. The school week is over, and all I can think is, *So is my whole life, if one day the sirens keep wailing and the Russians come with their bombs to get us.*

The Farmer from Independence

Harry S Truman was born in Lamar, Missouri, on May 8, 1884. He was a short boy with thick glasses, a little brother named Vivian, a little sister named Mary Jane, and parents who wanted him to grow up and take care of the family farm near Independence, Missouri.

"No roughhousing," his mother told him. "You'll break your glasses." So instead of roughhousing with the boys, Harry practiced his piano and read book after book and wished for friends.

He didn't want to be a farmer. He hated the smell and the feel of the farm, but Harry was a dutiful son and a hard worker, and after he graduated high school, he worked on the farm for ten years. Then his father died, and Harry tried new things. He tried being a timekeeper, a mail clerk, a banker, and a construction worker, but what he longed to be was a great soldier.

He had a chance, because, in 1917, America began fighting in a war in Europe,

World War I,
        The Great War,
                The War to End All Wars,

and Harry signed up. Now he would get to roughhouse. Now he would have friends. Now he would fight enemies.

Harry went to France as a captain in the field artillery, in a bloody, brutal war that was fought in trenches with mustard gas and bayonets and tanks and horses and machine guns.

He fought alongside the French in the bloodiest single battle in U.S. history. The Grand Offensive was a weeks-long engagement in the Argonne forest in France. It ended World War I and changed shy Harry forever. He wrote home to Bess, his only-ever girl:

The heroes are all in the infantry.

> *Don't worry about me because there is no German shell with my name on it.*

The outlook I have now is a rather dreary one. There are Frenchmen buried in my front yard and Huns in the backyard and both litter up the landscape as far as you can see. Every time a Boche shell hits in a field over west of here it digs up a piece of someone. It is well I'm not troubled by spooks.

It is a great thing to swell your chest out and fight for a principle but it gets almighty tiresome sometimes. . . .

If ever I get home from this war whole (I shall), I am going to be perfectly happy to follow a mule down a corn row the balance of my days — that is, always providing such an arrangement is also a pleasure to you.

And that might have been the end of that, except that

Harry didn't really want to be a farmer. So he married Bess and he ran for local judge, and he ran for the U.S. Senate, and he worked hard, a dutiful servant of the people.

America sank into the Great Depression and then rose into a second world war. Harry did such a good job as a senator that President Franklin Delano Roosevelt, who had New-Dealed the country out of the Great Depression and counseled it throughout World War II, tapped Harry on the shoulder in 1944 and asked him to be the vice president of the United States.

So that's what Harry did.

For eighty-two days.

Then FDR died suddenly, and Harry became the thirty-third president of the United States. (**Surprise!**) The farmer, the soldier, became president. And then the real roughhousing began.

As senator, Harry had looked at Germany and Japan and said,

We are facing a bunch of thugs,
and the only theory a thug understands
is a gun and a bayonet.

GIVE 'EM HELL, HARRY!

And that's just what Harry did.

If you can't stand the heat,
get out of the kitchen.

Here's what came next:

Harry directed the United States to drop two atomic bombs on Japan — one on Hiroshima, one on Nagasaki. Japan formally surrendered, and World War II was at an end.

But our ally Russia, which had become a Communist country after World War I, was not cooperative. We had to divide Germany, and half of it became part of the growing Communist bloc.

(what's a communist?)

Harry pushed through the formation of the United Nations — we'd protect the world.

Harry signed the papers that gave us the U.S. Air Force — we'd fight the Communists, who wanted to take over the world.

(why did they want to do that?)

Harry started the Central Intelligence Agency — we'd catch those Communists.

(because . . .)

The Berlin Airlift was Harry's idea. For a year we worked with our allies to parachute food to the West Germans and stymie those Russian Communists. We were heroes!

But then:

Those Russian Communists exploded their first nuclear bomb, and Americans got scared.

The Chinese became Communists, and Americans got scared.

North Korea — backed by the Chinese — invaded South Korea, and Americans got scared. Harry sent Americans to war again, into the bloody Korean Conflict.

Then U.S. Senator Joe McCarthy began pointing fingers at American citizens and calling them Soviet spies.

(Harry hated Joe.)

Americans were a scared bunch. They became so nervous about the spread of Communism, they began ducking and covering everywhere, anywhere, practicing to save themselves just in case the Russians decided to bomb the United States with their brand-new nuclear bombs and take over their country, too.

(such roughhousing)

And that's just for starters, during Harry's six years as president. It's enough to make a farm boy and his mule stumble.

But not Harry.

THE BUCK STOPS HERE.

That's what Harry Truman, that dutiful son and hard worker, said.

Some loved him for all he did. Some didn't.

Harry and Bess returned to Missouri in 1952. Harry never farmed again. He and Bess traveled. They became sensations in Europe, not far from the very fields that Harry had fought on in 1918.

Then, on December 26, 1972, when he was eighty-eight years old, farmer, soldier, president, hard worker, dutiful son, Harry S Truman died. He was buried at home in Missouri.

Long after he died, Americans learned that on the same day in 1945 that the Japanese surrendered in World War II, a man named Ho Chi Minh, in a little, faraway country called Vietnam, proclaimed Vietnam's independence from the French. He wrote —

We hold the truth that all men are
created equal, that they are endowed
by their Creator with certain unalienable
rights, among them Life, Liberty and the pursuit
of Happiness. This immortal statement
is extracted from the Declaration of
Independence of the United States of America
in 1776. These are undeniable truths.

Ho borrowed words from Thomas Jefferson in his letter. He declared himself president of the Democratic Republic of Vietnam and wrote to President Truman to ask for help for his fledging country. His letters were never answered.

The same year that Harry died, America was almost

finished burying the 58,209 soldiers who lost their lives in the Vietnam War.

Over four million Vietnamese, Cambodians, and Laotians perished.

The middle initial S in Harry S Truman's name stood for nothing.

3

I am dismissed ten minutes early, but I spend that time with some other kids and Jack in the nurse's office. The school nurse, Miss Gresham, dabs Mercurochrome on my knee and opens a Band-Aid with trembling fingers. Her voice shakes. "When you get home, have your mother take a look," she says, licking her lips, "and put a thin coat of Vaseline on the heels of those hands — it will soothe them." She straightens up, done with me, smooths her skirt, and moves on to the next kid.

"Yes, ma'am," I whisper to no one, even though I know Mom will put rubbing alcohol on all my scrapes. Mom loves rubbing alcohol as much as she hates germs. She puts it on everything.

The final bell rings and walkers are dismissed first. I feel like a privileged person — a *pudacrat*, to use Mom's word — with Jack in school, but nobody seems to mind today, not even the teachers, not even Mr. Mitchell, who also gives Jack a pat.

I put on my jacket, even though I don't need it this afternoon, slip my satchel strap over my head and onto my right shoulder, shove my hair out of my face — I feel undressed without my headband — and walk, in my dutiful way, on the right side of the hallway to the cafeteria. Jack's toenails click brightly across the tiles until we stop at the cafeteria doors, where we wait for Margie and Drew.

"Got your books?" I ask Drew as he quicksteps across the gleaming cafeteria floor toward me. His satchel is laden with the same science books he checks out of the school library each week. He's leaning to the left to keep his balance.

"Uh-huh." He looks determined and grim, but when he sees Jack, he lights up.

"Were you scared?" I ask him as he tousles Jack's fur and Jack circles around him, slobbering all over the place.

"Uh-huh."

Man of many words, Drew.

"Are you going to read all those books again?"

"Yep," he says. "In the tree house." The tree house is the first thing Daddy built for us when we moved here from Hawaii. We made umpteen trips to Pyles Lumber Company and hammered in nails wherever Daddy said to hammer them. There's even a rope ladder that drops through a hole in the floor. Drew and I tied all the knots in it with Uncle Otts's help.

"Hey, Pixie!" I shout as Margie comes through the cafeteria doors with a stream of other kids.

"Can you believe it?" she says, disgust shooting through her voice. "The siren! Right in school!"

"Weren't you scared?" I ask.

"It was the test signal, Franny!"

Who had the presence of mind to figure out it was the test signal? I didn't. But I don't say that.

"Did you see Mr. Adler try to save everybody?" I say instead. "He was like Moses trying to part the Red Sea!"

This makes Margie laugh, and suddenly she and I are yakking

ourselves silly about the air-raid drill as we walk through the playground and to the far reaches of the school yard, toward home. It makes us feel safer to poke fun at Mrs. Rodriguez running in those square shoes and Mr. Mitchell acting like John Wayne.

"They got it all mixed up," I say.

"Mr. Mitchell told Mrs. Scharr not to worry about it, that we'd start practicing what to do if we were caught outside when the siren went off."

Drew, huffing under the weight of his egghead books, joins in. "I helped Johnny Carmichael."

"You're a hero, Drew," says Margie, in her driest voice.

"I know!"

"Don't encourage him," I say, pushing the hair out of my face once again.

"You should stop trying to grow out your bangs," Margie says.

"I don't like bangs anymore."

"Then try using bobby pins," says Margie, "instead of a clunky plastic headband."

I don't answer Margie. I try to decide if she has hurt my feelings.

The walk from school to home starts in the playground behind school, wanders through a small stand of oak trees, then into the back of our neighborhood, where the clutch of us who live on Coolridge and Napoli Drives — two long, dead-end streets that cross like a capital T — can be seen every weekday straggling like sheep, down the road in twos and threes, walking home.

"Gale's going to be Marilyn Monroe for Halloween," says Margie, answering my ages-ago question as we step through the trees and make the right turn onto sleepy Napoli Drive.

"That's creepy," I say, "since Marilyn Monroe just died."

"It's Halloween," says Margie. "It's supposed to be creepy!"

"She doesn't look the least bit like Marilyn. She's got all that thick black hair."

"Gale's mother has a blond wig and says Gale can wear it."

"Really!" I am impressed. I've never met Gale's mother, but I heard Mom tell Daddy that she *dates.* "Does she have an evening gown and long white gloves, too?"

"Gale says her mother has a closet full of fancy clothes," Margie says with a sniff. "She even has a mink stole! I've seen it!"

I feel vaguely betrayed. What should it matter that Margie has been to Gale's? But it does.

"Well, I know something she can't give Gale," I say. I make a motion with my hands, wave them at my flat chest. Gale's chest is just as flat as mine.

Margie — whose chest is *not* completely flat — hoots. "I'll bet she's got socks!"

That makes us both laugh, and that feels good.

"What are you going to be for Halloween?" Margie asks me.

"I don't know yet — it's way too early to decide. What are *you* going to be?"

"Well, Gale says I should —"

Drew butts in. "I'm going to be an astronaut!"

"What else is new?" I say. "Don't interrupt, Drew."

"I'm gonna ask Dad to drive me around the neighborhood in a convertible, like John Glenn in that parade we went to, and I'll wear a space suit!"

"Good luck with that," says Margie. "How're you gonna get any candy?"

"I'm gonna parachute out of the car at every house!"

"That's stupid, Drew," I say. "You can't parachute out of a car — read your science books. Besides, Daddy'll probably be on a trip. He missed last Halloween, remember?"

"Yeah," says Drew. "I know." I have flattened him. He stares at the ground in silence.

"Here," I say. "Let me help you with your satchel."

Drew won't let me touch it. Instead he kicks a rock down the road ahead of me, zigzagging like a burdened loon to keep up with it. Jack tags along after him.

"He's home tonight!" I call in a helpful voice.

Drew turns around and brightens. "Hey — I gotta get home! Eddie's coming over! We're going to the gravel pit! Are you gonna come, Franny?"

I can't answer. I look past Drew and suck in my breath. *Look* what's coming our way: Uncle Otts.

Heavens to Murgatroyd, Uncle Otts.

It *can* happen Here

Where have all the flowers gone?
Long time passing.

Where have all the young men gone?
Gone for soldiers, every one.

Where have all the graveyards gone?
Gone to flowers, every one....

When will they ever learn?
When will they ever learn?

JOIN

Pete Seeger and Joe Hickerson 1961,
adapted from a Ukrainian folk tune

CIVIL DEFENSE

4

Uncle Otts weaves across the Moores' yard, where he has, no doubt, just accosted them with the latest civil defense literature, telling them how to keep our country safe and how to keep themselves alive if our country is attacked.

"Fall in line, troops!" he barks. He stuffs his pamphlets into his satchel and points at us like his arm is a bayonet. He's wearing his World War II civil defense helmet on his head and his World War I medals on his chest. "Fall in line!"

Twelve kids, previously scattered all across Napoli Drive and meandering home on a Friday afternoon, don't know what to do.

My face is scarlet with embarrassment.

"What's he doing?" whispers Margie, as Uncle Otts steps into the street and strides toward us.

"I don't know," I hiss. I am glued to my spot on the road. Even Jack sits.

"Come to order!" yells Uncle Otts.

Tom West makes a run for it. "Deserter!" Uncle Otts screams. "Yellow-bellied coward!" While his attention is diverted, I grab Margie and pull her behind the enormous honeysuckle bush beside the Ramseys' mailbox. We peek through the honeysuckle branches, and I telegraph Uncle Otts: *Go home! Go home!* But Uncle Otts stands in the middle of Napoli Drive with his hands on his hips and his feet apart, like General Patton in front of Third Army, daring anyone to move.

Kids are frozen in place. I can picture the dinners in their houses tonight, the talk around the table, all about the Chapmans, who moved in on the corner of Allentown and Coolridge two years ago, and their uncle, who has gone crazy. *Don't go to their house anymore, he might be dangerous —*

"What have we got here?" barks Uncle Otts. "A bunch of soldiers or a bunch of spies?"

Please stop! I telegraph Uncle Otts.

"Who's behind that bush!" He screams this, and the veins in his wobbly neck stand out like some grotesque comic book monster. My legs turn to jelly.

"Show yourselves! Spies!"

A crow calls from the yellow-leaved trees, and another answers it. A fat cloud covers the sun. I can hear Margie's breathing, hard and scared, next to me. I don't know what to do.

Drew does. He walks up to Uncle Otts, who towers over him. He leans far to the left with the weight of his satchel, but he still manages to calmly salute Uncle Otts and say, "At ease, Sergeant."

It's a line I've heard Daddy use a hundred times. And it works.

Uncle Otts peers down at Drew and blinks. The sun peeks out from behind the cloud as he slowly, painfully, recognizes Drew and salutes him back. "At ease, Private," he says softly. His shoulders slump and tears crowd his eyes.

Kids come alive again, start snickering, even laughing at the old man standing in the middle of the road wearing a battered old helmet and spouting like a madman. I telegraph them to *stop it! Leave him alone!* as they walk around him in a wide circle, as if he has leprosy.

Uncle Otts hugs Drew like he hasn't seen him for years, and Drew lets himself be hugged. He and Uncle Otts walk up Napoli, turn right at the corner onto Coolridge, and lumber toward home. Jack brings Drew a pinecone, Drew tosses it, and Jack scampers after it, happy.

I shove my hair out of my face and sigh.

"Whoa," says Margie.

I can't answer. I can hardly breathe. Then Margie says, "He's really gone psycho, Franny."

"Thanks."

"Sorry, Franny, but he's *really* weird now. He's scary-weird."

"I know, I know."

"What's wrong with him?"

Nothing's wrong with him! I want to scream, but that's not true.

"I don't know."

A fat blue jay lands on the top branch of the honeysuckle bush and eyeballs us.

"C'mon, let's go," says Margie.

I shake my head. "Not yet."

"Why not?"

"I just can't. I don't want them to make fun of me. I'm going to be the laughingstock of the neighborhood, if not the whole school, on Monday."

"Well . . . he's a nut, Franny. . . ."

"He's *not* a nut!" I swallow hard to keep the tears away. "And if you were really my friend, you'd understand that! And you'd understand why I'm embarrassed to death right now!"

Margie considers this. The October air is thick between us.

"I've got to get home," she says. "My mom's taking me and the twins shoe shopping — I'm getting my first pair of penny loafers!"

Penny loafers. I stare at my brand-new black Buster Browns with the velvet sides and the long, skinny laces. Mom says they are sensible school shoes.

"Good for you," I tell Margie, but I don't mean it. "See ya, Pixie."

"Bye."

I have a little sinking spell, right there behind the Ramseys' honeysuckle bush. What's worse: your best friend doesn't feel like your best friend anymore, or the whole neighborhood thinks your family is an embarrassment?

Or maybe it's worse that you wouldn't acknowledge your uncle, Franny.

Maybe I'll just stay here, hidden behind this bush, forever.

In Flanders fields the poppies blow
Between the crosses, row on row,
That mark our place; and in the sky
The larks, still bravely singing, fly
Scarce heard amid the guns below.

We are the Dead. Short days ago
We lived, felt dawn, saw sunset glow,
Loved, and were loved, and now we lie
In Flanders fields.

Take up our quarrel with the foe:
To you from failing hands we throw
The torch; be yours to hold it high.
If ye break faith with us who die
We shall not sleep, though poppies grow
In Flanders fields.

Lieutenant-Colonel John McCrae
World War I veteran, May 3, 1915

5

I count to one hundred and come out of hiding. I walk to the corner of Napoli and Coolridge and look left toward Judy James's house, Tom West's house, and the big woods at the dead end — the woods that hide the gravel pit. There are no kids in sight. Then I look right. No kids. I turn right and walk up the long stretch of Coolridge Drive by myself, hoping that kids aren't peeking out from behind their front curtains, drinking a chocolate milk after school, pointing me out to their parents, and saying, *See? There she is, Franny Chapman. She ran and hid from her crazy uncle. He's a nut.*

I pass the Moores', where I practiced Christmas carols with all the neighborhood kids last December before I went caroling with them around the neighborhood — that was so much fun. Nobody even mentioned Uncle Otts, and we sang at my house, too — sang my favorite Christmas carol, "O Come All Ye Faithful," and then "We Wish You a Merry Christmas." Uncle Otts came to the door and listened with tears in his eyes. He was so proud of me. He was better then.

I walk past the Thornbergs' house — they are the oldest people on earth and never come outside if they can help it. I scoot past Lynn Treakle's house so she won't see me — we used to play canasta together when I first moved in, but Lynn is older than I am, and now that she's in junior high, she doesn't have time for me. Then I pass the house next to Lynn's that's been empty ever since Chris Cavas moved out a year ago. There's a moving van in the driveway, and two colored men are carrying an orange couch through the front door.

New neighbors! I wonder if they have kids.

Margie, who lives next door to me and across from the new neighbors, doesn't wave at me from her mother's car as they pull out of their driveway, so I don't wave at her, either. It's so warm, all her car windows are down. The twins are jumping in the backseat and throwing things at each other.

As soon as I open my front door, I hear the running of water, the clacking of dishes, and the sound of the vacuum cleaner. When you come through our front door, you're on a landing, and you have two choices: a set of stairs going up to the kitchen, living room, dining room, my bedroom, Jo Ellen's, and Mom and Dad's, or a set of stairs going down to the family room, laundry room, Drew's bedroom, and Uncle Otts's room. I take the stairs up.

Jo Ellen turns off the Hoover when she sees me. She's wearing one of Mom's aprons, and her hair is wound in pin curls that peek out from underneath a wispy green scarf.

"Red alert," she says. Her voice is low and her eyes are puffy. "Everybody left like they'd been struck by lightning as soon as Uncle Otts banged through the door, blathering about spies in the bushes and blueprints in the mailbox." Jo Ellen wipes her nose with her apron and pushes the vacuum cleaner toward the hallway closet. "Drew took him downstairs."

"Where's Jack?"

"He's downstairs, too."

"Have you been crying?" I ask.

"Of course not," Jo Ellen says.

Dishes crash against one another in the kitchen. The roar from the faucet is so loud it sounds like Mom is washing dishes in a typhoon.

"Was it bad?" she asks me, nodding toward the street.

"Terrible. He held everyone hostage. I'm embarrassed for life."

"I'm sorry, Squirt." Jo Ellen winds the vacuum cleaner cord around its knobs and sniffs. "Take heart. You weren't standing next to Mom when Mrs. Ross flew out of here like she was on fire. She almost ran over Mrs. Hornbuckle."

"Was it bad?"

"Mom had a stroke," Jo Ellen says, her delivery picking up speed as she winds the cord faster. "We heard the air-raid siren from school — it was clear it was a drill and not an attack, but that was bad enough — they've never used that siren during the week, and then when Uncle Otts came running in . . ."

Now Jo Ellen is putting away the folding chairs, and I help her — she sounds *compelled* to tell me this.

"You look like you've been crying," I say. "Is something wrong?"

"Everything's fine," she says. "Drew never should have checked the mail — it was the package for Uncle Otts that really set him off. 'My plans!' he kept yelling. 'I've got the blueprints!'" Jo Ellen takes a breath. "I told Mom it's just three tables of bridge, eleven silly wives, it's not important what they think, but she says Daddy's up for promotion, and this will reflect badly on him when it gets back to all those colonels at the air base."

"Really? How?" I have visions of Mrs. Hornbuckle telling Captain Hornbuckle all about it at dinner.

"I don't know, Franny. Everybody knows everybody's business in the air force. Thank goodness we don't live on base." Jo Ellen takes her apron off and drapes it over the banister. "I've got to get out of these clothes. I'm going to a meeting on campus tonight with Lannie, and I'm going to forget all this. Go put your stuff away and let Mom know you're home — she's been looking for you."

And then, like she does it every day of the week, Jo Ellen opens the cigarette holder on the coffee table, picks up the lighter, and . . . *lights a cigarette*!

"You're *smoking*?"

Jo Ellen shrugs and exhales. "Hurry up," she says, to the sound of dishes clattering onto the drainboard.

Jo Ellen is the smartest person in our family. She looks like that gorgeous Mary Ann Mobley, the Miss America from Brandon, Mississippi, the town where Aunt Beth and Uncle Jim live. All the boys in high school were in love with Jo Ellen, but she's taking her time finding a beau. Mom always tells me Jo Ellen is *level-headed*, in a voice that implies I'm not.

Jo Ellen spent all last summer in Mississippi — we came home and left her there. I don't know what she did, because there is nothing to do in that tiny town where Miss Mattie lives, nothing. I missed her like crazy, and I think Mom did, too.

Ever since she went off to college, there's been something strange about Jo Ellen. I can't say what it is, but I can feel it. Something different.

American U-2 spy-plane pilot Francis Gary Powers, who was shot down by a Russian surface-to-air missile and captured by the Soviets in 1960, was released from prison today in a spy exchange between the Soviets and the U.S.

Captain Powers walked into West Berlin across a bridge separating the city's east and western sectors. At the same time, Russian spy Colonel Rudolph Abel crossed in the opposite direction.

from *BBC Reports*, February 1962

QUE SERÁ SERÁ

Mary Ann Mobley
is crowned
Miss America

Students for a Democratic Society, or SDS, held its first convention in June 1962 and adopted a manifesto called The Port Huron Statement:

We are people of this generation, bred in at least modest comfort, housed now in universities, looking uncomfortably to the world we inherit....

COME LET US

NEW WORLD

BUILD A
TOGETHER.

Student Nonviolent Coordinating Committee

Over 11,300 U.S. advisors and troops are now in Vietnam.

The students have decided that we can't let violence overcome. We are coming into Birmingham to continue the Freedom Ride.

Diane Nash to Fred Shuttlesworth, May 1961

**THE FUTURE'S NOT OURS TO SEE
WHAT WILL BE WILL BE.**

AIRFORCE

Exit, Stage Left! **Snagglepuss**

6

Our kitchen is pink. Pink refrigerator, pink stove, pink walls, pink sink. The room looks like it's been hosed down with Pepto-Bismol.

Mom is wearing her party apron at the sink. "Where have you been?" she asks in her Spanish Inquisition voice. Mom used to sing when she washed dishes. Not anymore.

"Drew ran ahead," I say, careful not to mention Uncle Otts. I telegraph myself, *You ran away from your uncle and your brother.* But what I say is, "I . . . stopped at Margie's for . . . I left my Nancy Drew over there yesterday."

"I see," says Mom, totally unconvinced. "Haven't you been told to come straight home after school?"

"Yes, ma'am. I'm sorry. I won't do it again."

I admit it, I lie. I lie, smooth as butter, but only in times of crisis, and only because it is *expedient* (thank you, *Word Wealth Junior*). I mean, what else am I going to say to a dish-crashing, fire-fuming mother? Am I going to tell her I hid out in the neighborhood until the coast was clear because I was embarrassed to death by Uncle Otts? She won't care — she was embarrassed to death and back again.

Mom clacks a fancy coffee cup into the dish drainer and breaks it. "Dang!" she says, only it's not *dang*, it's *you-know-what,* and that's it, I don't need anything else to tell me that Mom's at the end of her rope.

"Go help your sister," she snaps. "And get a headband for that hair."

I'm a yo-yo.

Jo Ellen is collapsing the last card table in the living room. "Franny," she says, "put the cards away." An unopened letter falls out of her dress pocket, and I pick it up.

"Who's Ebenezer?" I say, staring at the flowing script of the return address.

She snatches the letter from me. The paper it's written on is so stiff and fine, it crinkles.

"None of your business," she says. Her eyes fill with tears.

"What is it?" I ask. "What's happening?" Jo Ellen cried when she took me to the movies to see *West Side Story*, but she's not a crier by nature.

Jo Ellen straightens her shoulders and sucks in a deep breath. "You know what, Franny? Sometimes you ask too many questions. Put the cards away."

It's amazing how you can feel sorry for someone one moment and contempt for them the next.

"Stop acting like Mom," I spit.

"Grow up," Jo Ellen snaps.

"I'm not a baby!" I snap back.

She's not going to tell me what's going on. And I realize I'm smack in the middle of my own Nancy Drew mystery. *The Clue in the Crinkly Envelope*. It may take me some time, but I will solve it. The key is to act cool and uninterested.

"You're not the boss of me," I huff. I take two chocolate-covered raisins from the dish of leftover bridge treats, pop them in my mouth, and then nonchalantly run my fingers over the gold-gilded edges of the cards. Jo Ellen shakes her head and walks out of the room.

I put the cards away in the dining room hutch. No one is allowed to play with these cards but Mom and Dad and their card-playing guests. I have a deck of my own for gin rummy and crazy eights, but those cards aren't fancy like these are.

I can't count how many times I have lain awake at night on a weekend and have heard Mom bring out the Sara Lee banana cream pie and coffee for dessert, and then I've listened, late into the night, while the Ramseys play bridge here with Mom and Dad, bidding and playing their hands, laughing about friends and talking so low I can't always hear what they're saying. But I get the gist.

> *"There's a sign there now, 'You are leaving the American sector.' I saw it last time I flew into Berlin. It's right at the Wall."*

Supposedly I'm sleeping, of course, but I have never been able to fall asleep easily, even after my prayers, even when I was little. Nowadays I lie there, looking up at my pink canopy, and I think about the end of the world and how we're all going to die soon, and I compose a letter to Chairman Khrushchev in my head, and I know I'll write it tomorrow and I never do, but I compose it anyway.

Dear Chairman Khrushchev,

> *If you would just listen to me —*
> *I could explain —*
> *I don't know why you can't understand*

I compose my letter while I lie there, listening to the grown-ups talk about things I can't understand. I fall asleep to the sounds of my parents shutting up the house and listening to *The Tonight Show* on their black-and-white television in their bedroom, which is next to my bedroom.

"Heeeeeeere's Johnny!"

But before sleep comes, I need to go to the bathroom, so I get up and tiptoe down the hallway, knowing that owl-ears Mom will hear me and come to the dark hallway and say something about how I should be sleeping already and why am I not, which she always does, and then I feel guilty and pad back to my bedroom, having hardly peed at all because I feel guilty before I even get out of bed, and it's no use, I'm a goner, a kid who stays up half the night trying to figure out the horror of the world and trying to survive it.

How Can I Keep from Singing?

Peter Seeger was born May 3, 1919, in New York City just after the end of World War I and just before the glory days of Babe Ruth and Charles Lindbergh. His ancestors came to America on the *Mayflower*, and his grandparents had Money. They wanted the best boarding schools and the best friends for Pete and his two older brothers.

Pete wanted to be an Indian.

He read all the outdoor books of Ernest Thompson Seton (who was the first Chief Scout of the Boy Scouts), and he spent hours in the woods creeping through bushes in a loincloth, making his own tepee, and sharpening sticks as arrows for stalking rabbits.

This was Living!

"Don't forget where you come from, Peter!" admonished his mother. She wanted her boys to have grace and class and style. The older boys took music and voice lessons. But Pete couldn't be bothered.

> *"Whistles, anything that made music I banged on. I didn't want to study, I was just having fun."*

A shy and self-reliant boy, Pete was so protected from the world that he didn't really know people.

Worse, he didn't know himself.

"I knew all about plants and could identify birds and snakes, but I didn't know about anti-Semitism or what a Jew was until I was fourteen years old.

> *"My contact with black people was literally nil. If someone asked me what I was going to be when I grew up, I'd say an Indian or farmer or forest ranger. Maybe an artist. I'd always loved to draw."*

Pete's father, Charles, was a pacifist — someone opposed to wars, who tries to find peaceful, nonviolent means to solve conflicts. He also had a deep sense of justice — he wanted the world to be a fair place. Charles sensed that his son Peter was a kindred spirit, so he began to educate him to the world as he saw it.

During the Great Depression, Charles took Pete to the Lower East Side in New York City, where they walked for hours along the streets next to buildings with their shutters hanging off, windows broken. They watched dirty children with no shoes play in the streets, with trash stuffed into alleyways.

"The streets aren't so well lit as where we live," said his father. Pete knew just what his father was trying to say and he wondered about the people who lived there. This was the beginning of his awakening.

When Pete was a teenager, his father took him to meetings of a club he belonged to in New York City called The Composers' Collective. The members of The Composers' Collective wrote songs that were meant to be sung on picket and unemployment lines. Some of the members called themselves . . .

COMMUNISTS.

"It was quite different from the cartoons
of a person with a beard and a bomb.
I found these were very organized,
very intelligent,
very argumentative people."

These were the great, heady days of working people — many of whom lived on the Lower East Side — organizing together into one big union, in order to ensure fair treatment from their bosses. They were factory workers and dockworkers and steelworkers and immigrants, men and women. They called themselves the IWW or Industrial Workers of the World. Their nickname was the Wobblies.

Pete loved their songs — **"Solidarity Forever!"** — and he liked their ideas. He signed on to do whatever he could to help the workers of the world. He wasn't a worker yet, so he couldn't be a Wobbly; he became a member of the Communist Party.

When Pete's father took him to the North Carolina mountains to meet some banjo pickers he knew, Pete heard the five-string banjo for the first time and fell in love. He practiced banjo so much it drove his family crazy! They would make him stop. Then he would go outside and practice some more. He practiced until his fingers were ready to fall off, but it was too hard for him until he found an instrument maker to whack off the end of the banjo neck and add three more frets to it. THEN he was able to play it like nobody's business!

So that's what he did.

He invented the long-neck banjo.
And boy, did he wail.

He also started singing and making records with some friends. First the Almanac Singers and then the Weavers.

Together they sang songs in concerts and on the radio, including "Goodnight, Irene," which was written by Pete's friend Leadbelly. They sang the songs of the working people, the songs of the folk — folk songs — and they were wildly popular.

Pete didn't care about being popular. He cared about the people, and he cared about the songs. He let his membership in the Communist Party lapse — he moved on. He had found his calling. With his banjo and his new friend, Woody Guthrie, Pete set off on a trip across America to collect the songs of the people. To sing with the people.

He and Woody sang for their suppers and slept under the stars and rode in boxcars from time to time, like hoboes. And all the while, Pete scratched down the songs he heard, collecting them. Singing them. Recording them. Sharing them. Bringing people together in song.

He found old, forgotten songs and brought them to the people:

> Michael, row the boat ashore, Hallelujah!

He reworked snippets of old poetry, turning them into songs: *Where have all the flowers gone? Long time passing . . .*

He wrote new songs for the people to sing:
> *If I had a hammer, I'd hammer in the morning,*
> *I'd hammer in the evening, all over this land!*

He had become, like his father, a pacifist, a lover of peace.

Then he heard from the U.S. government:

Are you now or have you ever been a
member of the Communist Party?

America had been through another war, World War II. Pete had served in it. He had married his wife, Toshi, a Japanese American, during the war. He had written to her while he was in the Pacific:

*After the war, I want to organize
a very large chorus of untrained voices.*

And that is what he did.

But during the war, spies had been caught — German spies and American spies. Russian spies, too. Communists. Were there Communist spies here in the United States? Might they be planning to take over our country? How might we find them?

It was a scary time. **Anybody could be a spy!** said the American government, so it began to look into people's pasts, to see what it could see.

Everyone was suspect. Everyone was afraid.

Pete was afraid, too. It was not against the law to be a member or a former member of the Communist Party. It was only against the law to betray your country. That was treason.

Pete had spent his life bringing the people of his

country together with songs. But fear does strange things to people.

When the government started asking questions of Pete, people stopped inviting him to play for them. They canceled his work. He couldn't work anywhere for many years in the 1950s while the government made up its mind about Pete and thousands of other good Americans they were suspicious of.

Pete went to Congress to talk to the House Un-American Activities Committee, which was doing this questioning. He said:

"I love my country very dearly,
and I greatly resent this implication
that some of the places that I have sung
and some of the people that I have known,
and some of my opinions, whether they are
religious or philosophical,
or [that] I might be vegetarian,
make me any less of an American."

At first the court found Pete guilty and sentenced him to ten years in prison. Pete appealed, and in the end, the courts acquitted Pete — he was not guilty. He took his banjo and emblazoned these words on it in a circle around the head:

THIS MACHINE SURROUNDS HATE AND FORCES IT TO SURRENDER

Then Pete got busy. It was the 1960s. Pete and Toshi went to Georgia and Alabama and Mississippi. Pete and his friends Guy and Frank wrote new verses for and sang "We Shall Overcome" with Dr. King, with Fannie Lou Hamer, and the other civil rights workers.

We'll walk hand in hand . . .
We won't be afraid . . .

People packed auditoriums and festivals to hear him sing "John Henry" or "Abiyoyo" or "Guantanamera." He made them sing, too.

"It's not what I sing, but what YOU sing!" he said.
and
"A good song reminds us what we're fighting for!"

SING OUT!

He sang out against the war in Vietnam. He sang for little children, he sang for old people. He inspired a generation of folksingers and songwriters.

He had the best education, just as his grandparents had hoped he would have, and he had found the best and most important friends: the everyday working people of this great nation.

7

Of course Drew steals the show at dinner with his rendition of the air-raid drill and how everybody in the third grade ducked under their desks and how Johnny Carmichael, who sits next to Drew in class, peed his pants under his desk, and how Drew helped him to the bathroom and even got him his extra pair of snow-day pants out of the cloakroom before anybody knew Johnny had peed his pants, not even Johnny's teacher, Miss Bourdon. I have to admit, even I am impressed.

"You're a hero!" says Mom, echoing Margie but with feeling. She sits back in her chair and lights a cigarette. Drew beams and takes another bite of his hamburger, and Jo Ellen smiles at him like *she* is his mother, too, instead of an eighteen-year-old sister. I sit up a little straighter and say, "I was *outside* when the siren went off!" but at the same time I say this, the phone rings and Daddy claps Drew on the shoulder as he jumps up to answer it.

"I'm on call," he says, as he snaps the receiver to his ear and says, in a completely different voice, "Major Chapman." But it isn't the air force, it's Eddie Owens, wanting to know if Drew can play ball after dinner in the back lot, and Daddy, back to his at-home voice, not only says Drew can play, but he'll come himself to pitch.

Drew drains his milk like he's thirsting to death, and with a rushed "May I be excused?" he bolts from the table. "Just let me get my glove!" he shouts as he thunders down the hallway. "C'mon, Jack!" Jack comes bounding upstairs, from his banishment during dinner, wagging his tail, happy-happy-happy to be going outside with the boys. He ignores me completely.

"I'm right behind you, son," says Daddy.

What is it about being a *son* that makes parents go gaga over your existence? No one was going to like my story as much because I didn't save anybody's dignity, and I'm not a saint. Big deal. Who wants to be a saint anyway? No respectable kid I know. My faraway friend, Mary Flood, is a Catholic — she told me all about the saints — they have the most miserable lives imaginable.

It's a good thing Uncle Otts didn't come to dinner. He would have pinned one of his medals on Saint Drew's scrawny chest and inflated his ego even more. Then he would have jumped around the table, waving magazines and pamphlets, preaching about impending nuclear doom, which is why Mom banished him from the table weeks ago unless he could talk about something — anything — else. Still, I would rather hear about my impending doom than hear one more heroic word about Mr. Perfect.

I heard Mom and Dad talking in terse parent Morse code about Uncle Otts when Daddy got home from work. I was hanging up my school dress, changing into my play clothes, and I wanted to press my ear to their closed bedroom door, but I knew that all I had to do was stand outside their bedroom and Mom would hear me breathing in the hallway, so I just lay on my bed and strained my ears. I thought about getting a glass from the kitchen and putting it against the wall, but Mom would have heard that, too.

And lucky thing I didn't try it, because as soon as I was lying there, telegraphing the words to make sense to my ears, Mom burst out of her bedroom door and circled to my room. "Frances, go help your sister put dinner on the table!"

I sat up so fast, I'd like to enter my time into the Olympics. I put my most innocent look on my face. "Should I set a place for Uncle Otts?"

"No." No explanation. "I'll take him a plate."

Drew's holler comes right through the kitchen windows as he runs across the backyard screaming for Eddie with Jack at his heels. Jo Ellen and Mom begin clearing the table, running the soapy water, clinking dishes into the sink. I slump like a forgotten waif in my chair, hoping someone will take pity on me and sit down and say, "Tell me about *your* day, Franny, about *your* life, about *your* feelings," but that prospect doesn't look likely, so I think about what might cheer me up.

"Can I listen to your records, Jo Ellen?" I ask.

"Nope," Jo Ellen says.

"Franny, put the condiments away," says Mom.

I am only good for chores in this household. I pick up the relish, the ketchup, the mustard.

"Please, Jo Ellen?" I beg.

"Nope. Busy."

Jo Ellen has the world's best 45-rpm record collection. Since I can remember, I've sprawled across her big bed when she's in her room doing homework or talking on the phone to her girlfriends, and Jo Ellen has let me play her records, as long as I don't get fingerprints on them or let the needle scratch them. I'm not allowed to touch her albums, but the 45s she lets me rifle through to my heart's content.

I've memorized the geography of every one of those records. "Johnny Angel" has a yellow label, "Twistin' the Night Away" has a tiny scratch at the beginning edge, and "Runaway," which is my current favorite, by my favorite singer, Del Shannon, has a heart drawn on the label — by me. Jo Ellen doesn't know this yet.

Nowadays, Jo Ellen *shuts her bedroom door* when she's home. Mom would never allow me to do this. — I tried and she said, "What are you *doing* in there?" as if I might be plotting the overthrow of the United States Government, but she hasn't said a thing to Jo Ellen about it.

It hurts my feelings.

Mom hands me a sponge. "Wipe off the table, Franny."

Be a slave, Franny.

"Why not, Jo Ellen?" I ask my sister.

"Buy your own records, Franny," she replies.

"I don't have any money!"

Mom hands me a dry cloth and I take over drying the dishes from Jo Ellen, while she takes over washing the dishes from Mom. All three of us look out the big kitchen window where we can see the back lot and a bunch of boys who are gathering in the slanted light of early evening, ready to play ball. Eddie's father is there, too, talking with Daddy about something. They look serious, with their arms crossed at their chests.

You are leaving the American sector.

"You get an allowance," says Mom. She opens the refrigerator and finds a place for the leftover green beans.

"I save it to buy the next Nancy Drew!" I spurt. Nobody knows how hard I have to work to stretch my measly allowance. Margie gets twice what I get for an allowance, and she doesn't have half the chores.

"We all have to make choices," says Jo Ellen, letting the water out of the sink and wringing out the dishrag, which puts me in mind of Mrs. Rodriguez and my poor heart — only it's ten times worse at home. Jo Ellen dries her hands on my dish towel and tousles my hair with such friendliness you'd think she hadn't just turned down my simple request.

I stiffen, shake my head free, and telegraph my sister, *Just because you're all puffy-eyed from crying doesn't mean you can yell at me and pretend you're Mom.* I take my headband off and fix my hair. Jo Ellen sashays out of the kitchen in her old checkered dress, plucks her letter out of its pocket, swishes down the hallway with a walk that looks just like Mom's, and *shuts her bedroom door.*

What does she *do* in there? I clack the last dried plate onto the pile in the cupboard and sigh.

"Your sister's growing up," says Mom in a flat, authoritative voice that sounds like Walter Cronkite delivering the television news. "She's going to do what she's going to do." Not one thought for my feelings, of course. "Don't forget to sweep the floor."

Call me Cinderella.

Mom picks up the tray of food she has prepared while putting away the leftovers. "I'm going in," she says. She gives one nod to the stairs, toward Uncle Otts's downstairs bedroom. "Come get me if I'm not out in five minutes."

"Yes, ma'am." And that . . . is that.

The *craaack!* of a baseball bat smacking a ball pops the air, followed by the whooping of the neighborhood boys. Saint Drew is rounding the bases, and my father is leaping into the air with glee. Larry Stoffle races into the outfield to get the ball. Jack gets to it first. There is cheering, laughter, fun.

And here I stand in the kitchen, with a broom in my hand. And no friendly mice to help me.

Then I have a thought, a great idea.

I have five minutes. The floor can wait. I have something more important to do. I can take matters into my own hands, like Nancy Drew.

I can spy on my sister.

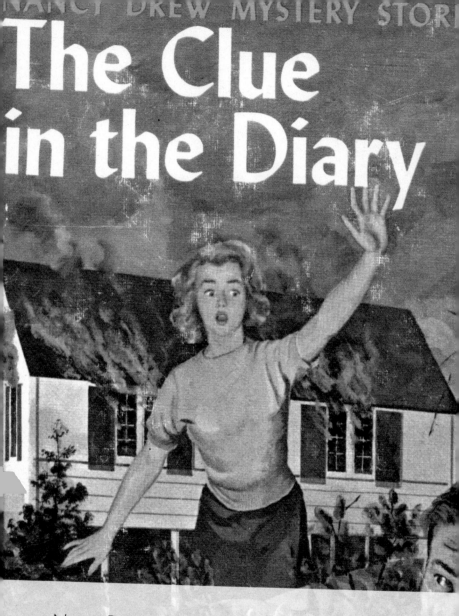

The Clue in the Diary

Nancy Drew, an attractive girl of eighteen, was driving home along a country road in her new, dark-blue convertible.

8

Jo Ellen has ESP.

"Sweep the kitchen floor, Franny!" she calls before I'm three steps down the hallway. So I walk right into her room, I don't even knock, because she knows I'm there anyway.

"How do you do that?" I ask.

"Knock!" she says. "Do what?"

"How do you know I'm there?"

Jo Ellen shrugs. She's wearing her bathrobe and is covering the telephone receiver with her hand. "I used to be eleven. You'd better go sweep." Into the telephone she says, "I'll see you in an hour," and she hangs up.

I snatch the mirror off Jo Ellen's dresser and flop on my back across her big bed. I'm trying to decide whether or not to forgive her for being such a rat fink of a big sister. But when I peer into the mirror, I forget all that; instead I gaze upon my plain, freckled face and blurt, "I can't stand it."

"What?" Jo Ellen has the ironing board in her room and begins ironing a black, short-sleeved blouse. The steam from the iron hisses and sizzles as she works, and the whole room smells like spray starch. The overhead light blinds me, so I roll over onto my stomach and grab one of Jo Ellen's pillows.

"Being homely."

Homely. That was a *Word Wealth Junior* word last week. When we had to write the definitions for homework, I almost wrote my name beside that one.

Homely: Not attractive or good-looking. Lacking elegance or refinement.

"For heaven's sake, Franny," says Jo Ellen. "You have a *winsome* face — go look it up. And you're about to have a red bottom if you don't go out there and sweep the kitchen floor — you know Mom can tell if you don't do it."

"Look here," I say, pointing to my chin. "I've got pimples starting here!"

"Wait until you're fourteen," Jo Ellen says.

"I'll be one big pockmark by then!"

Jo Ellen turns off the iron and slips her bathrobe over the bedpost. She's wearing pedal pushers and a black bra. It makes me blush.

Jo Ellen sticks her arms through the sleeves of the blouse she just ironed and turns her back to me. "Help me with this, will you?"

"Where are you going?" I fumble with the buttons in the back.

Jo Ellen pulls the pin curls out of her hair and begins to brush it. "I told you, to a meeting on campus with Lannie. And some friends."

"Lannie, the girl from Boston?"

"How many other Lannies do you know?"

"Just checking," I say. "You've got a lot of new friends."

"College is like that," Jo Ellen says. She sprays her hair to death with Aqua Net. It mists onto my skin. The sharp smell makes my nose water.

"How can you stand that stuff?" Jo Ellen doesn't answer. "What are your new friends like?"

"Hmmm . . ." says Jo Ellen. She picks up a silver comb and begins teasing her hair. "They're thinkers," she finally says.

"Everybody thinks."

"Not like they do," says Jo Ellen. She eyeballs me, as if she's deciding whether or not to tell me, then goes back to her teasing. "These friends are going to change the world," she says. "And I'm going to change it right along with them."

"How?"

But that's as much as I'll get. "It's complicated, Squirt," Jo Ellen says.

It sounds dangerous to me. "Who are these people?"

"Just people." By now, Jo Ellen's hair billows out from her head like an enormous bird's nest. She studies it for a moment in the mirror and says, "You know . . . I don't know why I bother."

"Then don't go!" I say, suddenly anxious for her. "You could stay home with me and Drew and watch TV. Drew wants to watch *The Flintstones* and I want to watch *Sing Along with Mitch*. You could break the tie so Daddy doesn't have to."

"I meant my hair. I don't know why I bother with this hair." She combs it into place, then drops her comb into her purse. "Anyway, I'd watch *Route 66*. You should let Uncle Otts decide about television tonight — he's had a hard day."

I lick my lips and feel a tingle of shame.

"Is he all right?" I ask.

"He's all right."

"Gale Hoffman told Margie that her great-grandfather got put into an old-age home."

"Uncle Otts isn't going to any home. He helped raise Daddy, and Daddy's going to keep him forever, so you'd better get used to him." She smiles a genuine, loving, big-sister smile. I forgive her for all her Mom-like trespasses, and suddenly I want to share a secret with her, a secret I haven't told anyone.

"I'm going to change the world, too," I say.

"What's your plan?"

"I'm writing a letter to Chairman Khrushchev."

"You are?"

"I am. I'm composing it at night, in bed."

"What does it say?"

"It says I want to meet him. If I could just talk with him, I know I could convince him to stop scaring the pants off everybody."

I can't help it—I cringe, waiting for Jo Ellen to laugh at me. Instead she says, "That's a good idea. How would you convince him of that?"

I will never be angry with Jo Ellen again. I sit up straight to make my point.

"I would tell him we're all just people, here in America, and we don't want to hurt anybody. We just want to live and be happy."

"My thoughts exactly," says Jo Ellen. "But don't you think he knows that, Franny?"

"Well, evidently not! If he knew it, he wouldn't behave like this."

"He knows it, Franny. It's complicated. I don't think anyone wants to bomb anyone else."

"How can you be so sure?"

Jo Ellen drops her compact into her purse, looks at me, and says, "There is more going on in the world than the Russians and the Americans screaming at each other about atomic bombs, Franny. Things that are just as scary, actually."

She sits next to me on the bed, takes my hand in hers, and says, "There are always scary things happening in the world. There are always wonderful things happening. And it's up to you to decide how you're going to approach the world . . . how you're going to live in it, and what you're going to do."

I don't know what the heck she's talking about.

"Are we going to get bombed by the Russians, Jo Ellen?"

"No."

"I'm not so sure. I'm still writing my letter."

"Good. That's one way to change the world."

I slide off the chenille bedspread. "Can I try your lipstick?"

"Sure. Not that one, though. It's new."

We stand in front of her dresser mirror together. She is gorgeous. I am not. I look like Popeye's Olive Oyl. Jo Ellen looks like the Breck Girl.

"Mom's had a hard day, too," Jo Ellen says. "I try to remember that when she's so . . . impossible." She sighs a long sigh.

"Nobody asks about my hard day," I say. I apply Jo Ellen's red lipstick thickly to my thin lips. "Nobody even cares that I was stuck outside during the air-raid drill and everybody panicked and cried and bled to death. But no . . . that's not important in this family, because I'm not important. Daddy hardly said two words to me today, but he plays a whole ball game with Drew."

I look in the mirror at my deep-red lips. I press them together and rub them back and forth. Jo Ellen hands me a Kleenex. I put it inside my lips and purse them. "Voilà," I say, holding up the Kleenex. Two perfect lips are on the tissue.

Jo Ellen rummages in her purse. I strain to the left, to see if there are cigarettes in there.

"Nobody's the favorite, Franny," she says. "Of course you're important. Just because they don't broadcast it —"

"You're not around enough to notice," I interrupt, standing up straight. "You're all grown up, you're in college — you have loads of friends — you even have new friends! You can do whatever you want."

"That's certainly not true," says Jo Ellen.

I sigh. "I just want to skip all these years in between and go off to college like you, only I want to live in the dorms like Lannie does."

"This, too, shall pass. You don't know how lucky you are, Franny. You go to a good school, your dad's an officer in the military, you eat, shop, play wherever you choose, you can go to any college you want when you grow up. You've got it made. You're privileged."

I toss the tissue in the trash. "I'm invisible around here. I could disappear for days and nobody would miss me."

Now it's Jo Ellen's turn to sigh. "Franny, you're eleven. That's the problem in a nutshell." She pulls an envelope out of her purse. "Everybody feels persecuted when they're eleven. It will pass."

It has passed already. My eyes are glued to the envelope Jo Ellen has in her hands. It's the exact one — or exactly like the one — that dropped out of her pocket earlier. A white envelope made of paper so crisp and fine it crinkles when you bend it.

The kitchen door opens, shuts — Daddy and Drew and Jack are home. I hear Jack slurping water from his bowl. His dog tags clink against the dish.

"I've got to go," Jo Ellen says.

I point at the envelope. "What's that?"

She smiles at me but doesn't answer. She takes a key from a chain around her neck and unlocks her hope chest. She slides the envelope into a drawer inside the chest. There are plenty of fat envelopes just like it in the drawer — lots of letters from someone named Ebenezer. Jo Ellen locks the chest and returns the key to her necklace.

Outside in the almost-dark, Lannie's car horn honks. Lannie drives a bright blue Volkswagen Beetle — it's brand-new. "There she is," says Jo Ellen. She snaps off the overhead light, and we are left in the soft glow from her bedside lamp.

"Can I sleep in your bed tonight?" I ask.

"Sure," Jo Ellen says. "Don't wait up, I'll be late. I like that color on your lips. And go sweep the floor!"

I go for broke. "Can I play your records?"

"Franny!"

"Okay, okay."

She tousles the top of my head, and this time I don't mind. Then she pats Jack, who has come to see us with a dog toy in his mouth, and she's gone.

"You just played a whole game of baseball!" I say to my dog. Jack drops his toy and flops himself onto the floor. I stare at my face in the mirror again. Even in the shadow-light, nothing has changed. I am plain, and soon I will be pimply, and there is nothing I can do about it.

Gale Hoffman attended the Melody Morris Charm School this past summer. She told Margie that it's inner beauty that counts, so I look deep into my eyes and concentrate on my inner beauty.

I can't see a thing. I'll never have a boyfriend. I'm going to be an old maid.

I run my fingers across the top of Jo Ellen's hope chest. I know about the salt and pepper shakers, the blue teapot, the handkerchiefs and doilies and treasures, all bits and pieces for Jo Ellen's future life after some boy sweeps her off her feet. But what I want to know now is, what's in those long white crinkly envelopes? Why is Jo Ellen being so secretive? What does she have to hide?

Early the next morning — a glorious, sunny, Saturday morning — Uncle Otts stands over my bed with a shovel in his hands. He's grinning at me like I'm the canary and he's the cat. "I heard you was grounded — again." *Agin* — that's what it sounds like.

I am not grounded. I forgot to sweep the kitchen floor, and Mom had a few choice words to say when she came downstairs to find me following the bouncing ball with Daddy and Mitch Miller, singing "Side by Side."

I had to go upstairs right that minute and sweep the dang floor. And then, as if that weren't punishment enough, I had to sleep in my own bed.

Now I pull the covers over my head. "Hi, Uncle Otts."

"It's reveille, Private," he says. "Come on." *Own* is the way he pronounces it. *Come own.* "We'll get 'er started today, Francine."

"I'm Franny," I say from under the covers. I have no idea what he's talking about and I don't want to know.

"A'course you are," he says. "Here's your shovel, Francine. Meet me at ground zero at oh-nine-hundred hours. That's an order." The shovel plops across the bottom of my bed.

He doesn't leave. I know what he's waiting for. I snake an arm out from under the covers and salute on top of my blanketed head. "Yessir."

Only when he's gone do I flip the covers off my head. Last night, Uncle Otts refused to come out of his bedroom. Today he's ready to conquer the world. He has lived with us all my life but I don't know who he is anymore. Nobody does. I'm not sure *he* knows, either.

Before I can even sit up, "Stars and Stripes Forever" blasts me out of bed. Mom and Dad cannot be home. I stumble toward the living room stereo to turn down the volume. Outside the picture window the sun drenches . . . Drew.

What? Drew is always in the tree house early on Saturday mornings. He gives up cartoons for the tree house and another casual reading of *Our Friend the Atom*. I blink and lean closer.

The front yard is littered with . . . stuff. And, yep, there's Drew, in his pajama bottoms and a Washington Senators baseball cap. He's shirtless, shoeless, and flitting from box to box like an overexcited chipmunk. Jack is running alongside him, barking, as if he thinks Drew is playing some fun new game. I rush back to my bedroom and throw on yesterday's clothes. I forget my headband. I stick my nose into Jo Ellen's room, but she's not there — did she even sleep in her bed last night?

"Hey, Franny!" Drew calls as soon I stagger out the front door. "Look at all this stuff!" He shoves a list into my hands, but before I can look at it, he races around the yard, introducing me to everything. "Generator! Water tank! Shortwave radio! *Blast door!*" Laid out in a neat line next to six stacked cots are flashlights, batteries, raincoats, boots, soap, towels, a first-aid kit, boxes of powdered milk, and cans of fruit and vegetables.

"Hey, lookit this!" yells Drew as he reads the label on an unopened box. "A chemical toilet!"

I'm dizzy. "Where'd all this come from?"

"Didn't you hear the delivery truck?" There's utter delight in Drew's voice. Christmas couldn't be more fun.

"Where are Mom and Dad?"

"They went to the airport. Dad had a trip — there's a note on the kitchen table."

"Did they see all this stuff?"

"No, they left early." Drew stands still for the first time. "Oh." Now he's thinking what I'm thinking.

Uncle Otts rounds the corner of the house, pushing an empty wheelbarrow. He's wearing a combat helmet and a green, button-up sweater over his flannel shirt. He has pinned his medals to his sweater. I look to see if any of the neighbors are outside yet; so far, the coast is clear. But we are the first house cars pass when they turn from busy Allentown Road onto Coolridge Drive. Anybody driving in or out of our neighborhood passes our house.

I push my hair out of my face. "Uncle Otts, what are we doing?" I try to sound nonchalant, even jocular (thank you, *Word Wealth Junior*).

"Stars and Stripes Forever" ends and "The Washington Post March" begins bleating from the stereo. "We're building a bomb shelter to protect this family," says Uncle Otts. "Starting today."

"Neat!" says Drew. I elbow him. "Ow!"

Uncle Otts hands Drew a shovel and glares at me. "Where's yours?"

"I left it inside," I say. "I'll just go get it."

"Double-time, soldier!" orders Uncle Otts.

I turn and almost trip over Jack, who has chosen to rest in the shade of the bushes in front of the porch. I sidestep him, run inside, turn off the record player, rush to the phone in the kitchen, dial Margie — it takes forever — and pray her parents don't answer the phone. When I hear Margie's voice, I spout, "Emergency! Hurry!" Then I hang up, grab the shovel from my room, and walk — I know it's dangerous to run with scissors *or shovels* — outside to find Drew much less enthusiastic now. Uncle Otts is gesturing to the ground in front of him and Drew is looking at me anxiously.

Think, Franny, grasp a straw, grab on to something.

"Right here, Private," says Uncle Otts, pointing to the green grass carpet beneath our feet. "Let's start her right here, Francine, and show the young private how it's done."

I blink. "Uncle Otts, I'm not sure . . ."

"A'course you are, Francine. You've just been given an order."

Pick a sturdier straw, Franny. "Uncle Otts, shouldn't we move all this stuff out of the way first?"

"I'll move it while you two shovel. I've got my handcart right here," he says.

Pick another straw. "How do we know this is the right place to dig?" I ask. "Or how deep to dig, or —"

"Francine, my blueprints arrived yesterday. I studied them all evening. I know what I'm doing."

"Uncle Otts, we haven't even had breakfast yet. Drew, did you eat breakfast?"

Drew shakes his head back and forth in an emphatic, frantic no. Drew doesn't do anything without eating breakfast. He eats breakfast before he goes to the bathroom in the morning.

I'm out of straws. Where is Jo Ellen? Where are Mom and Dad? It's up to me to say something grown up, or at least something sane. I draw myself up as straight as I can and I take a little breath. And here's what comes out: "Uncle Otts, Mom and Dad will kill us if we dig a hole in their yard. I respectfully decline. Sir. I'm sorry." I don't feel grown up or sane. I feel scared. Mom *will* kill me.

I glance at Drew. He is nodding like a bobble-head doll.

Uncle Otts takes my shovel and stares at both of us like he's Superman and can see right through us. "Insubordination," he says softly. "You are both insubordinate." He sticks the shovel into the ground and steps on it with his clodhoppered foot. The smooth steel point slices through the soft autumn earth.

"Go on," says Uncle Otts. "Git! War is not for yellow-bellied cowards. I don't need you! Git!"

I don't move, and Uncle Otts says, "You're catchin' flies," which is how I realize that I opened my mouth to protest but nothing came out. "Go on," he says, resigned. *Go own.*

Neither Drew nor I move. "Uncle Otts," I say, "can't we wait until Mom and Dad get back to start digging?"

He rubs a hand back and forth across his mouth, twice. Then he smiles at me, and for an instant I see the Uncle Otts I used to know.

"No, honey," he says, and he waves me and Drew away. Then he slices into the earth with his shovel and turns over the sod. All I can think about is how Mom and Dad work in the yard every single weekend, how Daddy mows and fertilizes and waters the grass — how proud he is of his lawn — and how Mom uses a special tool to weed out the crabgrass after she prunes the roses and clips the bushes. They love this yard.

"Go *own*," Uncle Otts says once more. He steps on the shovel again and upturns another chunk of the front lawn. Drew pulls on my shirt, and what am I supposed to do? Uncle Otts is a grown-up. I'm not.

"We'll be right inside," I say for some reason. I whistle for Jack as I take Drew with me into the house.

Margie meets us at the kitchen door. "What's the emergency? I had to do some fancy talking to get out of my chores —" Then she spies Uncle Otts and the mess in the front yard. "What's he doing?"

"He's building a *bomb* shelter," says Drew in a reverent voice, like Uncle Otts is on a mission from God that nobody else will understand.

"Where are your Mom and Dad?" Margie asks.

"They left a note," I say. "C'mon."

In the kitchen, I find the note printed in my mother's perfect penmanship.

> *Jo Ellen spent the night on campus with Lannie.*
> *She is on the way home. I am taking your father*
> *to Friendship Airport. Back before noon. Eat break-*
> *fast. Do chores. Don't bother your uncle.*

On the table are two bowls, two spoons, a box of Rice Krispies, and two peanut butter and jelly sandwiches wrapped in waxed paper.

"Your folks are gonna flip *out*," says Margie. "Should I get my mom?"

"No!" I try not to sound panicked. "Jo Ellen's on the way." I telegraph her to *get home this instant* —

Drew grabs a peanut butter and jelly sandwich from the table and sprints to the living room couch to watch Uncle Otts out the picture window. Jack follows him, begging for a bite, and Margie and I are right on his tail. Already there is a bare patch smack in the middle of the front yard. Mrs. Thornberg drives by in her old Buick and slows down to a crawl, then stops in front of the house. "Go away!" I hiss.

It's hot outside. *Indian summer*, Mrs. Rodriguez called it yesterday. Uncle Otts has an enormous handkerchief hanging out of his back pocket. He pulls it out and wipes off his whole face in big circles, like he's waxing a car. His medals gleam on his chest.

"Maybe I should take him some water," says Drew.

I issue an order. "Don't you move."

Uncle Otts fills the wheelbarrow with pieces of the front yard and struggles to the flower bed in front of the house, where he dumps the whole wheelbarrow next to the shrubbery that Jack was just sleeping under, on top of Mom's roses. He stumbles, rights the wheelbarrow, and goes back to his hole. He surveys it for a moment and then goes back to digging with a savage fury.

"He doesn't look so good," says Margie.

"He looks fine," I insist. But he doesn't. He looks like the workers do in that song we're learning in music, "Drill, Ye Tarriers, Drill."

> Every mornin' at seven o'clock,
> There's sixteen tarriers working at the rock
> And the boss comes along and he says be still,
> And come down heavy on the cast-iron drill,
> And drill, ye tarriers, drill!

Uncle Otts is digging like a tarrier. *Down with the shovel! Turn! Lift that earth! Heap it into the wheelbarrow! Repeat! Repeat! Repeat!*

> For it's work all day for sugar in your tay,
> Down, beyond the railway,
> And drill, ye tarriers, drill!

I should do something. I don't know what. Drew has forgotten his sandwich, and Jack is eating it in great big smacks, the peanut butter stuck to his teeth, oblivious to the scene outside.

I telegraph Uncle Otts to *just stop!* but he doesn't hear me. There's a crater forming in the front yard. Uncle Otts wipes his face with his handkerchief, loads up the wheelbarrow with chunks of our front yard, begins to roll the wheelbarrow toward the bushes, and then — he lets go of the wheelbarrow handles. The wheelbarrow topples onto its side. Uncle Otts staggers backward several steps, drops his shovel, and topples like a domino, flat onto his back. Dead as a doornail.

We shoot like missiles out the front door.

"Uncle Otts! Uncle Otts!" All three of us are shouting.

The next minute is a blur. Drew is on his knees next to Uncle Otts, fanning him with his baseball cap. Jack barks and runs in circles around all the stuff piled on the lawn. He runs right in front of Lannie's Beetle as it pulls into our driveway, but Lannie doesn't hit him.

Margie races for her house. I race for the watering bucket Mom keeps filled at the end of the rose bed, hoist it from under the bushes, turn, and stagger back like a maniac, water sloshing everywhere. I almost run into Jo Ellen racing toward us from Lannie's car.

"Take off his hat. Unbutton his sweater." Jo Ellen gives quick, sharp orders, and we follow.

"Give me that," she says, grabbing the bucket. "Franny — take off his shoes. Drew — run into the house. Get some pillows off the couch. *Go!*"

Drew scrambles for the house, and I frantically pull at Uncle Otts's shoelaces. He still hasn't moved or uttered a sound. Jo Ellen pours some water in her hands and slaps at Uncle Otts's wrinkled cheeks. "Uncle Otts! Wake up!" Nothing.

Drew slams out the front door, races across the porch, and jumps the low hedge. I hoist the water bucket and pour its entire contents into the middle of Uncle Otts's face.

"Franny!" screams Jo Ellen. Even Drew stops cold. But Uncle Otts comes to life. He sucks in a great breath and begins coughing violently, sputtering and spitting water.

"He's alive!" I shout, jubilant. Jack barks.

"He's drowning!" shouts Jo Ellen. With a great heave, we pull Uncle Otts to a sitting position and Jo Ellen begins pounding him on the back. Uncle Otts coughs like he has tuberculosis, then begins waving us away.

Drew has brought a whole couch cushion. He throws it behind Uncle Otts, who closes his eyes and lies back on the cushion, soaking it.

Lannie, who has stayed near her car, now steps across the yard toward us. She's wearing all black, like Jo Ellen, and has cut her hair into a boy's haircut. "Is he all right?" she asks.

"I think so," Jo Ellen reports.

"He got too hot," I say.

Jo Ellen leans into Uncle Otts's closed-up face. "Uncle Otts. Say something."

We all wait for confirmation from Uncle Otts that he's all right. The way we're gathered, we form a little ring around him, as if to protect him, like angels surrounding a manger. Mr. Gardener heads our way with Margie, walking briskly.

"Here come the neighbors," I murmur.

Then we hear from Uncle Otts. It's a whisper.

"This trench is full of the dead."

Drew's face turns the color of sheets drying on the clothesline.

"Uncle Otts?" Jo Ellen puts her hand on his arm.

"We got to bury the dead!" *Burry.* Uncle Otts sounds like a scared kid. His eyes are closed. What does he see? I telegraph him: *Open your eyes. See us.*

Jo Ellen gives Uncle Otts a gentle shake. "Uncle Otts! It's Jo Ellen. Can you hear me?"

"I can't find Nicky!" says Uncle Otts. His voice is edged with hysteria. His eyes are squeezed shut tight. He sees something horrible. "I can't find Nicky!" He lifts his arms and crosses them over his eyes.

Margie buries her face in her father's chest, Jack puts his head between his front paws, and Drew claps his hands over his mouth as Uncle Otts yells, "I'm burning! Everything's burning! Stop the burrrrning. . . ."

I try hard not to cry.

Uncle Otts's voice winds down until it is as silent as a clock that has finally stopped ticking. None of us breathes. A lawn mower starts up somewhere in the neighborhood.

"Who's Nicky?" whispers Drew.

"He's out of his head," says Jo Ellen. She holds Uncle Otts's hand and murmurs to him. "C'mon, Uncle Otts."

Mr. Gardener puts a hand on Jo Ellen's shoulder. "Give him a minute," he says. So we do. And after what feels like forever, Uncle Otts puts his wrinkled hands to his face, then slides them back along the sides of his old head. Fat tears slide out from his closed eyes as he comes back to himself. He heaves a sad sigh.

"Terrible to burn like that," he says in a small voice. He opens his eyes and looks right at me. He smiles a withered-old-man smile. I smile back. He is gray, ashen. He looks like he is a hundred years old.

The October sun washes over us, warm and sweet. Birds are singing as if nothing out of the ordinary has happened. I feel as if I am in a movie and I haven't memorized my lines. I don't know my part.

Mr. Gardener breaks the silence. "Mr. Chapman? Let us help you inside, sir."

Uncle Otts speaks slowly, as if he's just learning to talk. "Think I'll just stay here awhile, son."

"It would be good to get out of those wet clothes," says Mr. Gardener.

"Please, Uncle Otts," Jo Ellen pleads. "Before Daddy and Mother get home."

Even that doesn't move Uncle Otts. He looks like he might go to sleep right there, maybe for eternity.

An idea comes to me. "Uncle Otts," I say, hesitant. "I haven't seen those blueprints yet . . . and we've still got work to do."

He looks at me with questioning eyes, and my voice finds authority. I push my unruly hair out of my face. "We've got to get 'er started, remember, Sergeant? I've got my shovel right here. We need a leader, Uncle Otts."

Then, because it seems like the thing to do and I don't know what else to do . . . I stand and salute him.

Drew watches me a few seconds, then he stands and salutes, too. Jo Ellen makes a little groaning sound, but she salutes, too. So does Mr. Gardener and then Margie and even Lannie. We are lunatics, standing in our front yard, saluting a wet old man lying on the grass on a soaked couch cushion.

Lunatics, maybe, but it works. Slowly, slowly, Uncle Otts looks at each of us. Then he raises his right hand to his brow. "Yessir," he says in a soft, gruff voice. And he salutes. He is back with us.

Mom makes the turn from Allentown Road onto Coolridge Drive and swings the station wagon into the driveway at the speed of light. She pounds on the brakes so hard the car rocks as she parks it. She doesn't even bother to pull up behind Lannie, she just stops right at the mailbox and jumps out of the car.

I can't imagine what trouble we are all in, but I don't care. I have never been so glad to see my mother in my entire life.

FALLOUT SHELTER HANDBOOK

By CHUCK WES[T]

Diets and Food Kits

Surviving an Atomic Attack

Evacuation Techniqu[e]

Sources of Water Supply

Underground Shelters You Can Build or Buy

Basement and Garage Shelters

Above-Ground Shelte[r]

Medical Hints and First Aid

Fallout Detection Devices

THE WORLD
IS A CAROUSEL
OF COLOR

A TREASURE TROVE OF FACES!

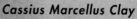

FOUR
4

I AM THE GREATEST!

Cassius Marcellus Clay

35

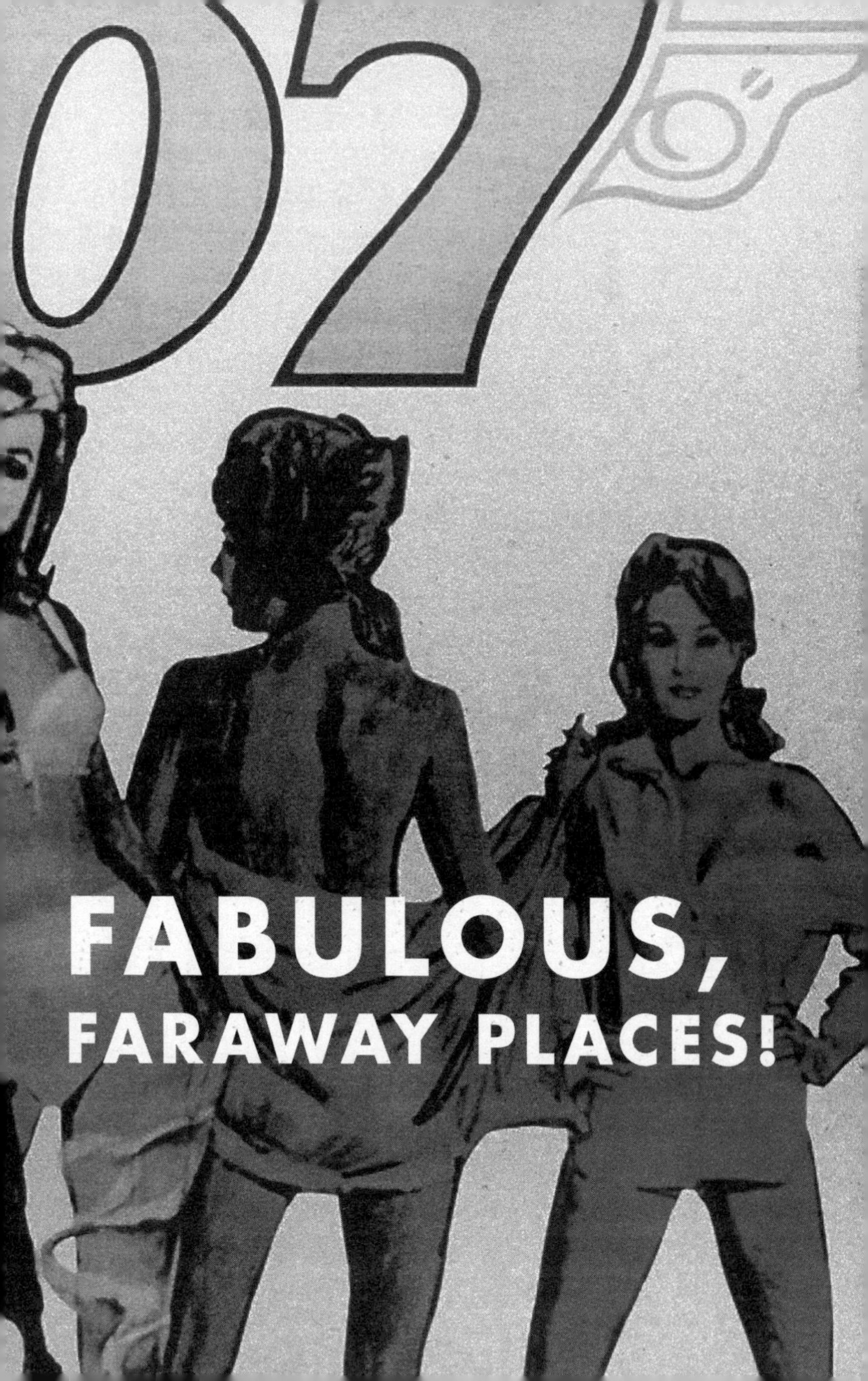
007
FABULOUS,
FARAWAY PLACES!

FAMILY IN THE SHELTER, SNUG, EQUIPPED, AND WELL ORGANIZED

LIST OF MATERIALS
YOU WILL NEED

500 solid concrete blocks, 4"x8"x16"

12 bags of prepared mortar mix,
one cubic foot per bag

3 support posts, 4"x6"x5'10"

1 beam, 4"x6"x8'4"

6 joists, 2"x8"x10'4"

3 joists, 2"x8"x7'8"

3 lengths, 2"x8"x8' for bracing

95 board feet of 1"x6" sheathing boards

3 pounds of 16-penny nails

3 pounds of 8-penny nails

Posts, beams and joists should be of
Construction Grade Douglas Fir

*Bricks can be used in place of blocks to construct this shelter.
In this case the walls and roof should be 10 inches thick
to provide the same protection as the 8-inch blocks.*

THE WONDERFUL
WORLD OF COLOR!

10

Who can concentrate on homework?

It's Saturday afternoon, and the house is as quiet as a tomb. We are holding a vigil without saying so. Eddie hasn't come over, and neither has Margie. Lannie has gone home. I've started my science fair project, a huge display of the solar system made with different sizes of rubber balls to represent the planets.

I'm working in Daddy's basement workshop, which is also the laundry room, next to Uncle Otts's bedroom. I've cut each ball in half (Daddy helped me with this last week), and I've been painting each ball a different color — Earth is blue, of course — and next I'll need to paint the backdrop and glue the half-balls in place on my backdrop, which Daddy made out of plywood at his table saw. It has two sides with hinges and folds flat when I store it, only it won't fold all the way once I glue on the nine planets.

I have changed into clean clothes. I found an extra-thick string of blue yarn in my sock drawer, and I'm using it as a headband. I tied it with a bow at the top. I like it. I'm working at Daddy's long worktable, surrounded by a scattering of screwdrivers, hammers, and C-clamps. I have one dozen tiny glass jars of paint, too. I feel rich.

Mrs. Rodriguez hates my science fair project. She says I don't have a hypothesis or an experiment, but I just can't be bothered with that, because I don't get it. I don't understand what the heck she wants me to do, and when I ask her (I do ask), she doesn't explain it — partly, I'm sure, because of her need to skip me. But I ask again anyway.

"What kind of experiment?" I ask her. "I can't experiment with the solar system, I can just show it to you." So Mrs. Rodriguez is frustrated, and I'm frustrated, and I'm creating a model of the solar system, even though I know it's going to cost me points because I'm not following the scientific method. I can't help it — I don't have a problem with the solar system and I can't just make one up.

I'm morose about this, but not nearly as morose as I am about Uncle Otts and the whole world falling apart around me.

At ten o'clock this morning, Mom put Jo Ellen in charge and told me and Drew to help her and Lannie lug all the boxes and cots and cans and stuff to the carport and out of the yard. Mr. Gardener volunteered Margie, too, and she was not happy about that. In the time it took Drew to get dressed, Mom and Mr. Gardener put Uncle Otts in the car, still sopping wet but wrapped in a blanket, and zoomed him off to the base hospital.

"Okay, let's get this stuff moved," says Jo Ellen.

Lannie chirps, "Oh! Jo Ellen! I almost forgot!" She grabs her purse out of the Beetle, opens it, and hands Jo Ellen an envelope. A white, crinkly-enveloped letter. "I checked campus mail early this morning."

Jo Ellen takes the letter and everything changes. "Listen, I'll do your chores, Squirt," she tells me, "if you take over for me, and

I'll get lunch ready." Before I can even answer, she and Lannie disappear into the house, whispering.

"Okay . . ." I say. But she's not fooling me. She's got another letter from Ebenezer.

"What about *my* chores?" asks Drew.

"You have half the chores I do," I say. I long to follow Lannie and Jo Ellen. They will smoke cigarettes and read that letter, I just know it.

A half hour later, Drew, Margie, and I have everything from the front lawn stacked neatly in the carport. We stare at the chewed-up lawn.

"I don't think we should touch that," I say.

"I agree," says Margie. "Look . . . I gotta go."

I don't stop her. I don't know what to say about Uncle Otts or what just happened, so I just say, "Thanks for helping."

She doesn't even say "you're welcome."

I don't feel like lunch, so I flop across my bed, with Jack on the floor next to me, and read some *Word Wealth Junior*. Now I know how to spell all of next week's words and can work toward my goal of 100 percent in every spelling test this year. So far I am seven for seven.

Time slows to a crawl. There is nothing good on television on Saturday afternoon. I have practiced my piano. I have finished *The Clue in the Diary*, which gave me some ideas about how to solve *The Clue in the Crinkly Envelope*.

Still no word from Mom.

Drew is in the tree house organizing his baseball cards. Jo Ellen plays weird new records in her room, *with her door shut*, and I work on my science fair project downstairs, worried sick that I'm the cause of Uncle Otts's collapse.

If I had chopped up the yard for him, he wouldn't have keeled over. Of course, I would be dead, but still. Maybe Uncle Otts is dead. *No, he's not — get hold of yourself, Franny.* If I hadn't thrown all that water in his face . . .

Even though I'm not supposed to use the phone without permission, I call Margie. I don't know why. I'm mad at her, I think. She's mad at me, I think. Her mom says she's over at Gale Hoffman's house. Well! No wonder she had to go. I'm dying to call Gale and ask to be invited to come over, too, but I've said all of four sentences to Gale in my entire life, and I've never called her ever, and anyway I'm not allowed to go to her house.

"Have you heard from my mom?" I ask Margie's mom.

"No, sweetie, no word yet. Try not to worry."

"Thanks."

I can't stand it any longer. I knock on Jo Ellen's door.

"Just a minute!" There's too much rustling and then Jo Ellen opens the door.

"What's that record?" I ask.

" 'Green Onions,' " she says. "Do you like it?"

"It's weird," I say. "Jo Ellen, am I a bad person if I go out and ride my bike until Mom comes home?"

"Take Drew and Jack," Jo Ellen says, "and stay in the neighborhood."

So that's how Drew and I are on our bikes at 3:13 P.M. on Saturday afternoon, October 20, 1962, when I remember — we've got new neighbors. We sail down the driveway on our bikes, we veer right onto Coolridge Drive and — instinctively, without saying a word to each other — stop one house up and across the street. Jack stands dutifully with us.

"I wonder if they have kids," says Drew, looking at the house like it might hold a present for him.

"We deserve kids," I say, "after the Fieldings." Besides Margie, we're the only kids on this end of Coolridge.

"I could go knock on the door," says Drew. We've done it before.

But Drew doesn't need to knock on the door. We stand there, astride our bikes, like we belong there, rooted to the street, hoping someone will notice us and, like magic, the front door opens. A boy stands there, a boy who looks familiar. I squint and squirt my head forward like a chicken. The boy smiles! Lifts a hand! And then, just as it all comes tumbling back to me, he says, in a much older voice than I've ever heard him use, "Hi, Franny!"

I have goose bumps — I actually shudder. Our new neighbors are our old neighbors. Chris Cavas is the new kid. And the old kid. Chris Cavas moved out of this very house a year ago, and now he's back. Chris Cavas, who . . . I can't even say it.

Heavens to Murgatroyd, Chris Cavas.

11

"Chris!" It's Drew who speaks first as Chris struts himself down the front steps and across the grass. "Hey!" He's a dead ringer for my favorite singer, Del Shannon. I expect him to warble "Runaway" any minute.

"Hey, Drew," he says. And to me, in a voice like velvet, he croons, "Hey, Franny."

"Chris?" I ask, as if I can't believe it's him. Mostly, I can't.

He laughs, and I can't believe that's the sound of his laughter. "Long time no see," he says, as if it were last week we last laid eyes on him. "You, too, boy," he says to Jack as he scratches his back.

"I thought you were in Pakistan," I squeak. I telegraph my voice to *calm down*. "Didn't your dad get transferred to Pakistan?" Chris's dad is in the foreign service. All the kids at Camp Springs thought Pakistan sounded so mysterious.

"He got transferred back," Chris tells me.

"Wow!" says Drew. "Where's Bobby?

"He's with my mom and dad. They took him to astronaut school."

"What? Where?"

Chris laughs. "I'm kidding, kid. They went to the commissary for groceries. You still want to be an astronaut?"

"I'm the next John Glenn," says Drew.

"And I'm Rocket J. Squirrel," I say.

"And I'm Chris Cavas." Chris grins. Grins. At me. His teeth are very white. His hair is very black. He is positively debonair.

"C'mon, I'll prove it," says Drew. "Remember the gravel pit, Chris?"

"Yeah. Is it still there?"

"It's better than ever. Some big kids hung a rope swing from a tree at the edge, and now you can swing out and over the whole thing — it's like being weightless, like one of the Mercury astronauts."

"Well!" says Chris. "This I gotta see!" He turns his big brown eyes on me and asks, "You comin', Franny?" I feel weak in the knees. It's not just Chris, it's the gravel pit. It gives me the creeps. Of course I'm coming.

Half a minute later, the three of us are biking to the end of Coolridge Drive, where the big woods hide the cavernous gravel pit that every kid knows about and no one tells his parents about. I make sure I travel last down the narrow dirt path through the woods. I want to get a good look at Chris without him seeing too much of me. Drew leads the way and sings, at the top of his lungs, "Off we go, into the wild blue yonder!"

"You'll have half the neighborhood there in a minute!" I yell. I hope I don't sound shrewish. I hope my yarn headband is attractive.

We don't know who excavated the gravel pit. All we need to know is that if we follow the path through the brambles and ferns and poison ivy, we come into a clearing so suddenly it takes our breath away every time. Here, hidden and surrounded by scrub pines, is a crater carved into the earth, so wide and deep we can't see the bottom in places.

We didn't even know what it was until some neighborhood kids told us it was a quarry long ago. Trucks haven't hauled rock out of it in decades. There is no way a truck could get into this part of the woods now, and no way it could drive to the bottom of the gravel pit by using the spiraling dirt road that was fashioned along the sides of the pit, which curls down to the bottom — the road is nothing but crumbles and ledges now.

There is stone on some of the houses in our neighborhood, and a stone wall at Camp Springs Elementary School, and sometimes I have visions of men deep down in the pit, blasting at the stone with dynamite, shoveling the gravel into dump trucks, and lifting the heaviest stones out with a giant crane long ago, and I wonder what happened to those men and all those stones.

This past summer, someone — maybe one of the high school kids — suspended two thick ropes from a sturdy oak at the edge of the pit, stuffed each end of the rope through holes on either end of a board at the bottom, and knotted it off tight.

Drew shows off the swing to a hesitant Chris. "That's a bowline below and a half hitch above — they're good knots," Drew says. "I know my knots."

"He does," I say. "He taught me." I don't want to mention Uncle Otts so I don't say that he's the one who really taught us both, and Drew doesn't correct me.

Chris inspects the knots like he's from Scotland Yard. "I see," he says.

"Watch!" shouts Drew. He doesn't hesitate — he never does.

He takes hold of the swing, turns his back to the pit, and runs as far as he can into the woods, screaming the countdown at the top of his lungs. "Ten-nine-eight-seven-six-five-four-three-two-one!" The swing gets higher and higher as Drew runs up the slope, and then, with a whoop that sets my ears ringing, Drew twists and makes a great leap backward onto the wooden seat. He takes off, facing forward, sailing out of the woods, through a rush of leaves and wind, and over the wide pit. It terrifies me, every time.

Drew laughs and laughs. "We have liftoff!" he screams. "Zero G and I feel fine!" His voice echoes across the woods. "I'm going to the moon!" There isn't another soul here this afternoon but the three of us and a barking Jack, a thousand birds and bugs, and the ghosts of all those who came before us.

The branch of the rope swing creaks and groans mightily, swaying in a way that makes my stomach quease and long for Mom and Dad, as Drew sails away and birds fly from the trees. Drew is part of a slow-motion movie, the rope and the swing floating over the pit, right toward the middle of the deep, gaping hole, suspending itself for a second, then deciding to calmly swing back onto land.

Now it's Chris's turn to say "Wow" in an awe-filled voice.

Drew flops back to earth like a fish — there is no graceful way to land — picks himself up, and brushes pine needles off his T-shirt. All his bony ribs stick out around his heart. His knees knob under his shorts . . . shorts that balloon around his matchstick legs. Jack runs to him and gives him slobbery dog kisses, which Drew swats away.

"Your turn," he says to Chris, panting. He flaps down next to me.

Smooth as a new puppy's ears, Chris says, "Ladies first."

I almost choke. I have never flown on this swing. I would never fly over this gravel pit in a million years. But do you think I can say that to Chris? No. Instead, like I do this every day of the week, I say in my most nonchalant voice, "In a minute," while I scan my list of excuses to see what I can come up with.

"Oh, not *Franny*!" says Drew, sounding exactly like the rat fink he knows how to be. "She never rides. She's chicken!"

"I am not! I ride all the time! Just because you're not here to see me —"

But Drew's not buying it. "You're nuts!" he says. He holds the rope swing toward Chris. "Here — your turn, Chris. Franny's a girly girl! She can't do it."

Chris takes a hesitant step, reaches for the rope, and I tele-graph myself to *get up! get up!* and then I telegraph Chris — *Wait!* — and I jump to my feet, grab the rope from Chris's hands, and run hard, back toward the woods, and leap and twist onto the seat.

And it feels good! Until the swing starts its forward journey toward the gravel pit and my heart stops.

I can't do it. *Get off! Get off! Get off!*

12

NO!

I wriggle and twist myself in an effort to rid my legs of the seat of the swing. I hear a mighty tearing sound and have a wild thought that I've managed to rip my legs off, but no, they are still attached to me and still attached to the swing as well.

Drew is screaming, Chris is yelling — I don't know what they are saying. The swing takes on speed and height. I thrash against the seat. The ropes fly out of my hands and my body swoops backward. I am upside down, and the back of my head drags the forest floor, bumping across pine needles and roots and rocks. I am going forward, forward to the pit, upside down. One more time I flail my legs upward, sideways, every which way as I twist my body in ways it was never meant to bend, and at the moment the swing begins its sail over the gravel pit, I free my legs and flop in a heap near the edge of the pit.

I don't want Chris to see me. I don't want to see Drew. I flip myself over, onto my stomach, and bury my face in the earth. My back is broken. I don't care. I am alive. I think.

Chris and Drew are on either side of me. "Franny! Franny!"
I don't move.

Drew scoots to my left shoulder. "Franny, say something," he whispers, but I don't have any air in my body, I can't say a word.

Drew bursts into tears. Chris says, "Let's get your mom."

"No," I manage to puff out. It's a groan.

"Franny?" asks Drew. He sniffs.

"Am I dead?" I take a breath, then two. I find my arms and use them to push me up enough so I can spit the pine needles out of my mouth. My bangs sweep the dirt beneath me, and a blue piece of yarn — tied into a bow — is tangled in them.

"You look bad," says Drew. "I'll see if Mom's home yet." He grabs his bike.

"Don't you dare," I say, surprised at how strong I sound. I face Drew and don't look at Chris, but I can feel him studying me. "It's okay. Nothing's broken." I am getting my breath back.

"Your shorts are ripped up," says Drew. "Your nose is bleeding."

I touch my nose. It *is* bleeding.

"Here," says Chris. He produces a handkerchief from his pocket. A *handkerchief.* He's a regular Prince Charming. And very tall.

Drew lets go of his bike. "Why'd you do that?"

"Are you impressed?" I take the handkerchief from Chris without looking at him. "Thanks." My universe is a six-inch square between my nose and the earth.

"Franny," says Drew, never one to mince words, even when his voice shakes. "You are so stupid."

"And you're an astronaut." I turn onto my back so I can breathe. I use my feet to scoot myself away from the edge of the pit.

"She's not stupid," says Chris. He looks at me with admiration

119

in his eyes. "I didn't want to swing across that pit, either — it's dangerous. Don't swing if you don't want to, Franny."

I am bleeding, and I am in love. "I won't," I say, and I telegraph myself, *Say something smart here, say something casual . . . insouciant.*

"I'm having a Halloween party next weekend," I say.

I am not having a Halloween party. I am not having a party of any kind, and certainly not a boy-girl party. No one has boy-girl parties.

Drew scratches his eyebrow. Chris looks at me like I've lost my marbles. I look at me, too. My hair is falling all over my face, it's full of leaves and sticks and a loose piece of blue yarn with a bow in it, my legs are scraped up one side and down the other, my shorts pocket is torn off, and my nose is bleeding. I lie back on the pine needles. Nobody would come to my party anyway.

"You're nuts," says Drew, in a kind way.

"Pistachio," I answer. Everybody breathes. I am okay.

Jack, who was nowhere around when I landed, suddenly shows up with a smashed pot lid in his mouth. He hovers over me, offering it to me. It's covered with damp leaves.

"Where did you get that?" I ask him. He just wags his tail and grins like an idiot. Drew takes the lid and spins it off into the woods, and Jack bounds after it.

"Am I invited to the party?" asks Chris. A breeze sways the pine branches above us. I close my eyes and imagine my wedding dress.

"I do," I say.

"We should go home," says Drew.

"You have to wear a costume," I say. I smile like a fool.

We walk our bikes out of the woods and up Coolridge Drive.

No one feels like riding. I guide my bike with one hand and pick leaves and sticks and pine straw off me with the other. I'm a mess. I have to come up with a story that will satisfy Mom. The only problem is, Saint Drew cannot tell a lie. So I may have to tell the truth and be grounded for life — or at least for Halloween. And if Uncle Otts is dead or brain damaged or dies of pneumonia because of me, I might as well lock myself up in a tower and throw away the key.

Chris reads my mind. "Does your uncle still live with you?"

"As far as we know," I say. At the same time I say it, Drew says yes, and of course that confuses Chris, but he doesn't pursue it.

It amazes me that Chris doesn't know all about what happened across the street this morning. Or maybe he does know and he's fishing for information. I decide he isn't. He's making conversation. Drew lags behind us.

I make conversation back. "Did you go to school in Pakistan?"

"There was an American school there. Kids came from all over the world, just like a base school."

"I've never been to school on base," I say. "We've always lived off base and gone to the neighborhood school. But there are lots of air force kids at Camp Springs."

"Lots of foreign service kids, too," says Chris.

I like making conversation with Chris. "We go to the base all the time, though — to the commissary and the PX and the movies. . . ."

"We do, too. Especially to the pool."

"You know, the first time I went to the movies off base, I was surprised to see they didn't play the National Anthem, with the flag waving on screen. I was all ready to stand up and put my hand over my heart, and then there were coming attractions instead! Not even a newsreel!" I'm talking too much. I'll stop.

"I register for school on Monday." Chris just keeps on making conversation — he is a confabulator. "Maybe we'll be in the same classroom."

I play it cool. "Maybe," I say. My nose has stopped bleeding. I don't offer to give back Chris's handkerchief. I may have to keep it forever.

"Does Margie still live across the street?" he asks.

She died, I say. No, I don't. But I think it. Margie is every bit as beautiful as Jo Ellen — they could be sisters. "I've got to go," is what I say. And the reason I say it is because our station wagon is pulling into our driveway.

I scramble onto my bike. "My mom's home and she's . . . I've got to go. See you." I pedal the three houses more up to my house. Drew sees what I see and races past me with Jack.

Mom is standing outside the car. She's looking at us. Waiting for us.

Uncle Otts is not with her.

She has news.

13

Observation. Uncle Otts is in Malcolm Grow Hospital, at Andrews Air Force Base, under observation. I am flooded with sweet relief that, first of all, he's not dead, and that, second, *observation* means they're just keeping an eye on him overnight and we can have him back tomorrow or Monday. Mom is as cool as a cucumber when she delivers this news — crisp, controlled, and curt.

I have a million questions, but I don't get to ask them. Mom takes one look at me and marches me and Drew into the bathroom, gets out the alcohol and the cotton balls, and starts asking questions.

I go for broke. "I fell off my bike going downhill too fast." No problem. I'm not trying to deceive my mother, it's just that the truth is so complicated, and it isn't . . . necessary. I'm fine, I learned my lesson, I'm not going to try *that* again. I telegraph Drew, *Don't say a word. Just keep your mouth shut.*

Mom begins the assault of my skin with alcohol, killing every last germ that ever lived on my legs. "Blow on it!" I hiss between clenched teeth, and she does. She blows and blows, and I blow, too, and soon the sting is gone.

"What hill, Drew?" Mom asks as she screws the top back on the alcohol bottle.

Drew stands there, just outside the bathroom door, and shuffles his feet. He won't look at my mother. The gravel pit is a secret, but it's not a lie; we just never mentioned its existence. I can see Drew chewing on his response, and I am certain we're about to get caught.

"Over by the school," he mutters.

I'm stunned — Saint Drew has told a lie. There's only one problem with it. It's flat as a pancake over by the school. I blink and stare hard at Drew, trying to get his attention.

"Oh," says Mom, as if there are mountains surrounding the school and she knows just which one Drew means.

"The Thornbergs' driveway, actually," I say. We aren't allowed on the Thornbergs' property. They're old and like their privacy. "Drew just doesn't want me to get in trouble," I say, "but nobody was home, and I just wanted to see what it would be like to speed down their driveway, it's so long and steep."

I already know what it's like — I've done it a hundred times.

"Are you fibbing to me, Drew?" asks my mother, clicking shut the door to the medicine cabinet.

"Yes, ma'am," says Drew. The truth rolls right off his tongue in a whoosh of relief. "I'm sorry."

"I never thought I'd live to see the day you would lie to me, Drew Chapman, not even for Franny."

Tears flood Drew's eyes. He won't look at me or Mom.

"You can't protect your sister from herself," snaps Mom. "Go to your room."

"Yes, ma'am." Drew turns to go and I desperately want to grab him and hug him, but I don't. Soon he's sobbing downstairs in his bedroom, a fallen saint.

Mom washes her hands. "You're lucky you didn't kill yourself, young lady." I'm not sure she believes me, but she's not going to press it. Her face is puffy with fatigue and her shoulders sag. I want to make it better for her.

"I'm sorry, Mom." I mean it, too.

She dries her hands on the small towel by the door and sighs. "It's time to grow up, Franny. Not only are you an example for Drew to follow, you represent your family when you are off this property."

"Yes, ma'am."

"I have enough to worry about without worrying about you when you are not home."

"Yes, ma'am."

"And I won't have you dragging your brother into a career of disobedience and lying about it."

"Yes, ma'am."

"Now wash up for dinner. And take a bath before bed."

"Yes, ma'am."

After Mom leaves the bathroom, I look to the ceiling and whisper, "I'm glad we had this talk, Mom."

The good news about Daddy being on a trip is that we have the following suppers, in this order:

1. Leftovers.

2. Scrambled eggs and biscuits with cheese.

3. TV dinners, of which meat loaf and mashed potatoes is my favorite. I try not to eat the rubbery green beans.

4. Grilled cheese sandwiches and Campbell's Tomato Soup. We also get this choice on Tuesday nights when Mom and Dad go to their bowling league in their red shirts with their names on them.

5. McDonald's, a restaurant. This is a sometime treat. There are no waiters and no waiting at McDonald's. When you get there, you go to a counter and order from a big menu on the wall, and the people behind the counter put the food, all wrapped up, on a tray. Then you take the tray to a table and eat it. The wrapper is your plate. You can dump your French fries on the wrapper and have a whole meal, just like that. There's ketchup for the fries in little pack-ets — everything but the tray gets thrown away at the end, and there are no dishes.

McDonald's is brand-new, and we've got one right outside Andrews Air Force Base, so how it usually works in my family is: We all go in the car to drop Daddy off at Andrews, and then Mom, if she's in a good mood or wants to do something at home, like yard work instead of messing up the kitchen, takes us to the Golden Arches. We go inside, Mom orders five hamburgers, five French fries, and five cokes. We eat. OH, how I want to try the fish sandwich! The chocolate shake! The apple pie! "NO," Mom says. Fine.

Uncle Otts always eats his hamburger and then walks to the counter and dumps twenty-five cents out of his pocket and buys a fish sandwich anyway, which he eats except for one bite, which he gives me first. I tear up thinking about that now.

Tonight should be leftovers night, the first night Daddy is gone, but Mom tells Jo Ellen she can't face leftovers tonight, and Jo Ellen offers to scramble eggs while Mom takes a shower. "Franny will help me," Jo Ellen says. And I do. I love popping open the biscuit can and putting the biscuits on the tray. Then I take square slices of American cheese and fold each one twice so that each slice is divided into fourths. When the biscuits are almost done, Jo Ellen takes them out of the oven and opens them up with a knife and inserts the cheese into each biscuit, then runs them back into the oven for another minute.

These are the world's best biscuits. And Jo Ellen makes good scrambled eggs. Annie Mae, the colored woman who works for my grandmother Miss Mattie, taught her how, when she was eleven. We spent two whole weeks in Mississippi that summer, like we always do. I was four years old and I ate so many scrambled eggs, Miss Mattie told me I was going to turn into an omelet.

"Get any good mail today?" I ask Jo Ellen as we set the table.

"None of your business," she says coolly. "What happened to you?"

"None of your business," I say just as coolly. "Tit for tat." Then, because I feel like it and it's a good idea to change the subject, I say, "Chris Cavas moved back in across the street!"

"Really!" says Jo Ellen. "I thought they were in Pakistan."

I put the jelly on the table. "They came back." My stomach grumbles at the smell of biscuits cooking, eggs scrambling. I missed lunch. I'm hungry.

Mom appears with Drew and Jack behind her. "Out!" she orders Jack. He slinks down the carpeted stairs, but only two steps, and sneaks the tip of his snout over the top step, so he can still be near us.

"Mrs. Cavas stopped by the hospital," says Mom as if she were part of our conversation all along and missed nothing. She's wearing her nightgown and bathrobe. Her wet hair is combed straight back. Her face is scrubbed so clean, it's red. It's six o'clock. The sun is still up. Well, barely . . . it's dusk.

Mom lights a cigarette and pours a cup of coffee from the percolator. She blows a stream of smoke to the ceiling and says, "Irene Cavas is the epitome of discretion, thank goodness, but this is going to be all over the neighborhood by tomorrow, thanks to Martha Gardener and her gossiping mouth. Pour the milk, Franny."

I pour three glasses of milk. I like Mrs. Gardener. She's nice. Jo Ellen puts plates of steaming scrambled eggs on the table.

"Your father comes home Monday," Mom tells us. "I don't know about Uncle Otts." Her voice cracks in the tiniest way, and we all lean toward her. She waves a hand. "I'm tired," she says.

"Franny's having a Halloween party!" says Drew in a cheer-you-up voice.

How is this helpful? I kick Drew under the table and pop up to serve the biscuits. Mom says nothing, and it's suddenly so quiet I can hear the tick of the mantel clock in the living room.

"I'm going to be an astronaut," Drew adds in a hopeful voice.

Mom rubs her forehead with her two middle fingers, like she's trying to force the right words to come out of her mouth.

"Drew, Halloween is the furthest thing from my mind right now. The front yard is a holy mess, your uncle is in the hospital, and your father is on a trip." Mom's voice rises with each thing

128

she ticks off on her list. "I'm the laughingstock of the entire neighborhood, if not the base, my children lie to my face, and no one understands the gravity of the situation in this family." She looks at Jo Ellen. "Nobody."

She takes another drag on her cigarette and blows the smoke out in a long, thin stream. Then she looks straight at me and sets her jaw.

"Franny, to even suggest a Halloween party at a time like this is the most insensitive thing you've ever done." She picks up her coffee cup, turns to leave the kitchen, turns back, and says in a rush, "No, I take that back. The most insensitive thing you've ever done is to allow your uncle to exhaust himself in the front yard in front of God and everybody. I hope you're proud of yourself."

To say I am stunned is an understatement. I am slapped. I am slugged. I am guilty, a horrible person.

"I'm sure you can finish dinner without me," says Mom. She looks at Jo Ellen, who stares at her shoes. "Am I right, Jo Ellen?"

"Yes, ma'am," Jo Ellen says in a voice so quiet I can hardly hear it. Drew stares at Mom's plate, steaming with scrambled eggs she will never eat. I cannot breathe.

Mom sighs, as if she might reconsider everything she just said, and maybe she does, but she doesn't say so. Instead she says, "I'm going to roll my hair. Be ready for Sunday school and church tomorrow morning at nine sharp. We all need it. *Some of us* more than others."

I don't feel like cheese in my biscuits. I don't feel like eating at all.

Before anyone can say anything else, I take my dark heart to my room and stay there.

129

14

My first concrete remembrance of church is going to revival with Miss Mattie, in Halleluia, Mississippi. I like revival. It's entertaining. I know almost every hymn in the Methodist hymnal by heart, every verse, and I can play most of them on the piano.

Revival lasts two weeks, so we go every night to church, and every night there is tarnation preaching and seventeen verses of "Just As I Am," until someone walks up to the altar to be saved.

Trouble is, Halleluia is a small town, and most everybody in church has already been saved. So unless somebody new shows up, or an older kid is pushed into the aisle by his mother, we just sing and sing that hymn, until my grandmother stands up and ambles in her square shoes up the aisle with a half-exasperated look on her face, and gets saved once again. Mostly she is saving all of us, and she knows we know it.

I wish she would save me now. I think about calling her as I get ready for Sunday school, but I'm not allowed to make long-distance phone calls. If I could talk to my grandmother, she would make me feel better. She would talk to my mother and tell her I meant well — she always says that about me. But I'm not going to tell Miss Mattie, of course, because then she'll tell Mom, and

Mom will know I've told on her, because that's what it would be, telling on her, even if I wouldn't mean it that way.

I have two dress-up dresses. I wear them to Sunday school or for special occasions, like going out for dinner at the Officers' Club at Andrews on Sunday nights when Daddy is home. I miss Daddy. I don't know what I'm going to do when Mom tells him about what I did to Uncle Otts . . . and what I didn't do. I don't think he'll spank me, but it doesn't even matter if he does, because his disappointment is always worse than any spanking.

I button up my blue dress with the birds on it, put on fresh white anklets, and buckle my black patent leather shoes. I look in the mirror and run a comb through my ridiculous brown hair. I imagine Jo Ellen and Mom doing the same, right this minute. Both of them are beautiful. I'm not beautiful, but I think Chris Cavas likes me. I say to myself in the mirror, "Franny, you have a *winsome* face." I slide my white headband onto my head.

Mom steps out of her bedroom and stands in my doorway. She clips her purse shut. Her hair is perfect.

"Bring a sweater," she says. "It's chilly."

"Yes, ma'am."

We don't know how to act with one another this morning. Jo Ellen pats my arm as I walk past at breakfast, and I can tell, just from her touch, that she feels low, too. Drew, the new family liar, wears his shame all over his face and still won't look at me. I want to tell him that, as far as lies go, his was beige, not even close to black and evil. It was almost a white lie. But I know Drew won't care about that. He will care about his character. He probably can't even give me the definition of character, but he knows what it is. John Glenn has character. And that's what Drew wants.

We each pat Jack good-bye and slide ourselves silently into the station wagon. Drew has brought *Our Friend the Atom* to read in the car — he's beginning to remind me of Linus and his security blanket in *Peanuts*, which reminds me of how Uncle Otts always reads the funny pages out loud on Sundays after church . . . except for this Sunday. *My fault, my fault . . .*

Andrews Air Force Base is on Allentown Road. Our house is on the corner of Allentown and Coolridge Drive. There are 1.4 miles of Allentown Road separating my house from Andrews Air Force Base — Daddy and I clocked it once on the odometer. We drive in utter silence past Camp Springs Elementary School, past Pyles Lumber Company, where Daddy bought the wood to make my doomed science fair project foldout, and past Bells Methodist Church, where we went to church the first year we were here.

We make a wide swing into Andrews Air Force Base and slow down at the open gates, where a soldier in uniform salutes our car. We're in, just like that, because we've got a sticker on our car that proclaims: *This Is the Car of Major Philip Chapman, Korean War Veteran and Now Chief of Safety of the 89th Sam Fox Squadron, the Squadron That Flies the President of the United States, John Fitzgerald Kennedy! This Is the Car of the Greatest Jet Pilot in the Air Force!*

Okay, it doesn't say that. But it does have some sort of fancy mumbo jumbo on it, some sort of secret code or something. Nancy Drew would know what it means.

Just being on base makes me feel better. There's something solid and safe about it, where everything is controlled and neat, everything is known, the rules make sense, and my whole family belongs. Every bush is clipped just so, not a blade of grass is too high, and on every sidewalk there is a man or woman in uniform, walking to wherever he or she is going. Every few minutes, a jet flies overhead. Sometimes lots of jets. Everything has a purpose.

I can almost forget about Uncle Otts lying in Malcolm Grow Hospital, right around the corner from the base chapel. But of course I can't forget. I stare at the hospital building as we get out of the car.

Mom says to me and Drew, "Come sit with us if you get out of Sunday school early." Usually I'm bored to tears in church, but after what happened last night, this feels like an invitation to the circus.

Drew's not in my Sunday school class, and I don't know many kids at the base chapel, because I only see them for an hour a week and none of them lives in my neighborhood or goes to my school except Bonnie Cross. Her dad is a navigator on Air Force One. The rest of the kids in my Sunday school class live on base. They go to school on base. They live in this little cocoon all the time. And they all go to church in the same place.

I used to think there were only Methodist and Baptist churches. Then I went to Vacation Bible School one summer at Aunt Beth and Uncle Jim's and found out they were Presbyterians. I couldn't tell the difference. Same Jesus.

Before we went to Mississippi this past summer, Mom let me spend a weekend at the beach with Mary Flood and her family. Mary has seven older brothers and she is the only girl. We all went to Mass on Sunday. It was in a foreign language. Same Jesus. And his mother, Mary, is in this church.

Gale Hoffman is Jewish. We went on a field trip to her church last year. It's called a synagogue, and the boys have to wear little

133

head caps. No Jesus. Lots of Moses. We have Moses, too. I'm not sure how this works, but the first five books of our Old Testament are part of the Jewish Bible, too.

Miss Creasy, my Sunday school teacher, is talking about the Old Testament Book of Psalms today. "Who would like to memorize Psalm Twenty-four for our parent presentation next Sunday?" she asks. My hand forgets that it's part of my body and shoots itself high in the air. "Why, thank you, Franny!" says a surprised Miss Creasy.

I'm surprised, too. I have no idea what Psalm Twenty-four is. But I am a good read-alouder, and I imagine I will be a good memorize-alouder, too. I hope it's a Psalm about goodness and mercy and forgiveness for a girl named Frances, who needs all the help she can get.

Psalm Twenty-four

1 The earth is the LORD's, and the fullness thereof; the world, and they that dwell therein.

2 For he hath founded it upon the seas, and established it upon the floods.

3 Who shall ascend into the hill of the LORD? or who shall stand in his holy place?

4 He that hath clean hands, and a pure heart; who hath not lifted up his soul unto vanity, nor sworn deceitfully.

5 He shall receive the blessing from the LORD, and righteousness from the God of his salvation.

6 This is the generation of them that seek him, that seek thy face, O Jacob. Selah.

7 Lift up your heads, O ye gates; and be ye lift up, ye everlasting doors; and the King of glory shall come in.

8 Who is this King of glory? The LORD strong and mighty, the LORD mighty in battle.

9 Lift up your heads, O ye gates; even lift them up, ye everlasting doors; and the King of glory shall come in.

10 Who is this King of glory? The LORD of hosts, he is the King of glory. Selah.

15

I can't wait for school tomorrow. Sunday afternoons when Daddy is home are fun. We come home from church, have tuna- or egg-salad sandwiches and potato chips and big glasses of milk. I read the funny papers with Uncle Otts. Daddy reads the newspaper, and then he and Mom work on a project, or Daddy disappears into his little office downstairs, where he edits home movies or organizes slides or reads from the forty-eleven million books he has on the shelves. Drew and I play with our friends.

Late in the afternoon, we pile into the station wagon and go for a drive. We just drive. Nothing's open but gas stations and 7-Elevens. We stop at model homes and walk through them in all the new neighborhoods that are being built around us. Mom and Dad talk about ideas for our house. We get ice cream. Sometimes we go to the Club for dinner, on base. We watch *Walt Disney's Wonderful World of Color* at 7:30, and then I go to bed.

I kneel beside the bed and say my prayers — always the very same prayer, always starting with "God bless Mommy and Daddy" and then listing everybody in our family including Miss Mattie, Jack, our dead dogs Flops and Pea Toe, always in the same order, and always ending with "and help me be a good girl, amen."

Mom listens to my prayers, and then she tucks me in. She kisses me on the forehead. It's nice. Then she goes to Drew's room downstairs and does the same thing, and I pull my Nancy Drew out of the nightstand and read with my flashlight. Mom comes upstairs in a little while and tells me that's enough — it's an unspoken agreement we have that I can do this — and I turn off the flashlight and lie there in the dark, contemplating the dangers of the world, until Mom and Dad come upstairs and go to bed, because there is no *Tonight Show* on Sunday nights.

But when Daddy's on a trip, like he is now, we don't do these things. Instead, Mom *works like a Trojan*, to use her phrase. She does the jobs that she never does when Daddy's home. She deep cleans. She super scrubs. She stays up until two A.M., ironing. And today, she spends the afternoon after church *fixing the lawn*. We are not allowed to help her. That's okay, we don't want to help her. We are all staying very far away from Mom this afternoon.

"No bikes. No woods. No friends," she says. "Stick around home and do something different. No television."

No Uncle Otts, either. "Children aren't allowed in the hospital," Mom declared as we pulled out of the chapel parking lot, as if we all had begged her to go visit. I fantasize about sneaking in. I dearly want to take a look at Uncle Otts and see that he's still there, that he's okay, and tell him I'm sorry. I hope he's not mad at me. Is he hooked up to tubes? Is a machine breathing for him?

I can't face my science fair project. I read Psalm Twenty-four from the Bible I got in the fourth grade and decide it's going to be hard to memorize. I write out the whole thing to help me get started.

I look out my bedroom window toward Chris's house — no car in the driveway. They must be gone somewhere, having fun, like Jo Ellen, who went off with Lannie after church. I go downstairs, set the timer for thirty minutes, and practice the piano with Jack at my feet.

I am always amazed at how long thirty minutes is when I practice my piano. Up and down the scales I go, over and over, louder and louder, and then I practice "Spinning Song." It is too hard for me, but I want so much to play it. Everyone wants to play "Spinning Song." It's in the *John Thompson III Piano Book*, and I am still working on *John Thompson II*. I play "Country Gardens" and another piece that my teacher, Miss Farrell, has assigned me. And then the timer rings, and I am done. Done!

Now I can play whatever I want. So I pull out Miss Mattie's *Cokesbury Hymnal*. It's old, thin, and brown, and I love everything about it. I love the way it smells, the texture of the pages, and the hymns on every page. I start with my favorites, "In the Garden" and "Love Lifted Me," which is almost too hard for me. I don't play any of them well — I start and stop a lot, but I don't care. I sing as I play — I'm a good singer. Soon I move to a new favorite, "Come Thou Fount." I love the words as much as the tune, so I play every verse, and I sing it loud:

> Come, thou Fount of every blessing,
> tune my heart to sing thy grace;
> streams of mercy, never ceasing,
> call for songs of loudest praise.
> Teach me some melodious sonnet,
> sung by flaming tongues above.

> Praise the mount! I'm fixed upon it,
> mount of thy redeeming love.

Melodious sonnets and flaming tongues! I feel great!

Drew flings open his bedroom door (yes, Mr. Perfect has his *door shut!*) and yells, "Clam up! I'm trying to read in here!"

"Can it!" I yell back. "I can't help it if the piano is down here!" It feels good to yell. It feels like we're washing away the bad feelings from last night and the strangeness of today.

"Here, Jack!" calls Drew, and I don't care. The two of them head outside. I watch them run toward the tree house, then I go on to verse two, even louder:

> Here I raise mine Ebenezer;
> hither by thy help I'm come;
> and I hope, by thy good pleasure,
> safely to arrive at home —

Wait a minute! Wait a minute!

I stare at the page. Ebenezer. *Ebenezer!*

Who is Ebenezer? *What* is Ebenezer? Who is writing to Jo Ellen? Now I've got something to do!

I slide off the piano seat just as Mom comes through the front door with Margie and her mother. Margie's mother is holding a casserole in her oven-mitted hands. Mom and Mrs. Gardener go up the stairs, while Margie comes down.

"Hi!" It feels like years since I've seen Margie, and I'm ready to forgive her.

"Shepherd's pie," says Margie, pointing up the stairs. "Mom

thought you could use it. She saw your mother out there working so hard. She says Uncle Otts comes home tomorrow."

I don't want to talk about Uncle Otts. "So does my dad," I say. "Can you stay?"

"I don't know . . . ," says Margie. "I'm supposed to go somewhere. . . ."

"Where?"

Margie changes the subject. "Have you seen Chris Cavas?"

I don't want to talk about that, either. "Have *you* seen Chris Cavas?"

"Of course I have, knucklehead — he lives across the street! My mom took his mom a welcome-back-to-the-neighborhood pie."

Of course. Great. And now he probably won't give me a second thought.

"Well?" says Margie. "What do you think?"

"About what?"

"About Chris!"

I shrug. I have perfected my nonchalant look. "He's okay."

"Okay? When he left, a year ago, he looked like Beaver Cleaver, and now he looks like Dr. Kildare!"

I shake my head. "Nope. Del Shannon." We laugh like old-lady friends, all the scritchiness between us gone. "Listen," I say, surprising myself. "I've got real, live detective work to do right now. Jo Ellen's not home and I want to —"

"Snoop?"

That's all it takes. We are on the case.

16

Mom can't refuse when I ask her in front of Mrs. Gardener. Mrs. Gardener seems relieved to unload Margie and says, "I don't know how you do it, Nadine, with Phil flying all the time. Plus, I'm a nervous wreck with all this nuclear news. Everyone must be on pins and needles at Andrews."

Mom doesn't divulge a scintilla of her feelings. She plasters Mrs. Gardener with a squadron-wife smile and says, "Phil comes home tomorrow — we're looking forward to it," and she guides Mrs. Gardener to the front door. "Thank you again for the shepherd's pie, Martha. So thoughtful of you."

"You're welcome," says Mrs. Gardener with a tiny pout. "Well, I've got to get back to the twins — they're down for a nap." She sashays out the door.

So Margie stays, Mrs. Gardener goes, and Mom goes back to work *fixing the lawn.* "Half an hour, Franny," she tells me, shooting me with a bullet stare.

"Yes, ma'am," I say. I telegraph her, *Don't come back inside for thirty minutes!*

I fill Margie in as we scoot down the hallway to my room. "Remember that letter Jo Ellen got yesterday?"

"Franny, I would need a scorecard to keep up with all that happened at your house yesterday."

"Right. Well, Lannie gave Jo Ellen a letter —"

"Oh, right," says Margie, "I remember —"

"— and Jo Ellen has lots of letters just like this one, and she won't tell me who they're from. She keeps them locked in her hope chest. It's a big secret, and I don't know why."

"Do you have a key?" Margie is nothing if not practical.

"I have my diary key," I say, "and my roller skate key. And . . . there's Mom's luggage key in her suitcase lock."

"Let's start there," Margie says. She's excited, I can hear it in her voice. "If they don't work, I have keys, too."

It's bad enough to sneak into Mom and Dad's walk-in closet. I know Mom can tell if someone has been in her room, and I'm sure she'll notice her suitcase key missing as soon as she steps into the closet again — nothing escapes her eagle eye. So I have to move like a ghost.

My heart beats like a timpani drum. "I'll do it myself," I tell Margie as she begins to follow me. "You watch out my bedroom window for my mom and tell me if she looks like she's going to come inside."

"Hurry," says Margie.

I take a deep breath and twinkle across the carpet in my flip-flops. Into the closet, out of the closet. I hold the key in my tight fist and look behind me to make sure I don't leave footprints. I can't be sure. I quickly walk to Mom and Dad's bedroom window and look for Drew. He's in the tree house, and Jack is sleeping, below him. Good.

I walk into the hallway and signal Margie. "Let's go," I say with a big exhale. I pull my diary key from my pillowcase in my room, and soon we stand in front of Jo Ellen's closed bedroom door.

We continue to stand there.

And stand there.

"Nancy Drew would open the door," says Margie. She says it with an edge of sarcasm to her voice — Margie quit reading Nancy Drew last year. She says she's gone beyond Nancy Drew, but here she stands, at Jo Ellen's door with me, ready for a mystery.

I take Chris Cavas's handkerchief out of my pants pocket and turn the doorknob.

"You don't have to be *that* dramatic," Margie whispers.

"No fingerprints," I whisper back. "This is a top secret operation." It feels good to flaunt Chris's handkerchief without telling Margie whose it is or how I got it. I've got a secret of my own — Nancy Drew would be proud.

I turn the doorknob and we are in.

"Close it?" Margie asks.

I shake my head. "We need to be able to make a quick exit."

Margie and I kneel in front of Jo Ellen's hope chest the way Mary Flood kneels in front of the priest at the front of the Catholic church. I work on the lock gingerly — I don't want to make a mark that Jo Ellen might notice.

My diary key doesn't work.

My skate key is way too big to work.

I telegraph Mom's luggage key to *work* . . . and . . . it does. It works like it was meant to open this lock. I tingle with delight

143

and dread, as I hear the clasp turn and the lock give. Margie whispers, "*Wowww*" . . . and together we push up and open Jo Ellen's cedar hope chest.

There are the saltshakers, the doilies, the pickle pickers, and the monkeypod salad bowls . . . all the trappings for a new life, saved in a holy place, for the wife that Jo Ellen will be some-day, as soon as she finds the picky man to match her picky woman ways.

"Don't touch!" I hiss as Margie reaches a hand toward the embroidered napkins. I don't want anything in here disturbed; it feels like we're rummaging through Jo Ellen's tomb, and for a moment I think I can't do it, I can't pull open the drawer that has the letters in it and let Margie see them — can I?

I can.

The drawer slides silently out of its cedar-lined pocket. There they are, gleaming like a crispy sea of sunshine, like the Sea of Galilee in *King of Kings*, the only movie I've ever gone to see by myself, because no one else wanted to see it this past summer.

"Hurry up!" snaps Margie. I come back to the present.

"Hold your horses!" I say. Now comes the question . . . what do I take? Jo Ellen would surely notice all of them missing. I slip my fingers under the bottom of the pile and inch the bottom letter out of its place. As I tug it, they all come toward me, but I push the rest of the letters back into the drawer and close it.

"Take the top one, too, you nut!" says Margie. "So we know the latest!"

"No! Jo Ellen might notice. I can't!"

"Don't be stupid, Franny!" Margie reaches for the drawer of letters and I push her hand away.

"No! Jo Ellen might keep track of dates or smudges. Nancy Drew would never take the top letter!"

"You're a *nitwit*, Franny!" says Margie, clearly irritated. "Nancy Drew is a nitwit, too."

Margie again reaches for the letters, so I grab the top of the chest to close it — but I lose my grip and the top bangs shut, just missing Margie's prying fingers.

"Franny, you're a moron!"

Hurry! Hurry! I fight the key in the lock, I turn it right and left, left and right, I tug on it like I'm a prizefighter, but it won't come out. I turn it some more, and now I'm frantic — *I've bent it!* — and I try to bend it back just as Margie shoots herself upright like a rocket and shouts, "Drew!"

I accordion to the floor and sit on the letter I have pilfered. It makes a muffled crunching sound. The suitcase key is still in the lock behind me.

"What are you doing?" It's a simple question, asked by a simple boy, and I need to find a simple answer.

"Nothing."

"Jo Ellen doesn't like people in her room."

"I know, Drew. I was putting some . . . napkins . . . in her hope chest. She asked me to."

"I'm helping her," says Margie, not helpfully.

"Oh," says Drew. He stares at me like Mom does when she knows I'm telling a whopper. He scratches his eyebrow. "Mom wants me to tell you your half hour is up."

"Okay," I say. "Margie's just going."

145

"I'll let Mom know," says Drew, and he flaps down the hall-way in bare feet.

I slip the letter out from under my bottom. I've squashed it — anybody with half a brain could tell it's been sat on.

"We've got to read it!" Margie says.

"You've got to go home," I say as I scramble to my feet.

Margie groans. "How can you leave me hanging like this?"

"I'll read it and let you know what it says," I tell her. "Hurry — you've got to go!"

"Oh-no-you-don't!" Margie grabs the letter from my hand, races to my room, jumps on my bed, and rolls across my pink bedspread.

"Give it back!" I try to snatch the letter from her hand, but Margie stuffs it under her shirt and won't give it to me. "Stop it, Margie!"

"*Stop it, Margie!*" she mocks me and laughs.

And then, out of nowhere, Mom appears.

"Frances!" Mom's short, but she sounds as big as Godzilla, standing in the frame of my bedroom door.

I stand as straight as an arrow — I have perfect posture for once, and it occurs to me, wildly, to hope Mom notices this. Margie scrambles to sit up on the side of my bed. The letter is crumpled beyond all recognition, but Mom doesn't notice. She's too busy noticing that I haven't sent Margie out the door.

"Yes, ma'am!" I say. And Margie crackles right out of my bed-room *with Jo Ellen's letter plastered against her left side* so Mom can't see it.

"See ya, Franny!" she says. "Bye, Mrs. Chapman! I've got company coming over, gotta run!"

The Long Stare of Mom is upon me.

"Sorry," I say. My shoulders sag.

"*Young lady,*" Mom starts, and I hear a lecture coming on. But then she falters. She's *bone-tired,* to use Mom's words. Her eyes have dark circles under them, her shoulders sag, and she looks more like Miss Mattie than Mom. "Wash up and come help me with supper" is all she says.

My mind whirls like an out of control blender. *When does Jo Ellen come home? When can I get back into her room without being noticed and get that key out of the lock? How can I return it to Mom's suitcase?* And, the biggest whirl of all: *What do I do about the fact that my sister's letter — my sister's secret — is now in Margie's hands?*

Poor posture is the cause of more ills than a cold. Learn to balance a book on your head, and glide, girls, glide!

— *Your Charming Self* by Melody Morris

147

17

We're having supper number three. Swanson TV Dinners. Turkey, dressing, peas, sweet potatoes. I loosen the foil and put three dinners in the pink oven in the pink kitchen. Twenty-five minutes at 425 degrees.

Sometimes we eat TV dinners on TV trays on Sunday nights and watch TV, but it's too early for Disney, so we eat at the kitchen table, just me and Mom and Drew. No Daddy, no Jo Ellen, no Uncle Otts. It's odd to have just the three of us, but tomorrow we will all be home, and Mom will cook meat loaf because it will be Monday, and things will be back to . . . well, normal.

"Did your sister say where she was going this afternoon?" asks Mom.

"No, ma'am," Drew and I chorus.

Mom puts her fork on her napkin and walks down the hallway. I crane my neck to see her and almost fall out of my chair. She walks into Jo Ellen's room, comes out, and I try not to panic. Drew and I look at each other. He shrugs.

I get my bath first so I can sneak into Jo Ellen's room while Drew is getting his bath, but Mom is upstairs, on the phone, calling people I don't know, so there's no way not to be seen.

* * *

We watch *Walt Disney's Wonderful World of Color* in the family room downstairs. It always starts with Tinker Bell and the castle and all that color that I never see because our television is only in black and white. Uncle Otts's bedroom door has been closed since he left, but I can still smell his Old Spice as I walk past it. I wonder what he will look like when we see him again, if he'll remember me dousing him with water, if he'll remember me at all.

I excuse myself to go to the bathroom twice. Each time I flush and then dash to Jo Ellen's room to give the key a tug.

The third time Mom gives me the evil eye and says, "Is there something wrong with the bathroom down here, Franny?" and I know I've got to stop. Jack happily chews on a fake dog bone and makes slobbery noises that Mom hates while we watch our show. Mom doesn't really watch; she stands at the ironing board, attacking the sheets with the iron.

At the end of the program, Mom sends us to bed. Jack always sleeps in Drew's room and I consider that unfair, but now is not the time to bring it up yet again. I trudge upstairs to prayers, reading, and lights-out when Mom shows up, and then I am in the dark again, stewing about how to get that key out of Jo Ellen's hope chest and back into Mom's suitcase before she notices it's missing, which will be any minute.

I am sick to my stomach about Jo Ellen's letter, and sicker still that Margie would just take it and not bring it back or call or say a word about it. I'll have to deal with that tomorrow when we walk to school — maybe I can go to her house a few minutes early. That's what I'll do. I'll just eat breakfast, grab my satchel, and run over ahead of Drew.

With that settled, I turn my attention to the letter I'm composing to Chairman Khrushchev.

Dear Chairman Khrushchev,

Are you crazy?

This won't do.

I try to concentrate, but Mom is back on the phone in the kitchen with Lannie's mother and then with someone else. She's murmuring in the kitchen, she's anxious, she's angry, she's . . . I don't know what she is.

I have to pee, but I lie in the dark, motionless, trying to hear what Mom's saying. I tiptoe to my open door, plaster myself against my desk, and peek down the lighted hallway. Jo Ellen's bedroom is to the right. Mom and Dad's is to the left.

Mom starts vacuuming the living room with a vengeance — the same living room Jo Ellen vacuumed on Friday — banging the Hoover on the floor when it coughs, moving furniture, slapping the stew out of the couch, and then suddenly there's a *pop!* and a shriek from Mom as the lights go out in the living room and the acrid smell of smoke hits my nose.

I race down the hallway. *Mommy!*

The streetlight illuminates Mom, who is sitting in the dark on the floor by the electrical outlet, holding her left hand with her right hand. The vacuum cleaner plug is beside her. "I'm fine, Franny," she says, her voice shaking. "*Fine*. It's just a shock." Mom's shoulders are shaking, too. "The circuit overloaded," she says, talking in quick time. "There's a short in the cord, or it isn't grounded, or . . ." She searches for another possibility, and as she does, her face begins to crumble — *my mother's face crumbles* — and she starts to cry.

I have never seen my mother cry. Never.

I don't know what to do.

"Go to bed, Franny," my mother says. She wipes at her nose and stands up. "Go to bed."

But I don't go to bed. I rush to my mother and hug her fiercely. I just have to do that. And she hugs me back.

"Everything's going to be fine," she says. "Go to bed, honey."

My heart melts. I tilt my face up to see my mother.

She smiles at me. Her eyelashes are coated with tears. She takes a gentle hand and pushes my unruly hair out of my face. And even with all that's wrong in my life right now, for a sudden, surprising second, I'm convinced that all's right with the world.

18

"So I hear you're having a Halloween party on Saturday night," says Margie as she opens her front door on Monday morning. "And you're inviting boys! Are you kidding? A boy-girl party?" Her four-year-old twin sisters are clinging to her dress, hugging her good-bye.

"Where's Jo Ellen's letter?" Yesterday, I was upset. Today, I am angry.

I was afraid to fall asleep last night, and every time I did, I jerked awake, dreaming the phone was ringing, dreaming Jo Ellen had come home and found Mom's suitcase key in the lock of her cedar chest. But Jo Ellen never came home. And this morning, when I checked, *there was no key in the lock.* Mom said nothing to me at breakfast, acted like it had never happened, was Mom in every way, including ordering me to go back and change clothes because my jumper was too wrinkled and she wouldn't have me looking like a hooligan at school. She doesn't seem the least bit worried about Jo Ellen now. Everything must be resolved, but I'm afraid to ask, so I don't.

"Bye, Mom!" Margie shouts to her mother.

"Bye, Margie!" sing the twins.

As we start down her driveway together, Margie asks, "Are you in trouble?" Drew catches up with us, leaning to the left under the weight of his satchel, so I don't answer. Both Margie and I gaze at Chris Cavas's house as we walk past. No Chris. His mother must have taken him and his brother, Bobby, to school early to register. And I won't get to see him after school, because Mom is picking me up to go get Daddy at Andrews. I don't know how Uncle Otts is getting home. Or Jo Ellen. Nobody tells me anything.

I decide to make conversation. "Have you got *Our Friend the Atom* with you, Drew?"

"Yep!" says Drew. "Did you know that carbon atoms have six electrons and uranium atoms have ninety-two?"

"No, I didn't know that."

"Did you know that a tiny piece of radium could keep a thimbleful of water boiling for centuries?"

"No, I didn't know that, either."

"Fascinating," says Margie in her best mocking voice. "You're a real egghead, Drew."

"Leave him alone!" I tell her.

"See ya, Franny," says Drew, who hates confrontation. He stumbles ahead to walk with Larry Stoffle.

"Excuse me!" says Margie. "You know, Franny, I thought I knew you better."

I practically grab Margie with my bare hands. "Where's Jo Ellen's letter?"

"Keep your pants on," Margie says in a cool voice. "I've got it right here." She pats her satchel.

"Give it to me."

153

"Now?"

"Now."

"What's the matter with you?" Margie asks. But she knows. "I'll give it to you at first recess."

"Why can't you give it to me now?"

"It's stuck in my satchel, inside the clip in my binder and under my homework — that's the way I got it out of the house without my mom seeing it. I'd have to unpack my whole satchel, right here on the street."

"I want it as soon as we get to school," I snap.

"Well, look who's being Miss Priss!"

"Did you read it?"

"Of course I read it." She doesn't even act embarrassed.

"It's none of your business!" I spurt.

"You thought it was my business yesterday," Margie says. "Do you want me to tell you what's in it? It's *very* interesting! I think you'd be surprised."

I won't give her the satisfaction of telling me what's in it.

"Why are you so mad at me?"

"I'm not mad," Margie says with more than a whiff of impatience. "Do you like my new shoes?"

Margie's new shoes are so shiny they hurt my eyes to look at them. I don't answer her. We turn the corner onto Napoli Drive. It's a chilly morning. Leaves dance around us as they fall from the trees. The air smells like wood smoke and leaves burning.

"Gale Hoffman is having a Halloween party at her house on Saturday night," Margie says. "I hope it doesn't interfere with *yours*."

I have nothing to say to that, nothing. I know it will be a boy-girl party. I know I won't be invited. I know Chris will be. And I know, even if I were invited, Mom would never let me go.

"Who told you I was having a Halloween party?" I ask as if I didn't know.

"Chris Cavas," breezes Margie. She actually sighs it. "Yesterday. He came over with his mom."

Stick a knife in my chest, why don't you?

Then Margie says, "Hey, Judy! Wait up!" and she runs ahead to catch up with Judy James. Judy James, who is about as interesting as a piece of shirt cardboard. Judy James, who is tone-deaf. Judy James, who doesn't even *read*.

I actually come to a complete halt right in the middle of Napoli Drive. I telegraph Margie: *Trip over your own two feet and go splat! Right here on the street!* But of course she doesn't. She cozies up to a surprised Judy James and the two of them waltz off to school together, chatting up a storm.

There they go, through the little stand of oak trees and onto the playground, and here I stand, all alone on Napoli Drive on Monday morning, October 22, 1962, without my best friend, and without Jo Ellen's letter.

By the time I've hung up my coat in the cloakroom and emptied my satchel into my desk, the bell rings, and I know I won't see Margie again until lunch and recess.

I slump into my chair and bury my head in my arms. It feels like a million years since I've last been in school. Then I have a thought — maybe Chris will be in my class! I sit up and see that Mrs. Rodriguez has already written our homework on the board:

155

Extra Credit:
Watch President Kennedy's address on television
this evening at 7 p.m.

I pull out my homework assignment pad and write this down.
I am an extra-credit fanatic. We are learning how to take notes
in fifth grade, and since Mrs. Rodriguez checks our assignment
books each Friday, I write my extra-credit assignment using my
best note-taking skills:

watch kennedy tv 7 p.m. 10-22-62

Then I erase it. I can do better than that:

JFK 7 p.m. tonight

I would stick with that, but it might look like I think President
Kennedy is coming over to my house at seven P.M., so I erase
tonight and add *TV* and I am done. *Good job, Franny.*

"Good morning, class," says Mrs. Rodriguez. She stands at
her desk, which is strewn with Monday morning presents: three
apples, a paper plate with brownies, a misshapen pinecone, and
a Dixie cup full of acorns. Lots of notes, too, which she always
opens and reads while the gifter is standing by her desk.

I used to bring my teachers presents, but I stopped. My favorite thing to bring — because no one could top it — was a rose
from Mom's garden. Mom would clip it and wrap the stem in wet
paper towels and then foil so the thorns wouldn't scratch me.
What I learned, though, was that presents didn't change anything. Not that I used them as bribes, but still, I was disappointed

when, after months of bringing Miss Bourdon roses in third grade, I still got a *G* instead of a *VG* in arithmetic. Once I even got an *NI* — Needs Improvement. Why?

"Because you need improvement," Jo Ellen had said. And then she worked with me on decimals for two weeks straight after school. I complained the whole time.

But now, I would do two weeks of nothing but decimals to know where Jo Ellen is. I'm sure the answer is in the letter in Margie's satchel.

Recess. I am living for recess.

FIRST, JACK: He was a sickly child, born upstairs in the master bedroom of his family's home. After his birth, his mother, Rose Kennedy, wrote on a note card:

> John Fitzgerald Kennedy
> Born Brookline, Mass. (83 Beals Street)
> May 29, 1917.

Rose kept note cards on each of her nine children so she could keep track of their shoe sizes and important milestones. Over the years, on her second child John Kennedy's card, she wrote:

> measles
> whooping cough
> chicken pox
> scarlet fever
> jaundice
> stitches

(This last after a bicycle collision with his elder brother, Joe. Joe was not hurt. Jack needed twenty-eight stitches.)

Jack (that was John's nickname) loved sports but was often bruised and hurt on the playing field because he was not bulky enough to compete.

"His smile was bigger than the rest of him," said a cousin.

Still, he was a good athlete and a fine sailor. All the Kennedys loved sailing and touch football. They were a large, loyal, chaotic, and wealthy family. Jack's father, Joe, challenged his children to be political and competitive, the best at everything they tried. His mother urged them toward a life of public service. The Kennedys were Catholics, and second-born John would become a War Hero at the end of World War II, a Senator from Massachusetts, and then the first Catholic President of the United States.

NEXT, JACKIE: Jacqueline Lee Bouvier was born into a wealthy Catholic family in Southampton, New York, on July 28, 1929. She had a younger sister, Caroline Lee, and then more brothers and sisters after her parents divorced and remarried.

When Jackie was a year old, her mother put her on her first horse. By the time she was eleven, Jackie was winning national championships.

She loved to read so much that she would sneak out of bed when she was supposed to be napping and make herself comfortable at the window seat with her white rabbit or her Scottish terrier, Hootchie. There she would read *The Jungle Book* or *Robin Hood* until nap time was over. Then she would scoot back to bed, after dusting off her feet so her nanny would not know that she had sneaked out.

Jack and Jackie were groomed — by their families, their Church, and their private schools — for great possibilities. They stepped into those possibilities with great smarts, great wealth, and the wide smiles of the beautiful people. And they *were* beautiful.

John Kennedy and Jacqueline Bouvier met at a swanky dinner party. Kennedy was running for the U.S. Senate. After he won the election, he proposed to Jackie, and they were married in 1953. Just seven years later, on November 4, 1960, John Kennedy was elected president. He was forty-three years old. His First Lady, Jacqueline Bouvier Kennedy, was just thirty-one.

THEN CAME THE SIXTIES:

"Let the word go forth . . . that the torch has been passed to a new generation of Americans."

Oh, yes, it had. Had it ever.

Not that we didn't like Ike and Mamie Eisenhower, but compared to the Kennedys, the Eisenhowers were bland. Old-fashioned. Tired. They represented the generation just before World War II that was graying and getting older by the minute.

Jack and Jackie were full of **pizzazz**. They moved their two small children, Caroline and John-John, into the White House with them, and soon there was a pony on the White House lawn, and a tree house, and a swimming pool, and two children jumping in the Oval Office, playing with their father, while a photographer from *Life* magazine took picture after picture for all of America to see.

Jackie refurbished the shabby-looking old White

House, then took Americans on a television tour in 1962. Women in America tried to dress like she did, wear their hair like she did, and move as gracefully as she did.

Jack took Jackie with him to Paris, where she wowed the French — she even spoke their language — and television captured it all. America swooned with delight whenever the Kennedys were caught on camera. Americans were inspired and came alive with a new spirit of swelling pride and youthful vigor.

> *"And so, my fellow Americans,*
> *ask not what your country can do for you,*
> *ask what you can do for your country."*

Such excitement!
Such charisma!
Such pageantry!
It was a time of blissful ignorance.
But not all was golden under the surface of the glimmering new America.

President Kennedy was not always well. After an injury as a young man and two back surgeries, he would never be free from back pain again. He moved his special rocking chair into the Oval Office, along with a doctor who would help him with special medicines for his pain. He often wore a back brace and needed long periods of rest after sitting or standing for too long.

And America had problems. Right off the bat, President Kennedy had to deal with a problem he inherited from President Eisenhower: the Bay of Pigs invasion.

It did not go well for Kennedy that we fumbled in Cuba and that hundreds of Cuban exiles were killed or captured.

But Kennedy learned from his mistakes. He became a better president with each passing crisis, each passing year.

He would not send U.S. troops to Cuba after the Bay of Pigs debacle. He would not start a war in Germany when the Soviets erected the Berlin Wall in 1961, and he did not authorize bombs to be dropped on Cuba or the Soviet Union during the Cuban Missile Crisis in 1962.

He did send more military advisors, but he would not approve the sending of American combat troops, to a little country in Southeast Asia called Vietnam.

He was slow to appreciate the suffering of black Americans and slower to understand that they could not claim the right to full citizenship in their own country without his help. But he did, finally, begin that work, too.

"We are confronted primarily with a moral issue. It is as old as the scriptures and as clear as the American Constitution."

He made hard decisions, and he showed the world that America could be a country of dignity and respect and endless possibility, that it could remember its best self and remake itself and that Americans could be proud to be Americans.

In December 1960, just weeks after Kennedy's election as the thirty-fifth president of the United States, the musical *Camelot* opened on Broadway. It was a retelling of the legend of King Arthur and the Knights of the Round Table, a tale of castles and kings, myths and legends, and above all, heroes, honor, and courage.

President Kennedy loved *Camelot*. He often listened to the music at bedtime in the White House. He memorized all the songs. He dreamed of the possibilities of peace.

Then, in November 1963, John Fitzgerald Kennedy was killed by an assassin's bullet while he rode next to Jackie in a motorcade through Dallas, Texas.

He had served as president for a little less than three glittering years. He had served for a thousand days.

America mourned the death of dreams and possibilities. In their place, Americans created a hero and a myth.

A week after her husband was killed, Mrs. Kennedy spoke to her friend, the writer Theodore White. She told him how much John Kennedy had loved the idea of Camelot, and she recited his favorite passage from the play:

> *Don't let it be forgot*
> *That once there was a spot,*
> *For one brief, shining moment*
> *That was known as Camelot.*

The rest is history.

"All this will not be finished in the first hundred days. Nor will it be finished in the first thousand days, nor in the life of this Administration, nor even perhaps in our lifetime on this planet. But let us begin."

19

Being in school is like living on another planet. A good planet full of information that you can't wait to find out about because you need it to survive and grow up and know how the world works.

School is a planet full of rules and schedules and organization, and I like that. Everything runs like clockwork at school and I know just when to expect what. The rules are the same for everybody, and I like it like that, too.

Rules that must be obeyed:

1. Walk in silence down the closed-in hallways, and stay to the right, single file.

2. No talking in the lunchroom during lunch. After lunch, scream all you want at recess. Oh, and at lunch, eat civilly. Eat all your lunch, even if it is a liverwurst sandwich (which I like, but Margie says is for nincompoops).

3. Never talk back to a teacher. Teachers are like God. Actually, teachers are God's boss.

Do whatever any teacher says. Behave yourself — mind your manners. Never, under any circumstances, get sent to the principal's office or have a note sent home about your behavior or, heavens to Murgatroyd, give your teacher a reason to Call Your Parents. That's like the end of the world.

4. Raise your hand if you want to speak in class. Wait until you are called on to speak. If your name is Franny and your teacher is Mrs. Rodriguez, expect to be skipped over three times during social studies because you are invisible.

That's about it.

I pride myself on being a good rule-follower at school. Next year I'm going to be a safety patrol.

Barely have I put my assignment book away when Chris Cavas walks through the door of my classroom. He wears a plaid shirt and a wide smile. His jacket is half-zipped. His shoes are Converse high-tops. Every kid in class (except me; I've already had my moment of delight) is all over him, slugging him in the arm, clapping him on the back — it's Chris!

"Settle down, boys and girls," says Mrs. Rodriguez, as the bell rings and it's time for the Pledge. Mrs. Rodriguez starts sniffling at "the United States of America, and to the Republic for which it stands." Sniffling! It's so unlike her. But by the time we get to "with liberty and justice for all," she is back in command and belting it out.

Then it's time for the Lord's Prayer, during which Mrs. Rodriguez remains firmly resolute, her voice mingling strongly with ours — all except for Chris Cavas, who I am watching as he stands next to Mrs. Rodriguez during the Lord's Prayer, and who *does not say the Lord's Prayer.*

Mrs. Rodriguez pretends not to notice this and assigns Chris the only empty desk, which is next to me and up one, so that he's sitting in the front row. It doesn't escape me that this is a reverse position of the way our houses sit on Coolridge Drive.

Glee! I can just sit here and stare at the back of Chris Cavas's head all day.

Which is what I do. I mesmerize myself into not thinking about the key, the letter, how weird Margie has become, where Jo Ellen is, how Uncle Otts is, and even what I'm going to be for Halloween. I completely miss my name being called during spelling, and it's not until Jimmy Epps pokes me in the back with his pencil that I wake up.

"Ma'am?" I say, realizing too late that Mrs. Rodriguez is talking to me.

"Where have you been, Franny?" she asks.

Kids laugh and I'm sure I turn as red as a fire truck.

Say something, Franny.

"*I* before *e* except after *c*," I say.

It's the dunce-iest answer ever, and even Chris laughs.

"May I be excused?" I ask in a rush.

Mrs. Rodriguez nods and I leave class, my ears burning with embarrassment. I have to leap across the whole room since my desk is by the window. I'm sure I set an Olympic record for the fifty-yard dash across the classroom, but I am out of there and into the closed-up hallway, where it is dark and cool and safe.

Until, that is, I see Margie walking into the girls' bathroom.

She is carrying Jo Ellen's letter.

"Hey!" I push the door open just as it closes behind Margie.

She turns around, startled, takes a step backward, and bumps up against the sinks.

I don't know why we're so mad at each other — we've been best friends since I moved in next door two years ago. That's what I want to say. But that's not what I say. I say, "Give me that letter." I sound like the Big Bad Wolf.

Margie gives me the kind of look that the Wicked Witch of the West gave Dorothy and says, "Gosh, Franny, get *hold* of yourself! It's almost first recess."

And you know what I do? I *push* her. I do. I can't help it. I'm just so *angry*.

She pushes me back with both hands. Jo Ellen's letter crinkles against my shoulder.

Now I'm *mad*. I *push* Margie again, harder. She stumbles against the sink, drops the letter, and pushes me back so hard my headband falls off.

"Stop it!" I yell. My voice echoes off the walls and sounds hollow. I push Margie as hard as I can. Her head knocks against the mirror.

"*You* stop it!" she yells back. But she doesn't push me again. She puts her hand up to her head and holds it.

I grab Jo Ellen's letter from the floor and scream into Margie's face:

"I hate you!"

"I hate you, too!"

The room vibrates with anger. We stare into each other's faces, at a standstill. I think I might explode.

And that's when Mrs. Rodriguez and Mrs. Scharr burst through the bathroom door.

"Franny!" says Mrs. Rodriguez.

"What's going on in here?" asks Mrs. Scharr.

"She started it!" yells Margie. Her voice has a ragged edge to it and her perfect hair is wild.

"Franny?" asks Mrs. Rodriguez.

"*She* started it!" I shout.

Mrs. Rodriguez picks up my headband and hands it to me. That's when we hear a flush and a click. The door to the farthest bathroom stall opens, and out steps . . . Gale Hoffman.

Let me sink right into the floor. It's bad enough to be caught fighting. Now there's a witness. Someone to tell everyone at recess. Suddenly I know why Margie has Jo Ellen's letter in the bathroom. *She came to show it to Gale.*

I hate her with all my might.

"What happened here?" asks Mrs. Scharr.

"Nothing," I answer immediately.

"Franny pushed me," Margie says.

"Is that true, Franny?" asks Mrs. Rodriguez.

I don't answer.

"Margie?" Mrs. Rodriguez peers at her.

Margie doesn't answer.

"Gale?" says Mrs. Scharr. "Help us out here."

Gale is washing her hands at the farthest sink. She turns off the water, yanks a paper towel from the holder, and says in a matter-of-fact voice, "Franny pushed Margie first."

What was she doing? Peeking through the cracks in the stall?

Margie does an instant recovery and smirks at me.

I will hate her forever.

"What's this about?" Mrs. Scharr asks.

No one answers.

"What's in your hand, Franny?" Mrs. Rodriguez chimes in.

"It's *mine*," I say, a hitch in my throat. "It's *private*." I telegraph Mrs. Rodriguez, *Please don't take it from me, please don't take it from me.* And, wonder of wonders, she doesn't. She and Mrs. Scharr exchange a look I can't decipher.

"Both of you to the office," says Mrs. Scharr.

I have never been to the office.

I have violated rule number 3. I start to cry. Here comes the end of the world.

20

Mrs. Scharr makes Margie see the principal. Margie marches into Mr. Mitchell's office with her chin jutting toward the ceiling, like she owns the place. At the last second, she turns and gives me a look that says, *you're gonna get it,* and I burst into sobs. Mrs. Rodriguez makes me see the nurse, Miss Gresham, because I can't stop crying — my face is completely wet with tears. While Miss Gresham is looking for the box of tissues, I stuff Jo Ellen's letter into my underpants and sit on it. It hardly crinkles anymore, it has been squashed so often.

I'm still sniffling when Miss Gresham ushers me next door into Mr. Mitchell's office, where Margie *sticks out her tongue at me.* Of course no one else sees her do it. I sit in the chair next to Margie's — we are both in front of Mr. Mitchell's desk — and I set my jaw. I am determined not to cry another second. I know Margie will be mean, and I am determined to tell my side of the story. So I go over it in my head.

Well, you see, Mr. Mitchell, I stole a letter from my sister's hope chest, and Margie took it from me and wouldn't give it back, and she's been taunting me about it — in fact, if I'm honest, she's been taunting me for weeks now and hanging out with Gale

Hoffman, and she doesn't want to spend the night anymore, she doesn't invite me over anymore, and she read my sister's letter and is going to tell everybody about it if she hasn't already, and I had to get it back — I don't even know what's in it — so no one would notice it's missing, especially not Jo Ellen (who has gone missing) or my mother. I'm a thief and a liar and I'm now friend-less, too, but I don't want anyone to know these things about me and . . .

Who am I kidding? I can't tell the truth. I'm scared to death — in fact, I feel queasy and sick and have a hitch in my side from crying so much. And I don't even have a good lie to get me out of this predicament.

"All right, girls," says Mr. Mitchell. He rests his elbows on the edge of his desk and clasps his hands together. He looks very powerful, like he could hand out death sentences if he wanted to. "You were fighting in the girls' bathroom. Is that correct?"

"Yessir," says Margie. She stares at her shoes.

"Yessir," I mumble. My breakfast burps into my throat, and I swallow it back down. My chest hurts.

"What this about?" asks Mr. Mitchell.

Neither of us speaks.

"Franny? Can you tell me what happened?" Mr. Mitchell's voice is deep and no-nonsense, and I realize I'm not about to tell him what happened.

"No, sir, I can't." Is there a punishment for saying that? My shoulders tingle and my head swims.

"Margie?" asks Mr. Mitchell. I feel the edges of Jo Ellen's let-ter poking my backside, and I fidget. My nose is stuffed up from all the crying I've done, and my stomach hurts. I can't sit here much longer. If Margie tells the truth, I'll faint. If I don't faint for real, I'll fake faint. That'll change things. I slump in my chair, to get ready.

But Margie doesn't tell. She says, "We had a disagreement. We used to be really good friends, but we've been having . . . an argument. I'm sorry, Mr. Mitchell. It won't happen again." She sounds very grown up and composed, although I can hear the shake in her voice. And I hear her, clear as day. Her words sting like a rope burn. We are no longer friends.

Mr. Mitchell looks at me, so I speak in a rush. "Yes, sir. That's right. It won't happen again, sir, I promise. I'm so sorry." I'm definitely swimmy-headed . . . maybe I've talked myself into fainting after all. That won't do. I hold on to the seat of my chair with both hands and push myself up straight.

Mr. Mitchell sighs and unclasps his hands. He picks up a pen and begins to write something on a piece of paper in a folder. I swallow and take a deep breath. My stomach rumbles up into my throat.

The bell rings — time for fifth-grade recess. Mr. Mitchell looks at his watch and sighs again. He puts his pen down and looks straight at me and Margie. "I usually send notes home to parents about aberrant school behavior, but you two have never been in trouble in school, you know the rules, you say you've been friends, and I think we'd all be better served if you spent some time talking this through during recess. What do you say?"

"Yes, sir!" says Margie in a bright voice.

And what do I say? "No, sir, I can't."

"Really, Franny?" asks Mr. Mitchell. "Why not?"

"I think I might be sick." I manage to croak it out around the acid taste in my mouth. I hate to throw up — I'll do anything to avoid it, but there is no avoiding this. I can feel my breakfast coming up and up, and I retch, right then and right there, on the floor of the principal's office.

"Miss Gresham!" shouts Mr. Mitchell. He's up like a shot and so is Margie, and I think I might really faint, but I don't. Before I know it, I'm next door in the nurse's office and my mother is being called to come get me.

"I feel fine," I say. "I feel *much* better." Mom will not be happy. "See?" I say, and I try a smile. "I'm fine."

I wipe at my nose with the back of my hand, and Miss Gresham hands me another tissue. I have a colossal headache. But I do feel better than I did before I threw up. "I'm fine," I say again.

Miss Gresham lets me go to my classroom to get my things. Kids are screaming on the playground, having all kinds of fun. Even Margie is out there. I'm sure she's with Gale, telling her everything — telling everybody her version of everything. There's nothing I can do about that. Now, on top of everything else, I will always be the kid who threw up in the principal's office. I stuff Jo Ellen's letter into the bottom of my satchel and hope Mrs. Rodriguez doesn't mention it to my mother.

Nothing says "potential" like a calm demeanor and the ability to accessorize. There is never a good reason for a temper tantrum.

Your Charming Self by Melody Morris

175

21

Mom is in the principal's office when I return, with Mr. Mitchell and Mrs. Rodriguez. Mr. Mitchell waves me in as Mom says crisply, "Thank you, Mr. Mitchell, and thank you all. I'll take Frances with me this afternoon."

I don't know what they've told Mom, but she doesn't pull me by the ear out of school, or shame me in front of everyone. She just says, "Are you feeling better?" and I nod my head. I can't look at Mr. Mitchell.

"Get some rest, Franny," says Mrs. Rodriguez. She pats me on the shoulder and that makes me teary again. Mom puts me in the front seat of our car and hands me a tiny pack of Kleenex tissues. She is wearing a weary look and says noth-ing — nothing — about my morning, and I'm left to wonder what she knows.

We drive in silence, except for my sniffing, and we don't go home. We go the opposite direction on Allentown Road, toward Andrews Air Force Base.

"How is your stomach, Franny?" asks Mom. "Do you feel like eating something?"

"I'm okay now," I say. "I was just upset."

"What were you upset about?" There's a hint of steeliness

176

in Mom's voice, but there's softness as well — she really wants to know.

"Well . . ." I take a breath and watch the sidewalk speed by. And it comes to me what's really upsetting me, so I say it. "Margie . . . Margie doesn't like me anymore." My eyes fill with tears, but I don't start sobbing again.

"Hmmmm . . ." says Mom. "What happened?"

"Oh, I don't know," I say. I feel one fat tear making its way down my cheek. "It's complicated. I don't know where to begin."

Mom nods her head, as if she understands completely. I wait for her to say more or to ask me more, but she doesn't. I want her to tell me I'm wrong, that Margie will come around, that it will all be okay, but she doesn't. There are lots of things I want her to tell me.

"Mom?" I hiccup and blow my nose.

Mom drives through the green light at Pyles Lumber Company and past Bells Methodist Church. She drives with one hand while she lights a cigarette.

"Yes?"

I wait for her to blow out that thin stream of smoke, which she does.

"Where is Jo Ellen?"

Mom rolls her window down a few inches and blows the rest of her cigarette smoke toward the opening. "Jo Ellen will be home soon, Franny," she says, the steeliness strong in her voice now. The October chill sneaks into the car and surrounds us.

I telegraph Mom, *What does that mean, "Jo Ellen will be home soon?"* but I don't ask.

Mom sighs. "Life turns on a dime, Franny." She flicks the ash off

177

her cigarette and says it again. "Life turns on a dime. And Miss Margie Gardener is getting too big for her britches. Mark my words."

Well! I feel like I hit the jackpot in some way I don't understand. Mom makes the wide right turn onto the air base. We get saluted by the same uniformed corporal, and then we swing right, drive past the chapel, and park in the Malcolm Grow Hospital parking lot.

"Are we picking up Uncle Otts?"

"Yes, we are," Mom says. "Wait here." And just like that, she struts off in her good shoes toward the hospital's double doors.

I stuff my used tissues into the little trash holder between the seats and look out my window. The trees are almost bare now. Two jets roar overhead, leaving thin streams of white in their wake. It's warm inside the car. The sun beams over everything, toasting me in a polite and comforting way. I lean my head against the car window. Just as I nod off to sleep, Mom opens the driver's side door, plops herself inside, and drives us to the front doors of the hospital, where, sitting in a wheelchair, looking like a shell of himself, is the old man I almost killed. My stomach does a flip-flop.

I roll down my window.

"Franny, give the front seat to your uncle," orders my mother.

"I ain't sittin' in no front seat," says my uncle. "I never sit in the front seat, and you know it, Nadine. It's not safe." My heart leaps — he sounds the same as ever.

Mom rolls her eyes. "Sit in the back with him," she tells me.

Two men dressed all in white help Uncle Otts out of his wheelchair and into the car.

"I can do it!" he protests. *I kin do it.* But they help him anyway. I climb in on the other side.

And now we sit together, side by side, the sunshine tripping through the empty tree branches and flashing in and out of our car while Mom drives us, like a taxi driver, down Allentown Road and to the McDonald's. McDonald's! I have never had McDonald's for lunch. But I find no pleasure in it today.

"Wait here," says Mom. "Both of you." An eternity stretches in front of me as I sit next to Uncle Otts and steal sidelong glances at him. His pants are baggy and he smells like antiseptic soap. His medals aren't pinned to his sweater, and I hope someone knows he went to the hospital with medals and came back without them.

I telegraph him like a crazy person: *Are you mad at me? Do you remember what I did? What happened in the hospital? How was the observation? Are you all right? Will you ever forgive me?*

My eyes well with tears again and I lick my lips to get hold of myself. Then Uncle Otts opens his mouth and says, "I hope she brings me a fish sandwich."

It makes me laugh, I can't help it. And as I do, Uncle Otts takes his long bony hand, puts it on top of my short, smooth one, and squeezes it.

I squeeze back.

Ten minutes later we are sitting together in the kitchen, eating hamburgers and French fries and washing them down with glasses of cold milk while Mom puts Mrs. Gardener's shepherd's pie in the oven, and Jack sits on the stairs, his snout over the top step, watching us.

Lunch has never tasted so good.

22

I am not sure, but I think I am babysitting Uncle Otts. I have never babysat anybody, not even Drew, and certainly not an old person.

"Look out for each other," says Mom. "I am picking up Drew, then your father, and coming straight home. The casserole is on warm in the oven and it will be ready when we get home. I'll make pear salad to go with it. Franny, set the table. We'll eat in the dining room. Arthur, take a nap, please — your doctor's orders. Franny, I'll pick up your homework assignments at school."

"Yes, ma'am," I say, and I brighten. "I already know my extra credit. We're supposed to watch President Kennedy give a speech on television tonight!"

Mom's shoulders stiffen and her mouth makes a tight, straight line. "That's past your bedtime."

"No, it isn't, Mom. It's at seven o'clock, and it's *homework*."

"I'll watch it with her," says Uncle Otts.

"We'll all watch it, I'm sure," says Mom in a grim voice. "Change your clothes, Franny — hang up your dress and put on your play clothes."

"Yes, ma'am."

"Arthur?" Mom says in her did-you-hear-me? voice.

"Yes, ma'am," replies Uncle Otts. No salute and no bravado.

He is snoring within minutes of Mom's departure — I can hear him all the way upstairs. I have the house to myself, which is an event as rare as Jesus walking on water. I have so much to do, I don't know where to start.

The most important thing has to be reading Jo Ellen's letter and putting it back where it belongs. Snooping in Jo Ellen's things was a stupid idea that has caused me nothing but grief.

I change clothes and search high and low for my satchel before I realize *I left it in the car. I left it in the car!*

I am dizzy with fear that Mom will open my satchel and find Jo Ellen's letter. I run all over the house on autopilot. I am through being careful. Jack follows me everywhere with his dog toy in his mouth and his collar jangling a tiny tune.

"Later!" I tell him.

I waltz right into Mom's walk-in closet and see that the key is not in the suitcase. I don't even worry about leaving footprints. I speed to Jo Ellen's room and confirm what I saw this morning, that the key is no longer in the hope chest. And then I do something I've never done before: I open Jo Ellen's dresser drawers. I open her closet. I look for her overnight case. It's gone. So are some of her clothes.

It's clear to me now:

Jo Ellen has run away.

My shoulders prickle with fear — I actually shudder. I need something to do. I run to the kitchen and set the table — how

181

many will be here for dinner? I count five of us with Daddy and without Jo Ellen. *Why would she run away?* I slap the plates on the dining room table, fold the napkins, and jangle the silverware, and I don't care if I wake up Uncle Otts or the whole neighborhood. *Where did she go?*

I run back to Jo Ellen's room. I play her new records — the ones I'm not supposed to touch. The Kingston Trio; Joan Baez; Peter, Paul, and Mary. Then I stumble on "Runaway" with its tiny heart on the label, the heart I drew. I put it on the record player, place the needle at the beginning, and listen to Del Shannon sing:

> Wishin' you were here by me,
> To end this misery

It's so romantic when Del sings it, and so sad when I think of Jo Ellen. I pad to my room with Jack, *shut my door*, and lie across my bed. Jack wags his tail, asking permission to come up on the bed with me. I give it to him, even though Mom doesn't allow it. Jack is shaggy and warm. The shepherd's pie in the oven makes the house smell cozy.

I could read my *Word Wealth Junior*. I could read a Nancy Drew. I could memorize Psalm Twenty-four. I could . . . I could. While thinking about my choices, I fall fast asleep.

The doorbell wakes me up. It takes me a minute to realize it's the middle of the afternoon and I'm asleep in my own bed on a school day. When Jack barks, I run to my bedroom window and look down at the front of the house. I can't see who's at the door, but there's a car in the driveway, a long blue car with tail fins.

The engine is running and a woman is behind the wheel. She's wearing sunglasses and a black scarf.

I take the stairs two at a time, open the front door, and there stands . . . Gale Hoffman.

Knock me over with a feather.

"Hi," she says. Close up, I can see light pink lipstick on her lips and shiny pennies in her penny loafers.

"Hi," I say back. I make sure to shut my mouth.

"I'm sorry if I got you in trouble in the bathroom."

I don't have a response to that.

"My mom got off work early and picked me up from school, and I wanted to bring you this. I gave them out at recess." She hands me an envelope.

What do you say, Franny?

"Thank you."

"I just told the truth, in the bathroom," Gale says.

I lick my lips. "I know."

"I always tell the truth."

I nod my head. "Okay."

"Well . . . see ya," says Gale, and she heads back to her car. She and her mother pull out of the driveway and turn left onto Allentown Road. I watch their car disappear and imagine them walking into an empty house every night, with no father, no brothers, no sisters, no uncles, just the two of them. I am almost jealous.

There is no name on the outside of the envelope. I open it. Inside is an invitation.

You Are Invited!
What: A Halloween Party!

Where: 2435 Avon Court, Westchester Estates
When: Saturday, October 27, 7 P.M. to 9 P.M.
Given By: Gale Hoffman

Special Instructions:
Wear a costume!
Bring your favorite record to dance to!

Please RSVP by Friday, October 26: 555-2388.

23

There is nothing like Daddy coming home from a trip — nothing. He is still wearing his flight suit with the zippers all over it, and his boots and his cap. He is carrying his flight bag, which will have a present for me tucked in it somewhere. When he sees me, he drops his bag, grins like he hasn't seen me for months, and scoops me up in his arms like he used to do when I was little.

"Franny!" He twirls me around twice, right there in the driveway, and laughs. He smells like everything good in this life, all rolled into one person. He can fix anything, Daddy can, and he does. Even Uncle Otts is all smiles, and hugs Daddy like he's a long-lost son. The mood at our house is suddenly lighter.

"Welcome home, Phil," says Uncle Otts as he takes his place at the dinner table.

"Same to you," says Daddy. "How are you feeling, Uncle Otts?"

"I feel good, son. Real good."

"How was everybody's day?" Daddy is obviously making conversation. Mom looks at me. I look at her. I don't mention my fight with Margie, and Mom doesn't bring it up. She doesn't mention my getting sick in Mr. Mitchell's office, either. I telegraph her a *thank-you*.

"You left your satchel in the car, Franny," Mom says. "I put it in your bedroom. There is no other homework except the spelling test on Friday."

"Yes, ma'am." I want to tell everyone that I've been invited to a Halloween party at Gale Hoffman's house, but now is not the time, and I don't want Mom to say no.

"How long is Jo Ellen staying on campus?" Daddy asks this as if it's the easiest thing in the world to ask.

"All week," says Mom. I notice how her mouth tightens, but she still smiles at Daddy. "She's staying with Lannie in her dorm room."

So! Jo Ellen *didn't* run away. I've been frantic for nothing! I decide right here and now that I'm officially angry with Jo Ellen. I'm officially hurt, too. Just wait until I see her again.

"Why is she there?" asks Drew.

Mom sighs. "There are lots of events this week at school, Drew. Lots of late nights. It's better for Jo Ellen not to be on the road so much or so late."

"Oh," says Drew.

Uncle Otts slurps his tea. "I miss that girl."

"Well, I don't!" I blurt. There is a moment of awkward silence, but no one says a word to me as I blow my nose on my napkin. "Sorry," I say. The inside of my nose stings as I stave off more tears.

Daddy, a bewildered look on his face, completely changes the subject. "Drew, I flew with a friend of Wally Schirra's on this trip — how about that? He was my navigator."

"Wow!" Drew splurts out some of his mashed potatoes. "Did he talk about the astronauts? Has he seen a Mercury rocket?"

"He gave me a Sigma 7 patch for you. Got it from Wally himself. He says Schirra's a fine astronaut and that his mission this month, from blastoff to splashdown, was flawless."

"I know!" Drew has studied the entire mission backward and forward in the newspapers with Daddy. "I'm gonna walk on the moon, just like President Kennedy said in his speech."

"Speaking of speeches," says Daddy, draining his tea, "what time is Kennedy speaking tonight?"

"Seven o'clock," I say in a bold voice. I have gathered myself back together. "It's extra credit homework to watch it."

"Is it, now?" says Daddy.

"I don't think it's appropriate for the children," says Mom.

Uncle Otts, who has been properly subdued through the entire meal, bolts upright in his chair. "Of course it's appropriate, Nadine. It's necessary!".

Instinctively, as if doing so will ward off verbal attack, I take a biscuit from the basket and feed part of it to Jack, who has managed to sneak under the table unnoticed.

"Why?" asks Drew.

"This doesn't concern you, Drew," says Mom. She shoves the biscuits at him.

"I'm telling you," says Uncle Otts, "you can shovel me into the hospital and you can call me crazy, but we would be better off if we had a bomb shelter on this property."

"Absolutely not, Arthur," says Mom. "Phil, say something."

"It would take a backhoe to dig a hole that size, Uncle Otts."

"I know that, son. I was just gettin' her started."

"We will not dig another hole in this yard," says Mom. "End of discussion."

"You won't talk like that when those Communists come knocking on your door, no sirree," says Uncle Otts. He pronounces it *Kommanists*. He's shouting. "And you'd better believe they're coming. Ten-nine-eight-boom!"

I am swimmy-headed, and then I realize: I'm holding my breath. I look at the faces around the table. We are frozen in time, in this moment, right here in our house on Coolridge Drive.

Dad clears his throat and Mom stands up. "Hush, Arthur," she commands. "You're scaring the children."

"I'm tellin' the truth," says Uncle Otts.

"I'm not hungry," says Drew. He doesn't look so good.

"Can we talk about this after dinner?" asks Daddy. He sounds perfectly calm. Drew and I lock eyes with each other.

Mom disappears into the kitchen, then returns with the iced tea pitcher. "We don't need to talk about it at all," she says. "I'm sure there are zoning laws, something sensible to prevent this. We will not be turning my yard into a crater, Arthur. You're overreacting."

"The Thornbergs have a bomb shelter," says Drew.

"They're overreacting, too," says Mom. *"Eat."*

Uncle Otts waves his knife in the air. Old Spice wafts all around him. "We're too close to Washington, D.C., not to have a bomb shelter. Where do you think those bombs are going to drop first? Right on the White House! Right on the Capitol! Ground zero! Practically next door!"

Drew puts his forkful of shepherd's pie back on his plate and looks at me. I can't take another bite, either. I almost ask to be excused, but I'm afraid I might miss something important.

"That's crazy talk," says Mom. Her voice is high and strident. She refills Daddy's tea and sits down again.

"Don't you read your *Life* magazine?" Uncle Otts waves a dog-eared copy of *Life* over the butter dish. The cover reads HOW YOU CAN SURVIVE FALLOUT. "Ever since that Bay of Pigs debacle I don't feel safe!" he crows. "Those Communists are out there watching us." He plops another helping of shepherd's pie onto his plate and passes the casserole dish to me.

So of course I have to open my mouth. Truly, I'm trying to be helpful. And I want to know.

"I was reading to Jo Ellen about Cuba in *My Weekly Reader* last week, and she said that Bay of Pigs is us invading Cuba."

"We did no such thing!" says Mom. She gives me the Look of Death and I know to *just shut up*. Drew looks at me, wide-eyed. I shrug, but I can hear my pulse beating in my ears.

"Oh, yes, we did, little lady!" says Uncle Otts. "Bay of Pigs — that was our doing. The U-nited States of America. Don't you read the papers?"

"We were trying to free the Cubans!" Mom says.

Uncle Otts snorts. "That's propaganda! We want Castro out of Cuba. The Russians want him to stay put." He looks at Daddy for confirmation, but Daddy takes a bite of pear salad — he sticks half a pear into his mouth and lets the mayonnaise coat his lips. He blinks and chews and looks at no one.

Uncle Otts drops his voice and speaks in secretive tones. "There's spies among us — everybody knows this. We don't know who we can trust."

Mom shoves her plate away from her and lights a cigarette. "Arthur, I won't have you throwing such ideas into the children's heads!"

Is she kidding? We've heard this stuff all our lives.

189

Mom blows a stream of smoke toward the ceiling and says, in her don't-you-dare-cross-me voice, "I won't have talk like this at my dinner table."

So we eat in silence, those of us who can eat. Forks clack on plates, ice settles in glasses. The furnace kicks on in the basement.

"There's chocolate cake for dessert," says Mom, brighter now, trying to change the subject and the mood. "I bought pumpkins for carving, from the stand on Brinkley Road. Franny, what are you going to be for Halloween?" She sounds so conversational, I consider answering her until Uncle Otts stands up and throws his napkin on his plate.

"Nadine, if we don't build this bomb shelter, we won't be having chocolate cake for dessert or pumpkins on Halloween! We won't even *have* a Halloween."

Drew starts to cry.

Mom rockets to her feet. "That's it! Phil, I told you he wasn't ready!"

Daddy wipes his mouth with his napkin and stands up, too. "Everybody sit!" he orders in his Major Chapman voice. Uncle Otts sits on his *Life*. Mom sits on her napkin. Daddy grabs the arms of his chair and uses them to help him sit down slowly. He looks first at Drew and then me, then at Mom, and lastly at Uncle Otts.

"I will tell you what I know," he says to all of us, "which is that no one really knows what's going on. The worst thing we can do is panic. Uncle Otts, as a civil defense warden — and as a war hero — you know that."

Uncle Otts's face closes down and Daddy continues.

"We're going to stay focused on keeping ourselves ready for anything. We're not going to dwell on what we can't control."

"But—" Uncle Otts begins in that same small voice he used while lying on the front lawn just days ago.

"No buts." Daddy holds his hand up like it's a stop sign. "No more, Uncle Otts. Please. Let's watch Kennedy, and then we'll talk about it." He takes a sip of his iced tea and says to me and Drew, "There will be jack-o'-lanterns. There will be Halloween."

Then he says to Mom, "And there *will* be chocolate cake."

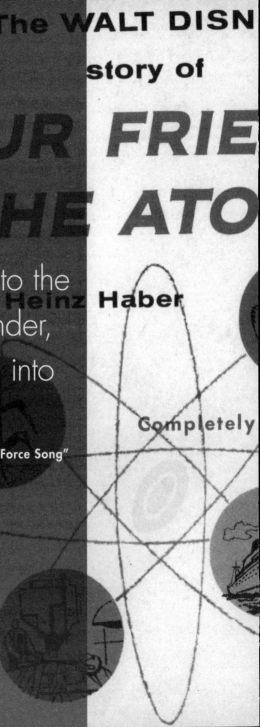

The WALT DISN

...story of

...UR FRIE

...HE ATO

Heinz Haber

Completely

Off we go into the
wild blue yonder,
climbing high into
the sun!

from "The Air Force Song"

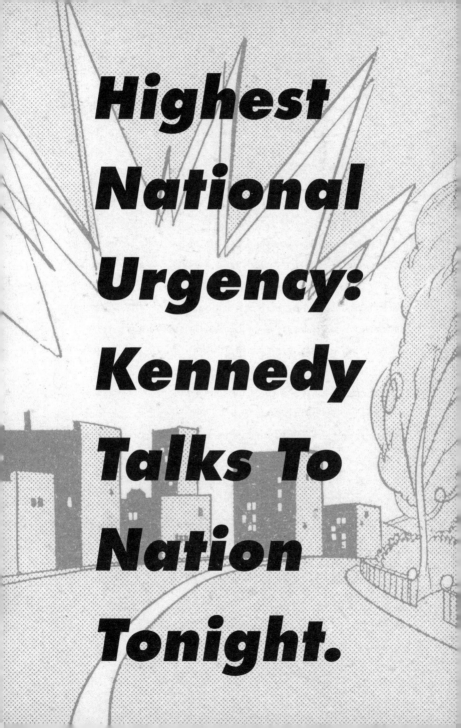

24

I help clear the table and dry the dishes without being told to do a thing. Mom and I work as a team, in silence. We are efficient. There is no baseball game outside, there is no noise at all but the sound of the rain that has begun to fall. The whole neighborhood is as quiet as a tomb. Maybe everybody is doing their dishes and getting ready to sit in front of the television to watch President Kennedy. I think about how I can soon cross this extra credit off my list, but it gives me little comfort.

Should we be worried? That's what I want to ask Mom, but she'd say no. I wouldn't believe her. And that scares me as much as what I don't know.

Drew appears in the kitchen, scrubbed clean after a shower and looking hangdog. He's got his arm looped around *Our Friend the Atom*. Jack is with him, wagging his tail and looking for dinner. "Feed the dog, Drew," commands Mom. "And take out the trash." She dries her hands on a dish towel. "Get a bath before you come downstairs, Franny." She hangs her apron on a peg by the door, then steps smartly down the stairs, to where Daddy and Uncle Otts are already camped out in front of the television.

"You okay?" I ask Drew.

"Did you know that every time you breathe you breathe in atoms?"

"No, I didn't."

"Did you know that the number of atoms in a breath of air is twenty-five with twenty-one zeroes?"

"That's a lot of atoms," I say.

"The paper in this book is made of atoms!" says Drew. "We're all made of atoms."

"That's nice," I say. I don't know what else to say.

"Galileo said there are countless moons and planets and stars in outer space. I'm going to see them when I grow up."

"Good for you," I tell him. "And I'm going to get a bath. See you downstairs."

When I get my bath, I don't bathe. I run the water in the tub, put the toilet lid down, and sit on the toilet to read Jo Ellen's letter. I have waited long enough. The letter is crunched and smudged and will never be the same, but I have it back. I slip it out of its envelope, unfold it in two places, and take a deep breath. I gaze upon the sturdy, dark-blue lettering and read:

SNCC
4043945593

CORE
2029353932

EBENEZER
9432843

FOR
3398452334

COFO
6013940259

I read it three times while the bathroom fills with steam. I am stumped. It's written in secret code, like the secret message on the carrier pigeon's leg in *The Password to Larkspur Lane*:

> *Trouble here.*
> *After five o'clock*
> *blue bells will be singing horses.*
> *Come tonight.*

But Nancy Drew figures it out handily. I will do the same. I'll start with Ebenezer.

I drain the bathtub, brush my teeth, and put on my pajamas. I pad down the hallway with Jo Ellen's letter, walk straight to her hope chest, and tug on the top, in case it might be unlocked. It isn't, and Mom still hasn't asked me about the key. Nobody can think of everything at a time like this, not even Mom.

I take myself back to my bedroom as the rain pours down outside. I stare at that Ebenezer address on the envelope. That's all it says. Ebenezer. There is no postmark. No stamp. I am officially stumped.

Even Nancy Drew is stumped from time to time. I slide the letter under my mattress. I miss my sister. If she were here, I could sit next to her when we watch President Kennedy, and she could tell me everything would be all right. I would believe her.

*   *   *

We are glued to the television as a family, at seven o'clock. Mom and Dad sit on the couch. Uncle Otts is in his chair. Drew and I are with Jack, on the floor, in our pajamas and slippers, in the same positions we take when we watch *Walt Disney's Wonderful World of Color*, only there is no Tinker Bell, no Walt Disney, no thrilling opening music.

But there is President Kennedy, and he is so handsome ... almost as handsome as Daddy. He's sitting behind his desk and he looks very serious. He doesn't smile or show his teeth. John-John and Caroline aren't there with him, and neither is Jackie — Mrs. Kennedy, the First Lady — who Mom says is *class personified*. It's just President Kennedy, the American flag, and us.

Good evening, my fellow citizens.

Mom whispers, "Look at the dark circles under his eyes."
"He hasn't slept for days!" snaps Uncle Otts.
"Shhh!" says Daddy.
Drew clutches his book while President Kennedy tells us shocking news. The Russians have been secretly shipping atomic missiles to Cuba, and we, the American people, need to know about it.

Each of these missiles, in short, is capable of striking Washington, D.C. ...

As if on cue, thunder claps outside our windows and we all jump. Even Jack whimpers.

In addition, jet bombers, capable of carrying
nuclear weapons, are now being uncrated
and assembled in Cuba . . .

Russian jets and Russian missiles in Cuba, with Russian
bombs aimed at us, right at Washington, D.C. Uncle Otts was
right.

I call upon Chairman Khrushchev to halt
and eliminate this clandestine, reckless,
and provocative threat to world
peace . . .

In fact, the bombs can reach the whole world, says President
Kennedy. He wants Chairman Khrushchev to stop trying to take
over the world. We are the United States, and we will not surrender. We're going to make blockades in the sea, and we will
fight back if anyone in the world is attacked.

The cost of freedom is always high, but Americans
have always paid it. And one path we shall
never choose, and that is the path of
surrender or submission. . . .

Jo Ellen was wrong. The Russians *are* coming to get us — they're
practically next door. My slippered feet are like ice and my mouth
is as dry as a cotton ball — I don't even have any spit to swallow.
I look at Drew, but he won't look at me.

There are no commercials after President Kennedy's speech,
just Walter Cronkite, to tell us what we already heard. We might

be at war with the Russians, any minute. Any minute those bombs might come roaring our way. We need to be prepared. We need to stay safe. And that's the way it is, Monday, October 22, 1962.

Daddy turns off the television. Drew takes Jack into his bedroom without telling anyone good night. He shuts his door, and Mom says, "I knew it was inappropriate." I look at Uncle Otts. His lips are pursed and he is deep in thought. I wait for him to say something.

"Bedtime, Franny," says Mom. *Bedtime?* Is she kidding? What if we don't wake up tomorrow? Besides, it's too early for bedtime. But as I look at each face in front of me, I know it's pointless to argue. It's bedtime.

"Everything will be all right, Franny," says Daddy. The phone rings. "Major Chapman," he answers. Then, "Yes, sir. Right away." He hangs up the phone and says, "I need to go to Andrews."

"Is it a trip?" asks Mom.

"No more trips for awhile," says Daddy. He gives Mom a lopsided smile. "You'll have to get used to having me around." Mom takes a breath and tries a smile back at Daddy.

Uncle Otts is strangely quiet and calm. His fingertips touch one another and make a tent in front of his lips. "You go on in, Phil," he says. "We'll be fine here." He smiles at me. "Let me tuck you in, little lady, while your mama tucks in Drew and gets your daddy off to work."

"Thank you, Arthur," says Mom.

"Yessir," I say. I don't know what else to say. It's obvious that

Mom and Dad want to talk. Uncle Otts hasn't tucked me in since I was six years old.

So I hug Mom good night, and she says, "I'll be up to check on you, too, Franny." I give Daddy an extra-fierce hug.

"You'll be back, right?" I ask him.

"Yes, I will," says Daddy. "It's just routine, Franny. Don't worry."

I am worried.

"Do you still say your prayers?" Uncle Otts asks me as we climb the stairs.

"Yessir." I get on my knees beside my bed and say the usual.

The rain sluices down my windows in the darkness. Thunder rumbles and crackles. Uncle Otts turns out my bedside lamp, tucks the covers around me, and kisses me on the forehead. I can feel his whiskers and smell his spicy smell. By the glow of my night-light, Uncle Otts says, "There was a time — I wasn't much older than you are now — when I was sure it was the end of the world."

"Were you afraid?" I ask him.

"Oh, yes," says Uncle Otts. "Very afraid."

"What happened?"

"I grew up to become an old man," says Uncle Otts. "That's what happened. And that's what will happen to you, too."

I think about this. "I'm not a boy," I say.

"Then you can become an old woman," says Uncle Otts.

I can't imagine being as old as Miss Mattie, as old as Mrs. Rodriguez, or as old as Uncle Otts. That's old.

"Are you sure?" I ask him.

"Very sure," he says. "Now go to sleep."

I lie in bed, alone in my room, and wonder what Drew is thinking. I want Jo Ellen to call home. I imagine the shape of her letter beneath the mattress, imagine I can hear its crinkle, imagine I can feel the emptiness of Jo Ellen's room down the hall.

Was it just today that Margie and I had that terrible fight, that I threw up in Mr. Mitchell's office, that Uncle Otts came home from the hospital, that Gale invited me to her party? All on the same day I found out that I might not live long enough to wake up in the morning? I'd better wrap up everything while I have a chance.

I crawl out of bed and get on my knees. I whisper, "Dear God: Thank you for not letting me kill Uncle Otts. And please, God, whatever Jo Ellen is up to, with those thinking friends of hers, please keep her safe. Please . . . let Drew grow up to be an astronaut. Keep Daddy safe. Keep all of us safe. And please . . . please talk to Chairman Khrushchev and help him understand."

I slip myself between the covers, too tired to work on my letter. I stare at my pink canopy while lightning sneaks like silver through the window blinds. I wait for sounds that my father is leaving, wait for my mother to come upstairs and check on me, but my eyes won't stay open. For once, I don't lie awake forever, I don't hear my parents' voices, I don't hear Johnny Carson on television, I don't hear another living sound. I sleep like the dead.

OCTOBER 22, 1962

Good evening,
my fellow citizens:

This government,
as promised, has
maintained the
closest surveillance
of the Soviet military
buildup on the
island of Cuba.

MISSILE ERECTOR

Within the past week, unmistakable evidence has established the fact that a series of offensive missile sites is now in preparation on that imprisoned island. The purpose of these bases can be none other than to provide a nuclear strike capability against the Western Hemisphere. . . .

CABLE

TRACKED PRIME MOVERS

Each of these missiles, in short, is capable of striking Washington, D.C., the Panama Canal, Cape Canaveral, Mexico City, or any other city in the southeastern part of the United States, in Central America, or in the Caribbean area.

Additional sites not yet completed appear to be designed for intermediate range ballistic missiles — capable of traveling more than twice as far — and thus capable of striking most of the major cities in the Western Hemisphere, ranging as far north as Hudson Bay, Canada, and as far south as Lima, Peru. In addition, jet bombers, capable of carrying nuclear weapons, are now being uncrated and assembled in Cuba, while the necessary air bases are being prepared. . . .

This secret, swift, extraordinary buildup of Communist missiles . . . this sudden, clandestine decision to station strategic weapons for the first time outside of Soviet soil — is a deliberately provocative and unjustified change in the status quo which cannot be accepted by this country. . . .

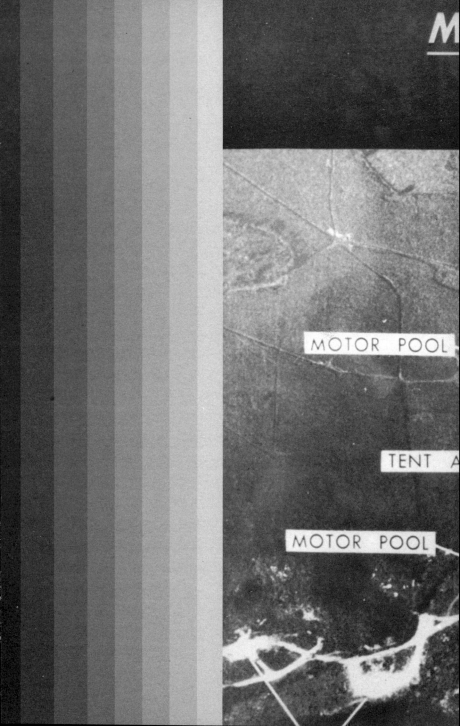

M

MOTOR POOL

TENT A

MOTOR POOL

?BM FIELD LAUNCH SI?

Sagua la Grande No. 2

17 OCTOBER 1962

3 MISSILE READ?

MISSILE CONTA?

A

ERECTORS

LDGS AND
63 LONG

CH PADS

To halt this offensive buildup, a strict quarantine on all offensive military equipment under shipment to Cuba is being initiated. All ships of any kind bound for Cuba from whatever nation or port will, if found to contain cargoes of offensive weapons, be turned back. This quarantine will be extended, if needed, to other types of cargo and carriers. We are not at this time, however, denying the necessities of life as the Soviets attempted to do in their Berlin blockade of 1948. . . .

IT SHALL BE THE POLICY OF THIS NATION TO REGARD ANY NUCLEAR MISSILE LAUNCHED FROM CUBA AGAINST ANY NATION IN THE WESTERN HEMISPHERE AS AN ATTACK BY THE SOVIET UNION ON THE UNITED STATES, REQUIRING A FULL RETALIATORY RESPONSE UPON THE SOVIET UNION. . . .

I call upon Chairman Khrushchev to halt and eliminate this clandestine, reckless, and provocative threat to world peace and to stable relations between our two nations. I call upon him further to abandon this course of world domination, and to join in an historic effort to end the perilous arms race and to transform the history of man. . . .

The cost of freedom is always high, but Americans have always paid it. And one path we shall never choose, and that is the path of surrender or submission.

Our goal is not the victory of might, but the vindication of right; not peace at the expense of freedom, but both peace and freedom, here in this hemisphere, and, we hope, around the world. God willing, that goal will be achieved.

Thank you and good night.

FINAL ★★★★★

DAILY NEWS

NEW YORK'S PICTURE NEWSPAPER ®

5¢

Vol. 44. No. 103   Copr. 1962 News Syndicate Co. Inc.   New York 17, N.Y., Tuesday, October 23, 1962*   WEATHER: Partly cloudy, windy, cooler.

WE BLOCKADE
CUBA ARMS

Red Ships Face Search or Sinking

(UPI Telefoto)

President Kennedy tells the world we will stop any vessel from taking nuclear arms or long-range rockets to Castro.
Stories on pages 2, 3, 4, 5; other pictures in the centerfold

Cuba reacted to the President's speech tonight by ordering all its armed forces on immediate alert. The U.S. is prepared to sink Soviet ships. The U.S. must assume it will face losses.

Douglas Edwards, CBS News

25

Everything has changed. I mean everything. President Kennedy's speech is all over the television and radio. Usually it's as quiet as the grave here in the morning. But this morning, no one can get enough of the news.

Daddy is still not home. Mom has the radio turned up high enough in the kitchen to hear it through the noise of making breakfast — so much for not scaring the children.

"Go get your brother," Mom says to me.

"Yes, ma'am." I troop downstairs, and I can't help it — I'm pulled to the television news. I stand silently next to Uncle Otts, who sits in a chair smack in front of the television. He listens, changes the channel, listens, changes the channel.

"The most ominous sign since the building of the Berlin Wall last summer," says one news anchor. "Khrushchev failed at seizing West Berlin; now he is after bigger targets."

Channel change.

"American U-2 reconnaissance flights over Cuba have shown that the buildup of missiles in Cuba over the summer has *not*, we repeat, *not* proven to be surface-to-air *defensive* missiles, but *offensive* weapons supplied by the Soviet Union, that can fire nuclear warheads at American cities as far away as Montana."

Channel change.

"As President Kennedy spoke to the nation last night, the American people were stunned to hear the breaking news that Soviet Russia has indeed armed nuclear warhead missile sites in Cuba, just ninety miles off the Florida coast, that can destroy United States cities within minutes. A presumed first strike would be Washington, D.C."

I try to swallow, but instead I start coughing, which breaks Uncle Otts's concentration. He wraps his long arm around my shoulders and says, "Come here, Private." And then he hugs me, just right. Not too hard, which would seem hysterical, and not too soft, which would seem uncaring. He hugs me with one of those it-will-be-all-right hugs, so I hug him back — too hard, of course, but oh, it makes me feel better.

Uncle Otts takes my shoulders in his big hands and gently pushes me away from him. I look him full in the face, asking questions I have no words for. He takes one finger and shoves my headband farther up on my head. "That is all," he says, and I am restored, for now.

I knock on Drew's bedroom door. He doesn't answer. I open the door a crack. "Drew?" It's dark in his bedroom and it smells overwhelmingly like Old Spice. I step inside. "Drew?" Jack comes to greet me with one of Drew's shoes. I take it from him. "No shoes!" I chide him. He wags his tail.

"I'm not coming out," Drew says from under his covers.

My nose crinkles at the Old Spice.

"Did Uncle Otts sleep in here?"

"No!" says Drew, and "Yes!" says Uncle Otts from the next room.

"You have to come out, Drew."

"No, I don't!"

"Believe me, when Mom has to come down here and get you, you'll come out!"

Drew scrabbles the covers off his body using his feet and lies there like a corpse with no covers. "We might have a real alert at school."

This is Drew, who sails across the gravel pit on a flimsy rope swing like nothing can hurt him.

"We might," I answer. Then I surprise myself and say, "But I know what to do."

I've always known what to do.

"What?"

"If the real siren goes off, I'm going to run right to your classroom and get you, and we'll race for home, how's that?"

"They'll never let us do that," says Drew.

"They won't have a choice," I say — it glides right off my tongue — "if we're brave. They won't be able to stop us."

Drew considers this. "I'll meet you outside by the kickball field, at the far end of the playground."

"Nope," I say. "What if your teacher hangs on to you or if there's a stampede and you fall and break your leg before you get there or something? I can't go home without you. I'll run from my hallway to yours, and you be ready for me, okay? Then we'll run together."

Drew sits up in bed. "Promise?"

"I promise. Now get dressed."

I feel like a smart big sister. I like it.

Drew scratches his eyebrow while he thinks about what I've just told him.

"Drew! Look lively! Astronauts always get dressed."

"Franny! Drew!" Mom calls from upstairs.

"Coming!" we chorus. Here we go.

I wear a soft blue headband today. It's a stretchy circle and it won't pop off my head, but it also doesn't hold my hair back as well, and sometimes it flops down onto my forehead. Sometimes it slips forward and bobs around my neck, if it's feeling real stretchy. I like it, though, and today I need the softness.

It's still pouring rain on this Tuesday morning. Thunder still grumbles in the distance. The sky is as gloomy as everyone's mood.

"How appropriate," says Mom as she lights a cigarette, stuffs us in the car, and drives us the two blocks down Allentown Road to school. Drew sits in the front, and I don't even argue about it. I'm a big sister. He hugs Mom as he gets out of the car, struggling with that hefty satchel, and she smiles and hugs him back.

Then Mom turns to me in the backseat, gives me her listen-to-me-very-carefully look, and says, "Look at me."

I look her directly in the eyes. She blows that long, thin stream of cigarette smoke to the ceiling, then gives me her you-know-what-I'm-talking-about look.

"Be good."

"Yes, ma'am," I give her the standard answer.

"You are better than that."

"Yes, ma'am." And I know, this is my talking-to for what happened yesterday in the bathroom with Margie. This is it. This is all. I don't know Mom anymore.

"Have a good day at school, Franny."

But I don't budge. "Mom?"

"Yes?"

"I love you."

Mom smiles a crooked smile. "I love you, too."

Of course she does. She waves at me as I turn around at the door, getting soaked. I wave back.

This is an official Civil Defense film.

When I get inside, Judy James smiles at me, and I smile back. That's nice. I want to ask her if she watched President Kennedy's speech, but no one is talking about it, no one, so I don't, either. In my classroom, I hang up my raincoat in the cloak-room, empty my satchel into my desk, and take my seat by the window.

Kids straggle in, damp and solemn. I watch their faces as they get settled. Nobody stares at me like I'm a weirdo after all that happened yesterday. They've all watched President Kennedy's speech, and they've got more important things on their minds. Denise Dubose says hi, and I say hi back. I wish I liked Denise more. I wish Mary Flood still went to school here at Camp Springs.

We all know the atomic bomb
is very dangerous.
Since it may be used against us,
we must be ready for it.

I sigh and open my assignment notebook and look at the rest of my week. I write everything down in my assignment book, everything I do for the week. I even write down what I have for lunch every day. I like to see the week go by as I tick things off the list. Now I just hope I get another week on the planet.

Before I can fill in "French" with Mme. Martin on Tuesday and "music" with Miss Farrell on Wednesday and "glee club" after school on Thursday, Mrs. Rodriguez steps smartly into class and claps her hands and announces that the entire fourth, fifth, and sixth grades will have an assembly program first thing this morning.

What a time for an assembly! But maybe that's good — it will take our mind off the Russians and their bombs in Cuba, and we'll miss arithmetic, too. Some kids clap, and we start to feel like ourselves again.

"Hurry, boys and girls!" says Mrs. Rodriguez. "We've got to have all students in the cafeteria by nine fifteen!"

**Getting ready means
we will all have to be able
to take care of ourselves.
The bomb might explode when
there are no grown-ups near.**

I can't even say hello to Chris as he splashes in at the last minute. After the quickest prayer and Pledge — I would like to enter our time in the Olympics — we troop, single file, to the cafeteria, where folding chairs are smashed up next to one another and we're all crammed together like sardines in a can.

It's raining so hard outside we can hear the roar on the roof. Mrs. Rodriguez puts a hand on each of our shoulders as she rounds us into our aisles. Mrs. Scharr seats her class on the opposite side of the room. Margie is whispering to Marcy Weaver, and Mrs. Scharr shushes them with her nightmare shush.

> Paul and Patty know this,
> and they are always ready
> to take care of themselves.
> Here they are on their way to school
> on a beautiful spring day.
> But no matter where they go or what they do,
> they always try to remember what to do
> if the atom bomb explodes right then.
> "It's a bomb! Duck and cover!"
> Paul and Patty know what to do.

Somehow — I did not do a thing — Chris ends up sitting next to me in assembly. He must have somehow figured out a way to sit next to me when we were lining up to walk down the hall to the cafeteria. Or maybe it was a mistake. Oh, I hope not. He gives me a quick smile of acknowledgment as he sits down. I give him a cool and composed nod and think, *You did that very well, Franny*. But in the next moment, all my composure evaporates.

Mr. Mitchell stands in front of us, clears his throat, and looks directly at me. No, he doesn't, but it seems like it at first, and I look away immediately. I will never be able to look Mr. Mitchell in the face again. But I can look at him from this distance, and I listen as he begins.

"Good morning, students and teachers. As many of you know, last night on television, President Kennedy spoke to the nation about the . . . situation . . . in Cuba."

223

Everyone starts gabbling like chickens — we've been bursting to talk about this — but teachers shush all of us at once.

"We are now living in a true atomic age," Mr. Mitchell continues. He wipes a hand across his mouth. "In an effort to make sure we are all informed and understand what to do in case of any . . . irregularities . . . we're going to show all students and teachers at Camp Springs a civil defense film that covers all areas of public safety and shelter. Please pay close attention. After assembly, you will return to your classrooms where your teachers will be available for further discussion."

Mr. Mitchell tugs at his tie uncomfortably. He has long forgotten my throwing up in his office. I am off that hook forever. I look around and half expect to see Uncle Otts running the projector. He would be in his glory here. He's been warning all of us for months.

The lights go down, and up comes Bert the Turtle on the screen at the front of the room. Bert wants us to *duck! and cover!* He tells us to do exactly what the kids in this movie are doing. *Ride your bikes! Play with friends! Have picnics with your family! Just be prepared! Okay?*

Here's Tony,
going to his Cub Scout meeting.
Tony knows the bomb can explode,
any time of the year,
day or night.
He is ready for it.

Duck and cover! Atta boy, Tony!
That flash means "act fast."
Tony knows that it helps
to get to any kind of cover.
This wall was close by,
so that's where he ducked and covered.

If you are not close to home
when you hear the warning,
go to the nearest safe cover.
Know where you are to go,
or ask an older person to help you.

Tony knew what to do.
Notice how he keeps from moving,
or getting up and running?
He stays down until
he is sure the danger is over.

When the film sputters off and the lights go on, there is not a sound in the room — not even a chair scrape. We are all officially scared to death, but we are going to go on with our lives because Mr. Mitchell tells us to. His voice has found a no-nonsense, I'm-in-charge-so-everything-will-be-fine tone, which I don't believe for one minute.

"Life will go on here at Camp Springs Elementary School," he says. "Glee club will meet after school on Thursday — we have a concert to prepare for. Safety patrols will report for duty daily. And on Friday we will have our annual Halloween parade. You may bring your costumes to school with you on Friday. It's going to be a great week here at Camp Springs School. Teachers, please dismiss your students. We've got the first through third grades waiting in the hallways."

Even teachers seem stunned. Maybe they won't dismiss us. Maybe this moment is frozen in time, and I can just sit here, pretending Chris and I will know each other forever, that his jacket sleeve will always rest against my sweater sleeve like it does now, still and safe.

"My class!" says Mrs. Rodriguez, and the spell is broken.

We don't speak to one another — those are the rules — as we file out of the auditorium. In the hallway we pass the third grade, and I give a thumbs-up to Drew, who looks so pale I wonder if he slept at all last night. He gives me a wan smile. If I were Mom and knew what Drew was about to watch, I'd write a note to Mr. Mitchell saying he wasn't allowed to watch it.

**The man helping Tony
is a civil defense worker.
His job is to help protect us
when there is danger of the atomic bomb.
We must obey the civil defense worker.**

As we take our seats in our classroom, Mrs. Rodriguez doesn't talk about atomic bombs or ducking and covering. She paces in front of her desk, back and forth, with her head down while we all stare at her and wait for the next thing. Then she looks at the clock. "Open your spelling books, boys and girls."

I've got all the words memorized, of course, so I don't have to even look at my words. Mrs. Rodriguez is much more interesting.

She doesn't sit down like she usually does as we go through our spelling words; she purses her lips and continues to pace. Denise Dubose spells *friendship* out loud and begins to use it in a sentence.

"Friendship!" interrupts Mrs. Rodriguez. "Put your spelling books away, boys and girls. Time for geography." And she pulls down the big map in front of the chalkboard.

Everyone is confused, but no one makes a peep. Mrs. Rodriguez takes her metal pointer out of her desk drawer, extends it to its longest length, and slaps at the map, just under the state of Florida. "This," she says, and we all look at where the red tip has landed, "is Cuba."

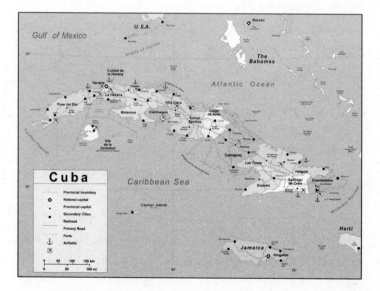

We stare at Cuba. We look at how close it is to the United States of America. And we talk, not about bombs and Russians, but about Cuba and Cubans.

"My husband is from Cuba," says Mrs. Rodriguez. Kids suck

in their breaths and lean forward in their seats. "He is a teacher in a college near here. He immigrated to America twenty years ago, and that's when I met him. Before I married him, my name was Miss Alberghetti. Gina Alberghetti."

We stare at Miss Gina Albergetti who became Mrs. Gina Rodriguez. No one knows what to say, but that's fine because Mrs. Rodriguez has plenty to say.

"Cuba is an archipelago of islands in the Caribbean Sea," says Mrs. Rodriguez. "*Archipelago* is one of your *Word Wealth Junior* bonus words this week — look it up, if you haven't."

Since I memorize the definitions of each spelling word, I know that an archipelago is *a chain or cluster of islands, usually in the open sea, that are formed by erupting undersea volcanoes.*

Jimmy Epps raises his hand. "Have you been there?"

"I have, many times," says Mrs. Rodriguez, "to visit my husband's family. But we have not been there since the Cuban Revolution started six years ago." She retracts her pointer, comes to the front of her desk, and leans against it. "Cuba is a beautiful country, full of beautiful people. Let me tell you about it."

We skip spelling and reading, and I begin to hope we'll skip social studies this afternoon — who needs to read about the explorers when we've got one right here in the room? The rain pours down like a monsoon, and we listen to Mrs. Rodriguez tell us stories through the gloom. Stories about beaches, mountains, music, food, tobacco fields, the city of Old Havana, and the stories of her Cuban family. She plays the mambo for us on the record player on her desk. She dances the cha-cha and we giggle in our seats until she makes us stand up and cha-cha at our desks. We laugh so hard our sides hurt.

When the bell rings for lunch, kids actually groan, and Mrs. Rodriguez has tears in her eyes. She pulls her handkerchief out of her pocket, dabs at her eyes and nose, and says, very quietly and resolutely, "I love my husband's country."

I have started to love it, too. How can I be scared of such a beautiful country full of people who are related to my teacher? I am weary of worrying, and maybe — just maybe — I don't have to.

Mrs. Rodriguez says. "You are dismissed for lunch. Remember, there will be indoor recess."

Kids make all kinds of noise as they get their lunches and lunch money out of the cloakroom, and Mrs. Rodriguez doesn't shush them. I open my assignment book and write *Cuba* on Tuesday morning. I telegraph Mrs. Rodriguez: *There must have been a reason you skipped me three times. I forgive you.* And then it is time for lunch.

A SUMMER PLACE

Bells will be ringing and birds will be singing if you and your lover should ever discover that

There's a summer place
Where it may rain or storm
Yet I'm safe and warm

For within that summer place
Your arms reach out to me
And my heart is free from all care

For it knows
There are no gloomy skies
When seen through the eyes
Of those who are blessed with love

And the sweet secret of
A summer place
Is that it's anywhere
Where two people share
All their hopes

ALL THEIR

DREAMS

Sundays, holidays, vacation time, we must be ready every day, all the time, to do the right thing if the atomic bomb explodes.

DUCK AND COVER!

This family knows what to do, just as your own family should. They know that even a thin cloth helps protect them. Even a newspaper can save you from a bad burn.

EAST
HAN
CU

STOP BASES
STOP
BLOCKADE

NO WAR
CUBA

ALL THEIR

26

"I'm not having a Halloween party."

I say this right away, as soon as we sit down with our lunches, because you should never keep secrets from boyfriends — well, he's not my boyfriend, he's a friend. But you should never keep secrets from friends, either. And my friend Chris Cavas is sitting directly across from me at the lunch table in the cafeteria.

Actually, I whisper this news, because we're not allowed to talk at lunch. Lunchtime is for eating. As soon as each table is finished eating, we are dismissed to recess. I want lunch to take all day. I don't have to talk to Chris. I just need to sit across from him.

But of course we are dismissed for indoor recess, in our classrooms, where we'll play hangman with each other, or board games, or read by ourselves (I don't keep a Nancy Drew in my desk at all times for nothing).

I manage to walk back to class with Chris, right past Margie's lunch table. She glares at me. I glare back. I don't see Gale with Mr. Adler's class. Maybe she's absent.

"Gale's having a Halloween party," says Chris.

"I know!" I say brightly, although I hope not *too* brightly.

"Are you going?"

"Oh — yes!" I answer as if the pope himself called me and told me I could go. "Are you?"

"I don't know," says Chris. "I've got another invitation . . ." He trails off.

Another invitation!

From Margie? I screech. No, I don't. I don't say anything. But I want to. Oh, I want to.

When we get to class, kids are already in a gaggle near the record player to listen to the Cuban music Mrs. Rodriguez brought in. Chris heads over there. I head over to Nancy Drew.

For the rest of the day, when I'm not worrying about the Russians, I worry about Margie and Chris. I worry about them right through the multiplication tables and right through the update on our science fair projects — I still have no problem with the solar system — and right through French, which I never fail to pay attention to, since I might grow up to be an interpreter at the United Nations.

"*Comment vous appelez vous?*" Mme. Martin asks me.

"*Je m'appelle Janine!*" I say. I like my French name — Janine — so much better than my real name.

"*Très bien,*" says Mme. Martin. And as she moves on, I do, too. I move on to thoughts about the weekend and Gale's party. I want to go even if Chris doesn't come. I want to be there, at that boy-girl party with music and dancing and food and costumes and games. I'll bet Gale has the same records Jo Ellen does. And . . . I'll bet Margie will be there.

"*Janine!*" says Mme. Martin.

"*Ici!*" I say. And the bell rings. It's the end of the day. Blessed end of the day that we lived through without a siren, without a bomb, without a drill. The sun has come out, blazing in the sky, as if to say, *You didn't forget me, did you? Here I am!* Now if I can just survive walking home with Margie.

> Yes, we must all get ready now,
> in case the atomic bomb
> ever explodes near us.
> If you do not know what to do,
> ask your teacher when this film is over.

But I don't have to worry about that. Margie walks home with Judy James. She doesn't even try to walk home with me. Good. She does try to walk with Chris, first, but Chris is walking with his brother, Bobby, and Bobby and Drew are friends, so I'm walking with Chris and Bobby and Drew, and that's just the way it happens.

"How are you?" I say to Drew in a peppy voice when I see him.

"Good," says Drew. Good.

"Where's your satchel?"

"I don't have homework," he says. He's holding only one book, *Our Friend the Atom*. Of course. "I just brought something to read," he says. I nod.

The rain has brought the cold, but my sweater and raincoat are plenty of cover. We step around puddles and soft, squishy, muddy places. Everything looks washed and new, and the earth smells clean. I love that smell.

When we reach the corner of Coolridge and Napoli Drives, Chris says, "Remember how the gravel pit filled with water when it rained hard and we used to see how high it would get?"

And before we even discuss it, all four of us, three boys and me, are turning left onto Coolridge instead of right, heading for the woods at the end of the road. I watch with great satisfaction as Margie stares after us then turns right, while Judy turns left toward her house.

"Wanna come, Judy?" I call, loud enough for Margie to hear.

"Sure!" she says. Margie keeps walking. Margie hates the gravel pit anyway, but I'm sure she hates me even more. I don't care.

"Don't you love that song about storms we're singing in glee club?" Judy asks.

"Which one?" I say. I know which one.

"You know" — and she begins to sing it! Tone-deaf Judy James begins to sing! And there's nothing I can do about it.

> When you walk through a storm,
> hold your head up high . . .

I am desperate. Her voice is like sandpaper on the blackboard. It's like a moaning, dying pigeon. It hurts to listen to it.

"It's great!" I shout, starting to run. "Come on!"

She runs to keep up with me and she can't sing while she's running.

> **Older people will help us as they always do,**
> **but there might not be any grown-ups around**
> **when the bomb explodes.**
> **Then, you're on your own.**

Everything — the whole world — is wet. I love the woods after a storm. Raindrops cling to every leaf and branch, and pebbles shine like they've been polished. Birds scream from the trees like they've been set free from prison. If you look closely, you can see insects crawling about, inspecting the new things the storm has brought, getting a drink of fresh water from a leaf, tiptoeing alongside the paths made by giants — us.

Water slicks off the branches and coats our hands and feet and faces as we walk in single file — Chris, me, Judy, Drew, and Bobby weaving down the path to the gravel pit. Suddenly, there is a shout up ahead, made by someone we can't see.

We all stop immediately, instinctively.

"We're not the only ones here," says Chris.

> But the most important thing of all
> is to duck and cover yourself,
> **ESPECIALLY WHERE YOUR CLOTHES
> DO NOT COVER YOU.**

We've always known we share the gravel pit, and we've seen the big kids who hang out here. We find empty soda bottles and occasionally a beer bottle on the tree stump that's as big as a table.

Sometimes we come at the same time as the big kids do, but we always leave without being seen. There's no reason for this, we just do. We don't know them. They don't know us. And they're older than we are. They got there first.

But today, Chris says, "Let's go! I hear Charlie Caldwell. We know him."

We follow Chris like he's the Pied Piper, but again we stop as one, before we come out into the clearing. The big boys are laughing and roping an enormous tree branch on a majestic old oak well away from the edge of the gravel pit. They are hollering directions at one another.

"What?" says Chris, turning to face us all.

"I don't want to," I whisper. I know Charlie Caldwell, and I don't like him. He's a year older than we are, and let me just say that he would never qualify to be a safety patrol.

"I don't want to, either," says Drew.

"Me, neither," says Bobby.

"Me, threether," says Judy.

Threether?

I sigh. "I'm supposed to go home straight home after school."

Drew is already beating a retreat.

Then — *craaaaack!*

The big boys whoop, Drew screams from down the path, and the rest of us jump out of our skins, like we've been shot. The huge old limb has crashed to earth with its branches and brilliantly colored leaves everywhere. It will die and decompose here, right on the forest floor, where the boys are hollering and clapping one another on the back, like conquering heroes.

When I can breathe again, I search for Drew. He's in a little ball at the end of the path.

"Go ahead," I say to Chris. "You go and tell us how deep the water is tomorrow."

"Hurry up, Franny!" calls Drew as he pops up and begins running, running, running for home, *Our Friend the Atom* close to his chest. I sigh and turn to follow my brother.

"Go on," I say again.

Chris takes a look at his little brother, who is looking up at Chris. "Nah," he says. "We'll come back later, too. C'mon, Bobby."

I do, I think, *I do*. This is the most romantic thing a boy — or anyone — has ever done for me. Chris Cavas is going to walk me out of the woods.

And right about then, I can see that Judy is mooning over Chris, too.

"Thanks, Chris," she croons. She almost swoons.

Oh, brother.

The four of us walk out of the woods. Judy breaks off at her house, with a dreamy smile. I can hardly tell her good-bye without the words curdling in my throat. Six houses later, Chris and Bobby wave good-bye at their house.

"Chris!" I say. I almost reach out and grab him.

"Hmmm?"

I'm thinking fast because I see Margie across the street, looking at us from her bedroom window. "I . . . I . . . I hope you do come to Gale's party on Saturday."

"Thanks," he says. That's it. *Thanks*. And he follows Bobby through the front door of their house.

I look up at Margie's bedroom window. The curtain is swaying, where she was standing. I smile to myself. I'm doing just fine.

No matter where we live,
in the city or the country,
we must be ready all the
time for the atomic bomb.

Duck and cover!

That's the first thing to do.

Duck and cover!

The next important thing
to do after that is to stay
covered until the danger
is over.

27

I walk through the front door, and Jack is there to greet me as always, so excited to see me. Mom huffs down the stairs ahead of me, with two bags of groceries.

"Go upstairs," she wheezes. "There's more on the kitchen counter."

Is there ever. Mom must have bought out the whole commissary. I bring down one bag—that's all I can carry. It's full of cans of tomatoes. I don't ask why we're bringing groceries downstairs. I don't ask these questions anymore.

"Change into your play clothes," says Mom, meeting me at the bottom of the stairs with a cigarette dangling from her mouth. "Where's Drew?"

"He came ahead," I say. "Didn't you see him?"

Mom shakes her head. "See if you can find him."

"What are we doing?" I ask. I can't help it.

"We're building your uncle's bomb shelter," says Mom. "In the laundry room. Hurry. And bring me another bag of groceries."

We're building a bomb shelter.

I jackrabbit up the stairs, change clothes, grab another bag of groceries, hand them off to Mom at the bottom of the stairs, and follow her into the only unfinished room in the house.

The floor is concrete, and the walls are concrete block with long rows of worktables that Daddy used to use for his projects before he built the shed last summer. Suddenly it seems perfect — why didn't anybody think of this before? It's a perfect space for a shelter. There is not even a window. Long fluorescent tubes of light buzz above us.

"Where's my science fair foldout?" I ask.

"It's in my room," says Uncle Otts. He stops stocking a shelf with canned peaches and says, "Francine! It's about time you got home from school. We need your help, Private."

"Arthur. . . ," Mom says in her cautionary voice.

Who'd have believed it? Mom and Uncle Otts are working together. The worktables are totally cleaned off and sleeping bags are rolled onto them. The supplies that Uncle Otts ordered for his bomb shelter — they're in here. There's the chemical toilet. There's the water tank. There's the shortwave radio. And Mom's radio is in here, too. It's turned on at fever pitch. Mom is consumed with our impending doom. Suddenly I understand why my theft of a suitcase key or my behavior at school isn't even on Mom's radar anymore.

"Where's Daddy?" I ask. "Is he coming home tonight?"

"He's home and he's taking a nap," says Mom. "It's our league bowling night."

Bowling? Last night we were worried about being incinerated, and tonight there is bowling?

"Find your brother," Mom repeats.

I know where to look.

Drew sits on the floor of the tree house, watching the cars whiz by on Allentown Road, clutching his copy of *Our Friend the Atom.*

I climb up the ladder carefully, inspecting every knot I made myself with Daddy and Uncle Otts. "Mom wants you, Drew."

"I don't care," says Mr. Perfect.

I no longer blink at anything anyone in this family says.

"C'mon, Drew, you don't want to get in trouble."

"I know all about atoms," says Drew. He turns his face to me. He's crying. "Atoms are supposed to be our friends," he hiccups. "I'm supposed to go to the moon! We're supposed to use atoms for peace — it says so right here in this book! An atom is like a genie in a bottle, and we can use that genie to go into space and make new discoveries. But we're making bombs to kill people! People who are made of atoms! It's all in this book — protons, neutrons, electrons, Madame Curie, Leonardo da Vinci, Galileo, reactors and rockets and spaceships and stars and planets and the moon!"

Drew is overwrought.

"I'm never gonna get to the moon, because we're all about to get blown up!"

He's completely overwrought.

"I'll be right back," I say. So much for being a smart big sister.

Back to the basement I go. "Mom, Drew is in the tree house. He's . . . overwrought."

"What?" Mom stops unpacking a box of batteries.

"He's upset," I say. I leave it at that. I don't know what to do.

Mom wipes her hands on her apron, stubs out her cigarette in an ashtray, then walks right past me and out the back door. "Help your uncle," she says. "I don't want him keeling over again."

Uncle Otts is sitting on the side of his bed, sweaty from

exertion, listening to his radio and staring at his dresser. Jack dozes at the door, one of Uncle Otts's socks in his mouth. He thumps his tail and I pat him on the head.

Uncle Otts's room is a museum of his life. It's packed with photographs and paraphernalia, and a zillion small mementos.

"Come here, little lady," he says when he sees me. He pats the bed. I step around my science fair project and sit beside him. And there we remain, listening to one dire prediction after another, until Uncle Otts reaches over, turns off his radio, and sighs. "Life is short."

What a thing to say.

"Yessir," I answer. And I telegraph him, *Please don't keel over right now, whatever you do.*

I am enveloped in Uncle Otts's Old Spice smell. I see his gas mask on the foot post of the bed and consider putting it on, but then I think better of it.

"See that picture yonder on the dresser?" Uncle Otts asks me.

"Which one?"

"This one." He leans over, picks it up, and hands it to me. "This is Tom Neibaur. He was a friend of mine in the Great War. We was in the Forty-second together, over in France. I was from the Fourth Alabama. He was from Idaho. We all got mixed together in France — we were called the Rainbow Division."

He takes a breath. "Fourth Alabama was originally part of the Confederate Army, did you know that?"

I didn't. I shake my head.

"Goes back to the Civil War. Back to the days of slavery. I don't, a'course. I'm not *that* old. But my granddaddy was in that

war—he fought for the Confederates, and my daddy fought in the Spanish-American War. Chapmans have fought in just about ever' American war under the sun."

"Yessir."

"Your daddy's daddy was killed in World War II—he was way too old for that war—and your daddy flew in Korea. Now he's involved in this Communist missile mess, and who knows what's next for him."

Kommanist.

I hold up the picture so he can see I'm interested. Uncle Otts points to it.

"Old Tom, he was a sharpshooter. He was wounded, he was captured, he escaped with his men, he killed scores of Krauts, and he saved scores of American—and French and Aussie and British—lives. He was decorated with the Medal of Honor. And he died of TB right after World War Two. I got a letter from his family. And I'm still here, all these years later. I'm still here."

Uncle Otts sniffs a big one, puts one hand on each knee, and pushes himself up straighter on the bed. I want to tell him that's great posture, but I don't.

"Old Tom, yessir, he was a hero."

I am supposed to say something.

"You're a hero, too, Uncle Otts. Daddy said so."

Uncle Otts stares straight ahead and says nothing.

"You've got medals and everything," I say. I look around the room, at all the memories stuffed everywhere. "I was wondering about your medals, Uncle Otts. I haven't seen you wear them since . . . you came home. You always wear your medals."

"I'll never wear them again."

I look straight into his face with surprise. Uncle Otts wipes a big leathery hand over his wrinkled face, up and down, up and down. "I should have been a pacifist," he says finally.

I am ashamed to say I don't know what a pacifist is.

"I could have broken the chain of war in this family, and that would have saved lives." He hands me a picture from his nightstand.

"Look at that boy," he says as his voice breaks. "Look at that beautiful, *beautiful* boy."

I take the photo from him. The boy is wearing a uniform.

"He looks like you," I say, "and you're right here."

"No, no . . . that's my brother," says Uncle Otts. "My brother Nicholas."

"I didn't know you had a brother Nicholas."

"He was sixteen. He was too young to enlist in the war. I told him he was too young, but he wanted to be like me. He worshipped me, and he wanted to be like me. A soldier."

I say it slowly, in a whisper. "What happened to him?"

Uncle Otts takes the picture from me like it's a baby and gently puts it back on his nightstand. "I killed him," he says simply.

I blink.

"God help me, I killed him."

C'MON,
C'MON,

DO THE LOCOM

KEEP DANCING!

U.S. military alert is set at DEFCON 3.
Fidel Castro has mobilized all of Cuba's military forces.

We are now in the most dangerous situation since the end of World War II. The next forty-eight hours will be decisive.

Richard Hottelet, CBS News

Today four Negroes were arrested when they refused to leave the lunch counter at McAdoo's Drugs in Leopold, Virginia, after being denied service. July 7, 1962

Discuss what you could do in different places if a bomb explodes.

U.S. sea and air patrols immediately will hail, stop, and search all ships bound for Cuba.

Roger Mudd, CBS News

28

Uncle Otts is not thinking straight. He would never kill a flea. But he's right about one thing: Life is short. It's time to take matters into my own hands, that's all there is to it.

The good news is that Mom and Dad do indeed go out to their usual Tuesday night bowling league. "Hornbuckle's covering for me tonight," Daddy says. And Mom says, "It will do you good to get some exercise and be with friends."

So Mom gets all heroic and no-nonsense and puts an exhausted Drew — who refuses to eat supper — to bed. She makes me a grilled cheese sandwich and tomato soup, takes a tray to Uncle Otts, and then off they go, Mom and Dad, wearing their red bowling shirts with their names on them. "We'll be back early," Mom says. "Bedtime at the usual time."

Uncle Otts is downstairs watching *Combat!* on television with Jack. For a murderer, this is a weird show to be watching. There is nothing good on television on Tuesday nights. I put my soup and sandwich on a tray, pour myself a tall glass of milk, and take my dinner to Jo Ellen's room. I retrieve Jo Ellen's letter from under my mattress and Gale's party invitation from my pillowcase. Then I go back to Jo Ellen's room and I *shut the door*, yes I do. I pull out Jo Ellen's box of 45s, and I fish through them. I play my favorites, one after another. They make me feel better than anything has felt all week.

I can tell my whole life story through Jo Ellen's records. These people understand me.

> That's the sound of the men
> working on the chain gang.

[Boy, can I relate]

> Are you lonesome tonight?

(Come home, Jo Ellen! Fall in love with me, Chris!)

> Hit the road, Jack!
> And don't you come back no more, no more,
> no more, no more!

(Hit the road, Franny!)

I pick "Runaway" out of the 45 box, with its little heart on the label. It's no longer my favorite. I tuck it back in its sleeve. Sorry, Del.

The music has worked its magic — I feel great. I have already done my homework. I have laid out my clothes for tomorrow. I am ready to take my life into my hands. I sit on the floor of Jo Ellen's bedroom, put her princess phone in my lap, and do three things.

1. I call Gale Hoffman.

"Hello?" It's Gale herself. I almost never answer the phone, and when I do, I have to say, "Chapman residence, Franny speaking." And Gale just says . . . hello. I imagine her mother in the background, wearing a Marilyn Monroe wig and a mink stole, lounging on the couch . . . with a date.

"Hello, Gale?"

"Speaking."

"Oh, hi . . . it's Franny. Chapman."

I am the only Franny in the fifth grade.

"Hi, Franny."

Silence. I telegraph myself: *Say something!*

"Hello?" Gale says.

"Yes." I clear my throat. "I was just RSVP'ing to your party on Saturday night. I'm coming."

Silence from Gale.

"You're still having it, right?"

"Yes, yes, I am," says Gale. "I'm just reaching for my list." She sounds secretarial. "I'm glad you'll come."

"Really?" I don't know what possesses me to say that.

"Really."

"Thanks for inviting me." My throat tightens.

"You're welcome."

This conversation sounds like something out of the Melody Morris Charm School.

"Were you sick today?" I ask. It comes out like a squeak. I tell myself I'm making conversation, but I know it's a nosy question to ask a girl I hardly know. But then, I am not Melody Morris.

"No . . . not really," she says.

"Oh." How do I get off the phone?

"Thanks for inviting me," I say. Again.

"Good-bye, then," says Gale. She knows how to get off the phone.

"Good-bye."

I can breathe again, and that's done. That is more words than I've ever spoken to Gale Hoffman at one time. What am I thinking? I will be so out of place. I don't even know who else is coming. I don't have a costume. I can't possibly show up in the hobo outfit I wear year after year for trick or treat.

Don't panic, Franny. Don't panic. You are taking your life into your own hands. I take a bite of grilled cheese and open Jo Ellen's letter.

I have been cogitating on this letter. I have pored over my *Arrow Book of Secret Codes* that Margie gave to me for Christmas in third grade. I have tried these codes, one after another, and they haven't worked on this letter, but I think I have finally figured out these numbers. I think they are phone numbers. And Ebenezer is the one I'm interested in.

SNCC
4043945593

CORE
2029353932

EBENEZER
9432843

FOR
3398452334

2. So I call it.

It rings! No one answers the first two rings. Then —

"Hello?"

"Hello?"

"Hello?"

"Yes."

"Who is this?"

"Who is *this*?"

Click.

My heart is in my throat, but Nancy Drew would be proud. I take a deep breath. I am taking my life into my own hands. I dial again.

"Hello?"

"Jo Ellen Chapman, please."

"Who?"

"Jo Ellen Chapman. She's my sister. I need to talk to her." I take a breath. "It's important." Another breath — I can hardly talk. "A family matter."

"Just a minute."

A minute later, I hear her voice. Jo Ellen.

"Hello?"

"Jo Ellen?" I try to sound strong, like Mom.

"Franny?"

"*How could you?*" I don't sound strong. I sound like a lunatic.

"Franny, are you all right? What's the matter, what's happened?"

"No! I'm not all right! What do you think?" I'm so angry, all I can do is shout.

"Franny, where are you?"

"I'm at home! Where are you?"

"I'm at school, Franny. I'm in the middle of a meeting. I'm —"

"You need to come home and right away! Right away! Tonight!"

Silence. I've shouted so much I hiccup.

"What's happening, Franny? Didn't Mom tell you I'm staying at school this week?"

"Yes, she told me. But you didn't!" My nose stings with tears. I will not cry.

Jo Ellen sighs through the phone lines. "I'm sorry, Squirt. I am. I didn't think."

"You sure didn't! We're falling apart over here, and you're playing around at school!" I sniff back my tears.

"I'm not playing, Franny."

"You've got *events*! You've got *late nights*! Well, guess what we've got? *Murder! Slap fights! Hunger strikes! MOM!*" I am furious.

"Franny! You're hysterical — take a breath and calm down."

"I need you, Jo Ellen. I need you now!" My nose starts to run.

"I won't talk with you while you're screaming at me," says Jo Ellen, in such an even voice that she surprises me and shuts me up. I blow my nose on her bed skirt.

"Tell me what's happening," she says.

And I fill her in. I tell her everything — everything but how I stole from her. It takes a long time, but Jo Ellen listens. She promises to come home by Saturday. I don't know if I can make it to Saturday, I tell her, it's only Tuesday. She tells me I can.

"The world may be blown up by then!" I point out.

But I can't make her come home. She says she has meetings.

"What meetings?"

"I'm joining a group here, a group that's going to do good work in the world, and I need to be here for training after classes every day."

"What kind of training?"

"It's too complicated for the phone — I'll tell you when I come home. But don't bring it up to Mom. We've disagreed about it, and I'm doing it anyway. I don't want to upset her."

I laugh — I actually laugh. It's one of those hooting, are-you-kidding? laughs.

"Listen," says Jo Ellen. "I can tell you what happened to Uncle Otts, so you don't have nightmares. . . . I can do that much right now."

"Tell me." I sit up straight. "Did he . . . you know. Did he?"

"No."

Relief seeps into my every pore. "I didn't think so."

"He blames himself, though. He and his younger brother and their division were gassed in the trenches in France during World War One. His brother didn't make it. He died in Uncle Otts's arms. I think that's why he's so obsessed with keeping us safe now. This craziness with Cuba and the Russians and their missiles has brought back all those memories."

Silence.

"Franny?"

Silence.

"Franny? Are you there?"

I am thinking. Nicholas is Nicky. Was it just three days ago that Uncle Otts was lying, soaked, in the front yard and calling for Nicky?

Terrible to burn like that.

I sniff.

"Are you okay?"

"I'm going to have nightmares."

"Call me if you do."

"Really?"

"Really. Use this number." Jo Ellen rattles off a phone number. I scribble it on the back of the envelope.

"How did you get this number?" she asks me.

"It's too complicated for the phone," I say. "I'll tell you when you come home."

"Tit for tat," she says.

"I'm playing your records," I inform her.

"That's fine," she says.

"Are you with your thinking friends?"

"Yes."

"Where are you, Jo Ellen?"

"I'm staying with Lannie. I'm really okay. And so are you. We're all going to be okay. I promise."

"When are you going to change the world?"

"Soon. Soon. I love you, Squirt."

With those words, my poor ragged heart gives in.

"I love you, too."

I hang up the phone and lean back against Jo Ellen's bed. Slowly, thoughtfully, I finish my cold soup and sandwich and drain my milk. Then:

3. I memorize Psalm Twenty-four.

Fannie Lou Townsend Hamer was child number twenty.

She had fourteen older brothers and five older sisters, so she was the baby, born on a farm in the Hill Country of Mississippi in 1917, the same year as JFK, more than fifty years after the end of the Civil War.

So Fannie Lou, a black child, was born into freedom. Or was she?

Her parents were sharecroppers on the farm. The whole family took care of one another and worked from daybreak to dusk to bring in the cotton harvest for the plantation owner. When Fannie was a baby, one of her brothers accidentally dropped her, and the fall broke her leg. There was no money for a doctor, so the bone wasn't set properly, and Fannie Lou walked with a limp for the rest of her days.

When she was two years old, her family moved to Sunflower County, to another plantation, this one in the rich soil of the Mississippi Delta, where Fanny Lou grew up and lived for the rest of her life. Ruleville was the name of the town.

The Delta land was as flat as a door as far as the eye could see. Every now and then, a tree grew in the middle of a field, like a scarecrow with eight or ten limbs, like arms, akimbo. "Hangin' trees," the sharecropper families called them.

Like other sharecropper families living and working on plantations, Fannie Lou's family was paid to bring in the cotton, but they weren't paid much, and they weren't paid fairly. They did all the work, but stayed poor, poor, poor. And in the Delta, there were no other jobs.

Most Negroes knew they were being cheated, but they rarely said anything when it came time for pay-day — it was too dangerous. White people owned the Delta, owned Mississippi, and owned the American South. They made the rules, and they depended on their cheap labor — the black sharecroppers — to make them their fortunes.

(There were poor white families, too.)

It had been that way ever since the days of slavery and most white people in Mississippi wanted it to stay that way. They didn't want the Negroes to have any power.

(What were they afraid of?)

So they made RULES.
Some were written into law.
Some were unspoken.

And the Negroes, who wanted to keep themselves and their families safe, learned to obey these rules.

Negroes were second-class citizens. They couldn't go to the same good schools as white children, couldn't eat in the same restaurants, couldn't swim in the town pools or shop in the same stores or use the same bathrooms.

They could cook and clean and sew and take care of white folks. And that's what many of them did, those who didn't work on the plantations in the fields.

Most of them were not registered to vote.

They knew that asking for change was dangerous. Pushing for fairness had found many a black man hanging by his neck from a hangin' tree, out in the middle of the Delta, or scraping the bottom of a riverbed nearby.

So there was no money for shoes. In the summer Fannie Lou went barefoot. In the winter, her mother tied rags around Fanny Lou's feet to keep them warm, but Fannie got so cold, she would stand in the places where the cows had been resting, in order to warm her feet.

Many black folks in Mississippi couldn't read or write or do their sums because they spent so much time in the cotton fields they didn't go to school. Even when they could go to school, they didn't have the proper books or clothes or shoes.

Fannie loved school. She was a spelling whiz and a fine reader. She loved to read so much, she would hop off the cotton wagon if she saw a scrap of newspaper by the side of the dirt road, and sometimes she'd go through the trash at the plantation owner's house, looking for words in print to read.

And she sang — my, that Fannie could sing! She loved church songs, she loved the songs of the cotton fields, and she loved to sing for her family at night after everyone got home and sat on the front steps shelling peas or roasting peanuts. Her favorite song was "This Little Light of Mine."

THIS LITTLE LIGHT OF MINE,
I'M GONNA LET IT SHINE!

She started working in the cotton fields when she was six years old. By the time she was thirteen, she could pick two hundred pounds of cotton in a week. She grew up, married Pap Hamer, and started sharecropping with him in the Delta. And she grew sick and tired of being treated like a second-class citizen. So sick and tired that, when the Negroes from the cities north and south began organizing for change, she wanted to hear what they had to say.

So, in 1961, the same year that Alan Shepard became the first American in space, the same year that John F. Kennedy was sworn in as the thirty-fifth president of the United States, the same year that the anti-Castro forces invaded Cuba at the Bay of Pigs, and the same year that the movie *King of Kings* was released . . .

Fannie attended a meeting at a church in Ruleville where she heard the speakers — black organizers she had never met (Bob Moses, Jim Farmer, James Bevel) — say that she, Fannie Lou Hamer, had a right to vote in this country and to make change in America.

"I didn't know that a Negro could register and vote!"

**Who will go with us on the bus,
to the courthouse, to register to vote?**

Fannie Lou's hand was the first in the air.

"Had it up as high as I could get it."

"I guess if I'd had any sense, I'd have been a little scared — but what was the point of being scared? The only thing they could do was kill me, and it seemed they'd been trying to do that a little bit at a time since I could remember."

Fannie Lou Hamer became a community organizer. The plantation owner kicked her off the farm, and Pap followed her as soon as the harvest was in.

"Find the lady who sings the hymns," said Bob Moses. The civil rights movement became her home.

After three tries, Fannie successfully registered to vote. Then she rode on the buses and helped others register. She worked as a field secretary for the Student Nonviolent Coordinating Committee — SNCC — and the Congress for Racial Equality — CORE — the organizations that had sent the organizers.

She was arrested,
   she was beaten,
      she was ridiculed,
         she was shot at.

She was GALVANIZED.

She spoke with fire from her heart in a voice that rolled like thunder. She sang to her compatriots, to calm them. She led them in the songs of the movement — the civil rights movement. *Ain't Gonna Let Nobody Turn Me 'Round!*

Fannie Lou became fearless.

HIDE IT UNDER A BUSHEL — NO!
I'M GONNA LET IT SHINE!

"We're tired of all this beatin', we're tired of takin' this. It's been a hundred years and we're still being beaten and shot at, crosses are still being burned, because we want to vote. But I'm goin' to stay in Mississippi and if they shoot me down, I'll be buried here."

She worked with the Freedom Riders who came to Mississippi for Freedom Summer in 1964 — most of them young white students from college campuses in the north. She helped train them, just as she had been trained.

Soon, everyone knew who she was, even President Kennedy and, after he died, President Johnson. Fannie Lou was indeed registered to vote, and she wanted all black people to have the right to register and vote. To vote was to have the power to change things. She traveled to the Democratic National Convention in Atlantic City, New Jersey, in 1964, and in front of television cameras so all of America could see her and hear her, she said,

"All my life I've been sick and tired. Now I'm sick and tired of being sick and tired."

and

*"I question America. Is this America? The land of the
free and the home of the brave?"*

Fannie Lou Hamer changed her destiny when she
raised her hand as high as she could get it that night in
Ruleville and said YES. She changed the destiny of thousands upon thousands of people, black and white, and
every color under the sun. She demanded human rights
for all. And because she did, she helped change the
world.

*"In 1962 nobody knew that I existed. Then one
day, the thirty-first of August, I walked off the plantation. From that time up until now I met a lot of
people. I met a lot of great people, both blacks
and whites. People that we have walked together,
we have talked together, we've cried together."*

Even of the people who beat her, she said, "Baby,
you have to love 'em."

*"I feel sorry for anybody who would let hate wrap
them up. Ain't no such thing as I can hate anybody and hope to see God's face."*

In 1964, President Lyndon Johnson signed the Civil
Rights Act of 1964, which assured every American,
EVERY American, the right to every public place — every
public drinking fountain, restroom, restaurant, school,
and more.

In 1965, President Johnson signed into effect the Voting Rights Act, which gave every American citizen of age the right to register and vote. He appeared on television and said,

> "I speak tonight for the dignity of man and the destiny of democracy. . . . The Constitution says that no person shall be kept from voting because of his race or his color. We have all sworn an oath before God to support and to defend that Constitution. We must now act in obedience to that oath. . . . Wednesday I will send to Congress a law designed to eliminate illegal barriers to the right to vote. . . ."

Fannie Lou had said it all along:

> "Live up to the creed, live up to the Declaration of Independence, the Bill of Rights."

In 1977, Fannie Lou Townsend Hamer died of cancer, and probably of complications from the beatings she had received fourteen years earlier as she struggled for her civil and human rights. She was fifty-nine years old.

> "Nobody's free 'til everybody's free."

And the struggle continues.

29

By the time Saturday rolls around, we're used to living like we're emergency room patients. Daddy leaves before dawn and comes home after dark. Drew has gone silent and no longer rides his bike or hangs out in the woods or the tree house. The only thing he really does is watch the news. Uncle Otts has stopped coming to the table for supper. He spends all his time in the workshop/family bomb shelter with the radio on. He tests everything. He rearranges everything. He sleeps in the bunker, as we've started calling it. So does Drew, because Drew sleeps where Uncle Otts sleeps. So does Jack. It's ridiculous.

That leaves me and Mom and Dad. And school and Margie and Chris and Gale. And a party tonight. I tried to ask Mom if I could go, I really did. But Mom has been so distracted she didn't go to bridge at Mrs. Hornbuckle's house. Maybe it was canceled. I'm afraid to ask for anything, so I just pretend I asked Mom and pretend she said yes. If I pretend long enough, I might believe it.

I can't help hearing the news wherever I go.

**Military forces go to
DEFCON 2,**

the highest level ever
in American history.

Soviet ships reach the quarantine line,
but receive radio orders from Moscow
to hold their positions.

*Now, what are you supposed to do
when you see the flash?*

School wasn't much better than home. Teachers listened to the news in the office, and Mrs. Rodriguez brought a transistor radio in to listen to the news during recess instead of coming outside with us. And, as if that wasn't bad enough, all week Margie and I battled.

On Wednesdays we combine classes for music. Miss Farrell played "In the Hall of the Mountain King" from the *Peer Gynt Suite* — I'm asking for it for Christmas, it's my favorite classical record, and Miss Farrell knows it. So when she asked who knew the composer and I shot my arm in the air, she smiled and picked me, but I pronounced *Grieg* improperly, so Margie immediately raised her hand and — without being picked on — said, "Not *Gregg*, Miss Farrell. *Greeeeg!*" Then she smirked at me. I smirked back.

In glee club we're working on "When the Red, Red Robin Comes Bob, Bob Bobbin' Along," and the alto part is sensational. I sing it all by myself in the bathtub at night. But I couldn't stay on my notes on Thursday after school because Judy James sang right in my ear. I finally complained to Miss Farrell, after practice. I spoke in hushed tones. I wanted a private conversation.

"Why does Judy always have to stand next to me? She can't hold a tune! Why is she even in glee club?" Miss Farrell smiled at me sweetly and said, "I depend on you to help her pick out the notes. Sing louder."

It's hopeless — Judy is hopeless — and I huffed and puffed about it — "Why me?" — and Margie, who had eavesdropped, laughed at me from the soprano section. It was one of those you're-so-stupid-Franny laughs. One of those I-can't-believe-you-take-up-space-breathing-on-this-planet laughs. It was also a you-get-stuck-with-Judy-James! laugh, and Judy heard it, too, because she had just walked in from the bathroom.

And yesterday, Friday, Margie pointed at me and laughed at my hobo costume when our class paraded through her classroom. She tried to trip me as I walked past her desk, I know she did, even though she looked as innocent as a baby when I looked back at her. I am ignoring her as best as can.

But she has also commandeered Chris after school, and this I cannot ignore. She can't get to him at recess, because he's playing with the boys, but Margie is willing to play kickball and dodgeball and whatever else Chris is interested in, and I'm not.

I should call Gale and cancel coming to the party tonight — it's not a good idea. I don't know how to talk to boys at all, except Chris. And Margie somehow figured out how to walk home from school with just Chris on Wednesday. I had to walk with the ever-silent Drew, the babbling Bobby (who turned *his* faucet on?), and the terminally tone-deaf Judy James. Margie ignored me as I walked past her to my house. I ignored her right back.

Plus, we haven't read out loud all week in social studies. What is the world coming to? Whatever it comes to, I have been to the dentist and I have clean teeth. And no cavities, I might add.

I would like to flash my clean teeth at Chris today and ask him if he's coming to Gale's party or not. I would like to unplug every radio in this house.

> The Soviet ship *Marucla*
> is cleared through the quarantine
> by American ships lying
> five hundred miles off the coast of Cuba.

> Aleksandr Fomin,
> KGB station chief in Washington,
> has met with ABC News correspondent John Scali
> and proposes the dismantling
> of Soviet bases under U.N. supervision
> in exchange for a
> public pledge from the U.S.
> not to invade Cuba.

I'm right in the middle of Saturday chores — I'm scrubbing the toilet and listening to the Top 40 Countdown on WPGC radio — when the doorbell rings. I rush to answer it. I love it when somebody rings the doorbell — there's always a little surprise waiting to happen as you open the door.

And what a surprise. It's Chris!

I smell like Comet cleanser and Pine-Sol. I smile widely anyway, so I can show all my teeth.

"Hey," he says, half raising a hand. Then, "Hey, Jack!" He pats my dog and smiles. I imagine his next words. *I just came over to see if you want to go steady.*

But that's not what he says.

"I brought a piece of your mail. The mailman left it in our mailbox by mistake. My mom asked me to bring it over."

"Oh! Thanks!" I hope I'm sounding bright, but not *too* cheerful; I want to be just cheerful enough.

Mom is right on my heels. I smell her cigarette smoke before I see her. I step aside and explain, "Chris brought over the mail that got left in his mailbox by mistake."

"Downstairs, Jack!" orders Mom. Jack slinks down the stairs. Mom blows her signature thin stream of smoke right above Chris's head and gives him the once-over. She hasn't seen him in more than a year. Her look says she thinks he might have turned into an ax murderer. But Chris just smiles. And then Mom smiles, too, one of her company smiles.

"Thank you, Christopher," she says. "It's good to see you again. How was your year in Pakistan?"

"Oh, it was great, Mrs. Chapman," says Chris. "We had a wonderful time." He sounds like Wally Cleaver's friend, Eddie, on *Leave It to Beaver*. Mom's baloney-meter is very high — she can spot an Eddie Haskell at ten paces.

"Good for you, Christopher," she says crisply. Yep. *Dismissed.*

Just as she takes the mail from Chris, the phone rings. Mom turns and quick-times it up the stairs, her legs pumping high like an athlete, her posture perfect, her time an Olympic record.

"My dad's on alert," I say.

Chris shrugs. "Who isn't?"

"Yeah." I notice I'm still holding a wet sponge. I put my hand behind my back. Nonchalantly.

"I'm coming to the party tonight," says Chris. "You asked, so I thought I'd let you know."

291

"That's great," I say. "I'll see you there."

I have six hours to learn how to dance.

"Are you sure you're coming?" Chris asks this as he studies his loopy shoelaces.

"Sure, I'm sure. Why?"

He bends down to retie his left shoelace. "No reason. Margie said you weren't allowed to go to boy-girl parties."

I can feel my face on fire. "Margie doesn't know everything about me."

And then there is an awkward silence.

"I think I'll check the mail," I say, "since the mailman came." I drop my sponge on the floor behind me and step out my front door. And Chris, that courteous knight in shining armor, *walks me to the mailbox.* We walk slowly. *We are sauntering,* I say to myself, and I pretend we're walking down the aisle, which is my driveway. I expect him to open my mailbox using a handkerchief. But he doesn't.

"See ya," he says.

"See ya," I say back.

But look who drives by before Chris can cross the street. It's Mrs. Gardener, turning off Allentown Road onto Coolridge Drive, with Margie in the front seat. *Tit for tat, Margie. Tit for tat.*

I need a new costume for tonight.

**An American U-2 was
shot down over Cuba today,
killing the pilot.**

30

When Jo Ellen comes home an hour later, I am still doing chores. I have dusted every ridiculous knickknack on the living room bookshelves, I have even dusted the books. I have been sent back to clean the bathroom sink — twice. The first time I couldn't even see the dirt Mom was pointing at, and the second time it was because I forgot to clean the mirror. But the moment Jo Ellen steps out of Lannie's blue Beetle, none of that matters.

Daddy is painting his new shed. He knocks over the paint can in a rush to hug Jo Ellen. Jo Ellen and Mom hug politely — they are obviously still disagreeing — but they hug. Drew and Uncle Otts are helping Daddy paint. They both stand at attention and salute Jo Ellen. Mom rolls her eyes, and Jo Ellen gives me a look that says, *Tough week*? I give her one back that says, *See? I told you!* And then we are in each other's arms.

"Finish your chores, Franny," says Mom. "Jo Ellen, we've got Dining Out tonight."

"I'll be here," says Jo Ellen as she waves good-bye to Lannie.

Dining Out is the most formal, most auspicious event of the year for the 89th at Andrews. But the news has been so dire, I wondered if it would be canceled, since everyone's on alert. Then I heard Daddy talking to Mom. "The whole squadron will be on base at the same time," he said. "We may as well dine together while we stay ready for anything."

So it's business-as-usual-but-not-really for the air force tonight, with all the officers dressed in their military dress uniforms, and all their wives wearing their best imitations of Marilyn Monroe or Jacqueline Kennedy. Everybody will drink fancy drinks with umbrellas in them and eat fancy steaks and sit at big round tables, listening to an important four-star general talk about important things.

And then there will be dancing. Ballroom dancing and a real band.

I know all about Dining Out. I've seen the pictures and have listened to Mom and Dad tell the stories. There are name cards with gold lettering at all the tables. There's a whole room set aside to store coats and hats and the occasional mink stole. Someone rings fancy chimes to call everyone in to dinner. An honor guard with flags marches in at attention, and a band plays the National Anthem. Manners are very important. There are toasts and awards and party favors, too, and even programs with so many names in them — it's a very big deal, and a very momentous night. The 89th always receives a safety award, and that makes me proud of Daddy.

When Mom and Dad are ready to go, Jo Ellen takes Polaroids of them standing in front of the fireplace. Daddy looks more handsome than I've ever seen him in his dress blues with bars and pins and medals and his shiny black shoes. Mom is wearing deep red lipstick, long white gloves, and an emerald green evening dress. And high heels. Also three strings of pearls, and pearl earrings. She's had her hair done up in a sweep above her ears.

"Look at yourselves!" says Jo Ellen, showing them their photos. "You'll be the most handsome couple there."

They look so glamorous, it makes my heart hurt with love for them. *This must be how they used to be*, I say to myself. They are smiling at each other as Jo Ellen snaps another picture. They smile at Jo Ellen, too, and she smiles right back at them, as if there had never been any disagreement. They tell little inside jokes. They hug me. It feels almost normal around here this afternoon, except that Uncle Otts is in the bunker, and Drew is refusing to eat again.

"See if you can get him to eat something," Mom says to Jo Ellen as they leave. "I'm worried about him."

"Don't worry," says Jo Ellen. "I've got everything under control."

Jo Ellen always babysits us on Dining Out night. She lets us have whatever we want for dinner, plays Scrabble with us and always wins, then walks with us on the sidewalk up Allentown Road to the brand-new High's Dairy so we can get an ice-cream cone for dessert. She also gives Jack extra dog treats, and she lets us watch television until we're sick of it. It's almost as much fun as New Year's Eve, when Mom and Dad don't come home until three in the morning and leave noisemakers and gold party hats for us on the kitchen table.

But this year things will be different. This year I've got a party to go to.

*   *   *

"What are we going to do with you?" says Jo Ellen.

"Well, for starters, I don't know how to dance," I say.

"There's no time to learn anything formal," Jo Ellen says. "You just move to the music, that's all. Just groove a little — you'll get the hang of it. Bop around. You'll be fine. Nobody else knows what they're doing either, believe me."

She puts a new 45 on her record player and dances! She looks like those kids on *American Bandstand*, only more beautiful. She's wearing black pedal pushers and flats, a white blouse, and a red scarf in her hair, tied like a present.

> Do you love me? (I can really move!)
> Do you love me? (I'm in the groove!)

"Come on, Franny! Do what I do — and sing after me! Watch me now!"

Jo Ellen wails! So I wail, too.

Then I get a glimpse of myself in the mirror. I look like a floppy albatross trying to dance, like a sick duck, staggering, stuttering, like I've got that disease — that tarantula disease. I stop.

"It's not ballroom dancing," I say.

And we both crack up. "Oh, heavens," says Jo Ellen, "and it's your turn this summer — you'll be twelve and ready for *ballroom dancing lessons!*" She laughs as she finishes dancing to "Do You Love Me?" doing the fox-trot, the rumba, the tango, the cha-cha.

"You're going to have *fun* tonight," she says when the song's over. "Come here."

I stand with her in front of her open closet. "You can't be a hobo," she says, flipping from hanger to hanger. "I've got just the thing for you in here. Let me see. . . ."

Soon I am wearing a bouncy skirt of red, yellow, blue, and green stripes that flow in circles around me, like Hula-hoops. "From one of Daddy's trips, years ago," says Jo Ellen. There's a petticoat underneath it that makes the skirt pouf like a dancer's. I twirl three times — what a skirt for dancing in!

I am overcome. I clutch Jo Ellen and hug her. Just hug her.

"I love it," I say. "I'm gorgeous!"

Jo Ellen laughs. "Of course you are! Look at that winsome face. And that winsome face with a little makeup — voilà! Gorgeous."

I'm wearing my own red shirt above the skirt — it's the only one that matches, and it looks just fine. "I'm a gypsy!" I say. My hair flops into my face and I shake it out.

"Exactly," says Jo Ellen. She starts fiddling with her necklace. "You're only missing two things. You need some long, dangly earrings and a set of fabulous scarves." She holds up the key to her hope chest and says, "I just happen to have some fabulous scarves right in here."

I feel the blood leaving my face. I hold my breath as Jo Ellen opens her hope chest as if it's the easiest thing in the world to do, as if she's spreading soft butter on toast, that smoothly. She opens the top and . . . nothing. She notices nothing. She doesn't open the drawer where her letters are, she doesn't count them, she doesn't look at me accusingly and demand: *Where is my letter, Franny? What did you do with it? Why did you steal it?* Nothing.

Jo Ellen rummages in the deep recesses of her hope chest and pulls out four beautiful, colorful scarves. "Are you sure?" I say, as she twists together a blue one and a red one and ties them around my waist.

"I'm sure." She ties a gold one around my neck, where it drapes itself dramatically over one shoulder.

"And the *pièce de résistance*," she says as she ties a billowing black scarf with silver moons and stars around my head, capturing my unruly hair, tucking it over my ears, tying it in the back with a flourish. It makes me look — I'll admit it — glamorous. Earrings from her jewelry box — big round ones — and a set of bangle bracelets complete the look.

"Where did you get them?" I can't take my eyes off the scarves.

"I'm saving them for my trousseau, for when I'm married," she says. "Miss Mattie gave them to me. They were part of her trousseau, when she married. She wore them on her honeymoon in Mexico. They are pure silk, spun by silkworms, very delicate and very strong at the same time. Aren't they beautiful?"

I rearrange my scarves in the mirror. I imagine myself as a young bride in Mexico, on her honeymoon. "I miss Miss Mattie," I say.

"Me, too," says Jo Ellen. "But I'm going to see her over Christmas break. I'll leave the day after Christmas."

"Why?"

"She understands," says Jo Ellen.

"What? What does she understand?"

"She understands what I want to do. And I'll spend next summer working in Mississippi."

"Is that what your training is about?"

"Partly," says my sister. "I'm learning a new way of looking at the world, Franny. And I'm going to work in the South to help change things. It's what I want to do."

"I don't want you to go." I don't know what else to say. I just want the world to be here tomorrow. I want it to be kind to me tonight.

"I'm not going forever." Jo Ellen begins putting away her makeup and straightening her dresser. "Time for your first boy-girl party! When you get back, I want to hear everything. And I'll tell you about my plans."

She fishes in her purse and comes up with a cigarette and a pack of matches. She lights up, takes a long drag, and blows the smoke out in a large, soft puff that envelops both of us.

"I shouldn't let you go tonight," she says. "Mom wouldn't allow it if she knew."

"I know. *Thank you* for letting me go, Jo Ellen. I promise, I'll be back early."

And with those words, I begin the longest night of my life.

MOON RIVER

AND ME

PERSONAL
PREPAREDNESS

in the

NUCLEAR AGE

DEPARTMENT OF DEFENSE
OFFICE OF CIVIL DEFENSE

DREAM MAKER

This will be the day when all of God's children, black men and white men, Jews and Gentiles, Protestants and Catholics, will be able to join hands and sing in the words of the old Negro spiritual, "Free at last, free at last, thank God almighty, we are free at last."

Dr. Martin Luther King, Jr., Dartmouth College, May 1962

HEARTBREAKER

TWO DRIFTERS

Friendship 7

little bit to fat
perhaps

31

I try to sneak out of the house without letting Drew see me. If Mom or Dad ever question him about this night, he won't have to lie. Of course, I don't think Drew will ever lie again. He is still recovering from his beige lie of last week.

"Where are you going?" It's Drew. He appears in the kitchen, out of nowhere. Jack is with him, ready to go out and play.

I attempt to sound nonchalant. In a gypsy costume. "So you're talking again?"

"I never stopped talking."

"You coulda fooled me."

"Where are you going?"

"Out."

"I have something for you," Drew says. "It's in my room."

I troop downstairs with my brother. Jo Ellen's bracelets make tinkling noises as I walk. *Chris will like this,* I telegraph to no one.

Drew's room is the picture of neatness. Baseball pennants line the walls along with his air force jet posters and his signed picture of John Glenn. He has Mercury rocket models on his bookshelves and green army men in buckets next to his toy box. His shoes are lined up perfectly in his closet. He has a teddy bear with perfect posture lying on his perfectly made bed.

"What have you got?" I ask.

Drew opens the top right drawer of his desk, takes out a small white box, and hands it to me. "In case we die before tomorrow."

"Jeez, Drew. What is it? All your millions?"

"Open it."

I do.

Inside the box is a key. A suitcase key. It had once been bent, and now is straight. It had once been lost, and now is found.

"How? What?"

"I took it," says Drew, "after Margie left that night."

"Why?"

"I knew you would get in trouble. I knew I could fix it."

I look at my brother's face, so full of character. I feel my face shaming into a deep red.

"I don't know what to say."

"I'll put it back in Mom's suitcase tonight," says Drew.

"Then why are you telling me this?"

"I don't want you to have to worry about it anymore."

I haven't one single clever thing to say, and I also know — and this comes to me like a brand-new thought — I'm not required to explain myself to my brother.

"Thank you, Drew," I say. And I mean it.

"You're welcome."

Just like that.

"You should eat."

"I know."

I give him back the box with the key.

"Don't you want to know where I'm going and why I'm dressed this way?"

"I already know."

Saint Drew.

The first thing I hear is the music.

> It was an
> itsy bitsy
> teenie weenie
> yellow
> polka dot
> bikini,
> that she wore
> for the first time today.

I consider turning around this minute. It's dusk. Golden lights shine from Gale's house, the house I've never been to, the house I'm not allowed to go to. There are kids inside — lots of kids. And I'm afraid. I feel like the lion in *The Wizard of Oz*.

I'D TURN BACK IF I WERE YOU.

Most kids in fifth grade who go to Camp Springs Elementary School can walk to Gale's house, like I just did. And, evidently, most of those kids' parents have no problem with (1) their kids going to Gale's house and (2) their kids going to a boy-girl party.

> She was afraid to come out of the locker.
> She was as nervous as she could be.
> She was afraid to come out of the locker.
> She was afraid that somebody would see.
> Two, three, four, tell the people what she wore!

It's a beautiful night. A fat, full moon hangs low in the sky. It's chilly but not cold. I don't even wear a jacket — I want to show off my beautiful scarves, and Jo Ellen has lent me a shawl. The storm earlier in the week shook a rash of leaves off the trees, and now they crunch underfoot, brown and wrinkled and ready to skitter down the street with the slightest breeze.

"Welcome!" says Gale's mother as I walk through the front door. "Happy Halloween! What a lovely costume!" She takes my shawl and gestures to the room with all the windows, where everyone is getting punch and hot dogs. She looks like everybody else's mom. No wig, no long gloves, no evening gown. No date.

There are no stairs in this house when you come through the front door. Instead there is a long hallway with large rooms to either side. I crane my neck to see into the back of the house. A kid comes out a swinging kitchen door carrying a bowl of candy. To the right there's a living room with a piano, a couch, a wall — it's just a regular house. It looks like anybody else's.

> She was afraid to come out in the open,
> And so a blanket around her she wore.

Across the hall from the living room is the family room, where most of the action is. There's the stereo, stacked with 45-rpm records, flipping, one after another, onto the turntable. The boys are standing at the food or around the edges of the room, looking shy and uncomfortable. I know exactly how they feel. The girls are giggling and gossiping and swaying to the music and eyeballing the boys like they're just waiting for them to make a move.

And here comes Gale. She is not Marilyn Monroe. She's a hobo. A hobo! She's wearing baggy pants and suspenders and her hair is in pigtails — she looks like Pippi Longstocking, but with thick black braids. She's got freckles painted on her face. She's grinning like she just won the big prize on a television game show.

"Mom, this is Franny from Coolridge Drive — remember, we took her the invitation. You've heard me talk about her," says Gale. And Gale's mother says, "Oh, yes! Franny, your *quiet* friend!"

Quiet? Who says?

And I wouldn't exactly call us *friends*. Yet.

"Come on, Franny, let's get punch," says Gale, and the next thing I know, she has elbowed three boys out of the way, and I am standing next to the punch bowl, trying to ladle lime sherbet and ginger ale into a tiny glass cup. It gets all over the place, but not on my scarves, thank goodness.

I am wearing my Buster Brown shoes, but Jo Ellen's skirt is long enough to cover them, so I pretend I'm wearing gypsy slippers. I stand straight and tall. I smile at Gale as she clinks her punch glass against mine.

"What a costume!" she says. "I love it!"

Suddenly, Gale is a fount of friendliness.

"Thanks," I say. "My sister helped me with it."

"Hmmm." Gale sips her punch. "She's got good taste!"

Now she is afraid to come out of the water,
And the poor little girl's turning blue.
Two, three, four, tell the people what she wore!

The boys are laughing at the music and pointing at the girls, who are blushing, even though none of them is wearing a bikini.

"Do you know Carol Moyer?" Gale pulls Carol over. I know Carol. She sits in front of me in Mrs. Rodriguez's class.

"Hey," says Carol. "Great costume."

"Thanks. You, too." Carol is some kind of Viking warrior. Warrior-ess. It suits her.

"Have you noticed how you get skipped over in social studies lately when we read?" Carol asks.

My face burns. "Maybe."

"Why don't you say something?"

I shrug.

"I think she can't see you," says Carol.

"I'm invisible," I say.

"No, really," Carol says. "The sun comes in that window like a heat ray in the afternoon, have you noticed? It cooks my back, so I figure it's coming right across your desk and blinding Mrs. Rodriguez."

I've never thought about it.

"You should speak up." Carol talks to me like she's giving stage directions. "Want to get a hot dog?"

The table is covered with food. The candy bowl is filled with Nik-L-Nips, candy necklaces, candy cigarettes, Mary Janes, Pixy Stix, and Tootsie Rolls. Every face looks amazed to see it, but everyone is politely eating pigs in a blanket like their mothers taught them to do. Dinner first, dessert later.

Two, three, four, tell the people what she wore!

I don't see Chris. I came on time so I could make sure to practice conversation with him, to make him fall in love with me, but he's not here, and now I'm faced with conversation with Gale and Carol and other kids I never talk to in school. Where is Margie? *With Chris*, says my dark heart. The two of them got me here so they could be alone somewhere, right now. They had no intention of coming to this party.

She was afraid to come out in the open
And so she sat, bundled up on the shore.

Carol is eating her third pig in a blanket, and kids are laughing so hard now, you'd think they were all wearing bikinis.
How do I leave?
Jimmy Epps is here. Jimmy Epps! He's a pirate. There's Denise Dubose. She's a fairy, with a wand. And Judy James — I don't know what she is. Please don't let her sing. Carol, Marcy, Laurie — I think the whole fifth grade has been invited to this party, and most of them have shown up.

"Beautiful costume, Franny," says Denise. She taps me with her wand and giggles. Denise, who I was afraid to say anything to or to touch when she cried during the air-raid drill. And now she has tapped me with her wand. And she giggles! She's so earnest about it, she looks so ridiculous, and she doesn't care. I take a breath and . . . I can't help it . . . I laugh. So Denise taps me again. And laughs. Suddenly, everything is fine. We're smiling at each other. Me and Denise Dubose.

At that moment, the next record falls onto the turntable, and kids squeal with delight.

I was working in the lab late one night . . .

"Dance, Franny!" shouts Denise, and she bops away, waving her wand. Boys peel away from the wall — here's a song they can get into. They immediately turn into monsters, every one.

He did the monster mash!

Gale pulls me by the arm. "C'mon!" Suddenly, I am . . . a changed person. I actually telegraph this to myself: *Franny, you are a changed person.* I am a gorgeous gypsy with beautiful scarves and dangling earrings and dark red lips, and I don't care about anything else anymore, I'm dancing.

I'm flopping around like a uncoordinated albatross, like a sick duck, like a winged dove with bangle bracelets, and I'm laughing with everyone else. The boys are bent over and stomping like ghouls, lurching after the girls, and the girls are shrieking and pretending to run away and be scared.

It's fun. It's *really* fun. I'm having such a good time. The petticoat under Jo Ellen's skirt fluffs out the skirt so it bounces and twirls with me. I am gorgeous.

The next record drops and all the girls shriek and form a circle

317

so they can sing to one another. Gale grabs me and pulls me into the circle. Even Judy James sings, and I don't care. What I care about is that I'm in the circle.

> Mister Postman, look and see
> Is there a letter in your bag for me?

I croon to the ceiling, right along with the Marvelettes and my friends. When the record ends, we keep on singing until we realize how bad we sound without the Marvelettes, which makes us laugh — oh, it feels fine.

Tom West — who is dressed like an overgrown bunch of grapes — restacks the 45s, and we all attack the punch and hot dogs. I reach for one, and someone reaches at the same time I do and we knock knuckles.

"Oh, I'm so sorry!" I say. I draw my hand back quickly and my bracelets twinkle together.

"'Oh, I'm so sorry!'" says the someone sarcastically.

I know that voice. It's Margie.

She's wearing a crown — a tiara — just like Miss America's, and she's dressed like Cinderella, like Sleeping Beauty, like the most beautiful princess in the world in a flowing blue gown with pearls in her hair. Her face, however, is all evil stepmother.

"Well, well, well!" she says. "If it isn't *Dixie*!" She eyeballs me. "Dixie the Gypsy!"

I don't know what to say. All my newfound friends must have heard her. I'm afraid to look at them to see if they've noticed. It's too quiet, while Tom West shuffles the records and gets a new stack ready to play.

Gale pushes open the swinging kitchen door and walks into the room carrying a bowl of Chex Mix.

"Something salty!" she proclaims, and then says, surprise in her voice, "Hi, Margie . . ." as she sits the bowl down next to the pigs in their blankets. Then, even more surprised, "Hi, Chris!"

Chris is here. And he came with Margie.

"Hey!" says Chris. I want to be furious with him, but he turns his brown eyes on me. "Hey, Franny. Great costume." Chris is dressed as — I kid you not — Superman.

"Want some punch, Chris?" croons Margie. She leans across the table toward Gale. "I see you had to invite her," she says in a voice that's just loud enough that it invites people to listen.

I look from side to side. Kids want to know who Margie's talking about. They must know it's me. I take two steps back, to distance myself from the conversation.

"What are you talking about?" asks Gale. She takes Margie by the elbow and walks her to the end of the table.

"Watusi!" shouts Tom West as the first record drops onto the turntable and "Do You Love Me?" starts to wail.

Was it just an hour ago that Jo Ellen was trying to teach me to dance to this very tune?

"Want to dance, Franny?"

Superman is asking me to dance. I can't get my mouth to open. My tongue is plastered to the roof of my mouth. I nod. But I know my feet won't move.

"C'mon, Franny!" shouts Denise Dubose as she joins a gaggle of kids in the middle of the room.

I look to see where Margie has gone — I can't find her. Tom slams into Chris because he's bopping up and down like a

319

deranged fruit, and Chris bumps into me, which gets my feet to move and the next thing I know, we're in the middle of a bunch of kids who have no actual partners but are all dancing together.

I try to move, but I'm scared of Margie and need to know where she is. *You had to invite her.* Gale was being nice to me because she had to be. Of course, of course — why can't I ever see these things? And of course, Gale has disappeared, back into the kitchen. Maybe Margie has gone with her.

"You okay?" Chris shouts above the music.

I stumble backward into Denise and Carol. I'm going to be sick. I scoot away from the dancers and to the side of the room, where kids dressed as Draculas and witches and cats and kings are milling around with punch and cookies, and fake spiders are dangling from the ceiling. A few dancers come to check on me, including Chris, who touches me on the arm and says, "Franny — you okay?"

"I'm fine. I'm just . . . I need some air. I . . . want to go home now."

"Want me to walk you?"

I look past Chris, and here comes Margie, storming out of the kitchen without Gale. Steam might as well be coming out of her ears. She's weaving like a maniac between dancing kids. She pushes Denise Dubose out of her way. She's not watching where she's going and she bangs into the stereo, which sends the needle *zzzzzzip!* across the record.

"Ow!" she shouts, and then stumbles sideways two steps. Her Miss America tiara falls off her head just as kids stop, mid-mashed potato, and turn to the source of the silence. Margie's anger takes up all the available space in the room — everyone can see it, feel it.

We are all standing there, waiting for the next thing to happen, and I am reminded of how eerie it feels to wait for that next thing to happen when you don't have any idea what it might be, like the day that we all — every kid in this room — were stuck outside, plastered against the playground, waiting to die.

Margie focuses her angry stare on me, standing next to Chris. "He came with me!" she says between her clenched teeth.

I lick my lips. I can feel lime-green punch swirling in my stomach.

My eyes are locked into Margie's; I can't even look at Chris. I can't say a word, either, but Chris can and does.

"My family ate dinner with your family at your house tonight." He says it loud and clear.

"So?" says Margie. She pulls her eyes away from me and glares at Chris.

"So that's why I came with you."

No one says a word.

Now Margie's face beets up, and like magic, I can look away from her.

"You stay," I manage to croak to Chris. "I've got to go."

"I'll bet you do," says Margie, taking a deep breath and one step toward me. "They don't let you Chapmans out on your own, do they? You never know when one of you might go crazy!" The words rush out of her mouth. I feel slapped.

Kids murmur and shuffle, and no one knows what to say.

"I'll go home with you, Franny," says Judy James in a resolute voice.

"Okay," I whisper. I start for the door.

"Watch out for her uncle!" says Margie. I whip around to

face her and see she can't stop herself. "And watch out for her sister — the *spy!*"

What is she talking about?

I'm dizzy as kids crowd around to hear more. The air is going out of the room, and Margie is like a rabid dog, chewing on her news. She speaks so quickly I can hardly keep up.

"Franny's sister is writing to spies, and they're writing her back! I've seen the letters — they're full of codes — she keeps them locked up in her room! Isn't that right, Franny? We saw one of them — she's working for the Russians! The Communists! She's a spy!"

All those numbers in Jo Ellen's letter. My mystery. Nancy Drew. The Russians. Kommanists. Spies.

Oh, Margie, you are so wrong!

I stumble to the door. My skirt catches on something and I hear a rip. Jo Ellen will be so disappointed. I grab the doorknob, turn it with a desperate twist, and yank the door open with both hands.

The cool October night rushes at my face and lifts me up. It gives me strength. It fills me with a power I didn't know I had. I drink it in, this potent night air, and I turn to face every kid in Gale's house. Every eye is turned on me. I am no longer invisible.

I speak slowly and clearly. "My sister is not a spy." My voice is strong and sure.

Chris's eyes don't leave my face.

"My uncle" — I catch my breath — "is a good person."

Judy James gives me a tiny nod.

322

"And so am I."

Gale and her mother push open the swinging door and walk

out of the kitchen, carrying a coconut cake shaped like a ghost with candles for eyes.

"What's happening?" asks Mrs. Hoffman. "Franny?"

"My sister is not a spy." I begin to repeat myself. I sound like a robot.

"Of course she's not, dear," says Mrs. Hoffman immediately. "What's this about?"

All heads turn to Margie, but it's Gale who speaks.

"I told you that you were wrong," she says in an even voice.

Margie looks at Gale as if she's just been shoved out into the snow with the door locked behind her. "I tried to show you," she says. "I tried to tell you." Margie lifts up her hands, pleading with Gale. "We had a plan!"

Gale shakes her head. "I just told you in the kitchen — *you* had a plan. I was never part of it."

I wipe at my eyes. My makeup is running all over my face.

Margie looks at Gale as her face crumples into a thousand pieces. "I just . . . I just wanted you to be my friend." Her voice is a whisper now, and for the first time she realizes . . . we are all watching her.

She opens her mouth to say something but changes her mind and bolts past the punch, past the chips, past the cake, where the ghost's eyes are now turning into puddles of molten candle wax. She pushes me out of her way and runs down the front steps, tripping and falling on her princess dress and sprawling onto the front walk, where she pops up like a jack-in-the-box and starts to run across Gale's yard and down the street, not toward the empty lot and home, but deeper into Westchester Estates. She's going completely the wrong way.

Mrs. Hoffman calls after her, but Margie won't stop. I have a wild thought that maybe she lost a glass slipper on the steps, but I telegraph myself — *Stop it!* Then I wish Chris would hand me his handkerchief so I could mop my face — does Superman carry a handkerchief?

I am insane to even think these thoughts — I'm a wreck. I start down the front steps as kids crowd the doorway, and Mrs. Hoffman says, "Come inside, boys and girls!" and I say, "I'll get her, Mrs. Hoffman, she'll listen to me!" and before she can protest I'm past her, and I hear Chris say, "I'll go with her, Mrs. Hoffman, it'll be fine," and in two seconds he's next to me and we're both running down the street to catch Margie.

I don't know why I said I'd do it.

She was my friend.

She is my enemy.

I don't know what else to do.

33

If I'd ever imagined walking through the dark with Chris Cavas, I'm sure I would have made it out to be swoon-makingly romantic. It isn't. It isn't at all. I have a hitch in my side, my nose is stuffed up, and it's starting to get cold. I left Jo Ellen's shawl at Gale's. I can't even look at Chris, who is ahead of me. I just want this part to be over.

And it's dark. Everything is different in the dark. Drapes are drawn, venetian blinds are closed, and soft yellow lamplight glows from house to house, like homing beacons signaling all the children safely home. It's eerily quiet except for the running of our feet. Everyone is shut in for the night.

Chris stops and looks back, so I stop and follow his gaze. Gale's front door is closed. No one is following us. We're on our own. Now what?

"I don't see her anywhere," Chris says. He bends over and tries to catch his breath.

"Neither do I."

"Do you think she might have run behind someone's house and circled back the other way?"

"I don't know." I hold the catch in my side and try to breathe calmly. Thousands of crickets chirp their end-of-season sounds, singing in those long, autumn chirps, one last song. The bright, round moon hangs at the tips of the treetops.

"There's a way to get home from here, going in this direction," I say.

"What is it?"

"There's a metal bar — a barrier — across the road up ahead to the left, where there was maybe going to be a road once, but they never built it. It dead-ends a little ways up. If you go past the barrier, you're in the woods."

We both think about this.

"Can you get over it?"

"You just walk past it, on either side."

"Would she have gone through the woods?"

"I don't know. She knows the way."

We've done it a hundred times, me and Margie.

If there is a warning, you will hear it
before the bomb explodes.
But sometimes,
and this is very, very important,
sometimes the bomb might explode
without any warning.
Then, the first thing
we would know about it would be
the flash.
And that means duck and cover fast,
wherever you are.
There's no time to look around and wait!
Be like Bert.

If there's a flash, duck and cover!
And do it fast.

Chris cups his hands around his mouth to make a megaphone and shouts: "Margieeeeeee!" On his third try, two porch lights flip on. We dash down the street.

"C'mon! Let's try the woods!" Chris says.

We aren't six steps into the woods before I reconsider.

"I don't think so." I'm out of steam.

"What?"

I shake my head. "Let her find her own way home."

"Why?"

"Why not? *You* go after her!" My good sense is returning. I'm a moron to run after Margie.

"She's really upset," Chris says.

"And I'm not?"

Superman doesn't know what to do. I cross my arms and stare at him.

"I'm going in," he says.

"Fine," I say. "Tell Her Highness hello for me."

Chris swallows hard. "What do I do?"

Oh, brother. "Stay on the path until you reach the fallen tree," I tell him. "That's where the path ends. Stay to the right — but not too far to the right or you'll wind around and come out back here again."

"Okay," he says, so easily, as if he's Margie's guardian angel. He licks his lips. "See ya."

And he is gone, Man of Steel, in his blue sweatshirt with the red *S* sewn on the front, swallowed up in the dark, walking alone inside the loblolly forest, his red Superman galoshes crunching into the pinecones and sticks on the path.

I turn on my gypsy heel and strut the six steps out of the woods, walk around the barrier, and stand on Westchester Road. I drink in the deep breath of visibility.

I'm not going to care what any of them think of me on Monday morning. I'm going to walk into school smiling. I'm going to talk to everybody. I'm going to go right up to Mrs. Rodriguez and tell her that she has been skipping me in social studies and ask her to please stop. I'm going to ignore Chris completely. I will hang out with Denise Dubose and Judy James. Margie will be like dust to me, like a speck I flick off my sweater as I sit in class listening to Jimmy Epps butcher the social studies textbook.

Smug. I am smug.

And I cannot walk forward.

My stomach, which gave me a reprieve when I stood up for myself at Gale's, is in a quease again, but it's a different kind of queasy. It hurts. It feels bad. It feels like the time Drew had been a rat fink to me, and I tricked him into searching for something in Daddy's new shed, and then locked him in, when Mom and Dad were gone. It was a hot August day. Drew panicked and beat on the door and screamed for me to let him out, and I wouldn't. I let him scream until, finally, a good ten minutes later, he got real quiet, and then I opened the door.

I thought I would laugh in his face — *Ha-ha! I got you back!* — but I couldn't laugh. Drew was covered in sweat. He stumbled as he clawed his way out of the shed. His face wore that horrible panicked look of a trapped animal, and all I could feel was guilt — guilt! I had hurt my brother — I had scared him to death.

And now, Margie is off in the woods, beside herself, alone, in the dark. Margie, who has been worse than a rat fink to me.

And Chris has gone after her, alone. He doesn't know the way. I do.

I can help.

I don't want to.

I will.

I turn myself around and run into the woods.

34

A minute later, I'm at the tree trunk. No Chris. I scramble over the tree, handily. My feet find the just-right path toward home.

"Chris!" I whisper into the silvery darkness. Nothing.

Every shadow looks like someone lurking behind a tree trunk, waiting to grab me. My heart begins that conga beat, and I quicken my pace.

"Chris!" I won't call for Margie. I won't.

I'm coming up soon on the gravel pit — I have never been near it at night. I slow down, begin to watch my step, and hear a distinct, dry *craaaack!* Someone is up ahead. And I am alone in the dark.

I take three steps and wait. Another *craaaack.* Three more steps, and wait. *Craaaaack!* Wait — it's behind me! I twirl.

"Chris!" It's a girl's high-pitched shriek in the dark.

"Margie!" I shriek back.

"You!" Margie screams. She starts pummeling me — pummeling me! With both fists!

"Stop it! Stop it!" I push her away from me. "Stop it!"

And here we go again, like wrestlers on Saturday morning television, rolling all over the forest floor, twigs and sticks and pine needles and rocks and dirt and — everything. We're rolling all over the place, one princess and one gypsy, both with poufy skirts and makeup.

We're not even hitting each other. We're just rolling in the dirt, hugging each other tight, like we're long-lost, angry explorers who have found each other, finally, in the jungle. We are ridiculous.

**But no matter where they go or what they do,
they always try to remember what to do
if the atom bomb explodes right then.**

Just when I'm wondering what we're supposed to do next, Margie pops up — her blue princess dress is as wrinkled and crushed and smudged as Jo Ellen's letter — and starts running away from me, as if I've suddenly contracted the Black Death and she doesn't want to catch it.

So what do I do? I pop up and stumble after her, my arms waving wildly as I try to keep my balance over roots and sticks. As we enter the clearing by the gravel pit, the moon pops on us like a cockeyed spotlight, and we just keep running like crazy people — and we *are* crazy, because the gravel pit is right ahead, yawning like a huge crater on the moon —

"STOP!" I scream at Margie, but she's not listening to me. We are too close, too close!

Then —

Pop!

Bang!

Pop-pop-pop!

BANG-BANG-BANG-POP-BOOM!!

"It's a bomb! Duck and cover!"
Paul and Patty know what to do.

Margie screams like she's on fire.

I dive for the earth and crawl to the nearest thing I can grab hold of, which is an old, gnarly tree trunk that looks like the Grim Reaper in the dark. I don't care what it looks like — I'm about to be blown to bits. I tuck my head against the tree trunk and begin to chant, against my will. "Ten-nine-eight . . ."

There will be no running to Drew's classroom and racing home together, no more walking home from school, no more Andrews Air Force Base, no more records with Jo Ellen, dinners with Uncle Otts flailing and Mom shushing and Daddy stuffing half a pear in his mouth, no more glee club, no more explorers, no more nothing. No nothing. *No nothing!* I squeeze my eyes shut and wait for the white blast so hot it will melt me, and so bright, I will see it through my eyelids.

But it doesn't come. Instead, I hear voices.

"Come ON!" shouts one.

"Hurry!" shouts another.

"Somebody's here — she saw us!" shouts a third. And I recognize that voice. It's Charlie Caldwell — big kid, non-patrol, troublemaker.

"She'll tell!" shouts the first voice.

"Let's go!" Charlie shouts into the blackness. "We can stuff these in mailboxes!"

Big feet and loud laughter pound the hard, woodsy path, and then the woods are quiet again. Cicadas begin that up-and-down song they sing from the trees, and the moon, round as a biscuit, floats over all of creation. It never blinks, not at anyone or any-thing. It just shines and shines and shines.

I let go of the tree I've been hugging. I brush bits of bark off my face and clothes and realize — I'm still not breathing.

Breathe, Franny.

Not a bomb. *Not a bomb.* But my heart can't wrap itself around this knowledge, it just keeps on running. I hold on to it — I actually press both hands to my chest, to cradle my racing heart — and make myself breathe again.

Firecrackers. Not bombs. Kids, not Communists. Life, not death.

I stand up so slowly, so carefully. It's strange to see the world still here, the whole Earth, still turning, still breathing. It smells and looks the same as it did when I said good-bye to it, just a minute earlier.

"Margie?" I step a tiny, baby step forward. One more step. One more.

"Franny!"

"Margie, where are you?"

"I'm over here — I'm in the gravel pit!"

No, she's not. She can't be in there. She'd be dead.

This trench is full of the dead.

"Where?"

"I slid in!" screams Margie. "Help me!"

You can't slide into the gravel pit. Then I remember the old dirt road that was constructed around the edge of the pit, spiraling down against the outside walls like a Slinky, the dirt road that the dump trucks took, eons ago, to the bottom of the quarry, where they were loaded with rocks and dirt and then made their slow trek up, around, and out of the pit.

3

A tingle starts at the top of my head and creeps across my shoulders, down my spine, and into my toes. Margie is in the gravel pit.

"Hurry!" she screams.

I run to the pit until I get so close it threatens to swallow me up. In the light of the moon, the hole is huge, gaping, and black. The earth here slopes toward the pit, so I drop to my hands and knees. "I'm coming!" I call. But I'm afraid to get any closer. I flop to my belly on the sloping earth — the petticoat of my skirt crunches underneath me — and slide like a snake across grit, moss, sticks, pushing with my toes, my head lower than my feet, reaching my arms out ahead of me, until my fingers grasp the fat, firm edge of earth that forms the lip of the gravel pit. I am light-headed. If I move too quickly, I might slide right into the pit. I inch forward until I can peek over the rim.

"Margie?"

"Here!"

There she is, to my right and down, bathed by the moon, silhouetted like something out of science fiction, like an astronaut tucked in a corner of a crater on the moon.

We choose to go to the moon.

She's crouched against the wall of the pit, perched on the spiral road that leads to the bottom. She's got both arms wrapped around a tree root.

"Can you see me?" she asks.

"I see you."

"Can I walk out?"

"I don't think so."

I know she can't. Drew and I have eyed this road many times, we've even stepped tentatively onto it, only to have the sides of it crumble away under our feet. The road has crumbled so much, all that's left of it are ledges. Some are wide, like islands, and some narrow, like shelves. Margie is on an island. She's got a good tree root to hang on to, but if she steps off the ledge, or if her tree root snaps, she's going down, into the abyss.

"Are you hurt?" I ask.

"I can't tell. I don't think so."

"Wait right there. I'll run get help!"

"Don't you dare!" Margie screams. "Don't you dare leave me here alone!"

"Well, I can't get you out!" I yell right back at her.

"Think of something!" Then she starts to cry. "Those stupid, stupid boys!"

I scoot myself backward, out of danger, and roll onto my back so I can think. My moon and stars scarf slides over my eyes and I pull it off.

They are pure silk, spun by silkworms,
very delicate and very strong at the same time.
Aren't they beautiful?

Yes! I telegraph *Thank you!* to Jo Ellen and apologies to Miss Mattie for ruining her honeymoon scarves. I sit up, use my teeth to make a tear in the moon-and-stars scarf, rip it in half, then rip each half in half, lengthwise. Then I knot each piece together. If there's one thing I know how to do, it's make a good knot.

"Are you there?" Margie calls.

"Just a minute!" I call back, my voice traveling skyward. "I'm

337

making you a rope!" I rip the gold scarf in half and in half again and tie it together, then tie it to the moon-and-stars rope. *Oh, Jo Ellen, don't be mad!*

"Hurry!" shouts Margie.

"Hold your horses! I'm working as fast as I can!" I rip the red scarf into four strips. *Oh, Miss Mattie — I'm so sorry!*

"I'm going to fall!" Margie wails.

"Shut UP!" I shout. "Just SHUT UP!" I tie the halves of the red scarf together.

"I hate you!" Margie shrieks.

"I hate you, too!"

"You take my friends!" Margie wails, as if she's got to have it out, right here, right now, with me, in the dire dark, in case she plunges to her death.

"I'm the best friend you've got!" I shout. It feels good. "You're a stupid moron!"

I finish tying all the scarf strips together into one long rope. Now what?

"You're a square!" Margie cries, and then she sobs again.

Yes, I am. I wrap a piece of the moon and stars around the palm of my right hand and tie it, using my left hand and my teeth. *Yes, I am.* I slide onto my stomach and inch sideways until I'm right above Margie. *Yes, I am. I'm a square, in my Buster Brown shoes and plastic headbands, with my Nancy Drews and my* Word Wealth Junior. *But you know what, Margie? You're mean. And that's worse.*

I scoot back far enough to hold on to a tree root with my left hand, and offer my right hand as far down into the pit as I dare let it go. I open my fist and let the scarf rope drop toward Margie.

"Can you see this?"

"What is it?"

"It's a rope!"

"I can't reach it!"

"Try!"

Silence. I can't hold on to the tree root and look down into the pit at the same time. I don't know what she's doing down there.

"It's way above my head!" Margie shouts.

"Can you stand up and grab it?"

"I can't move!"

"Try!"

I hear her getting to her feet. I hear the trickle of pebbles and dirt skittering into the pit below. Then, "It's too far out, into the pit — I can't reach out that far."

Neither of us speaks for a moment. Then Margie says, in the quietest voice she's used all night, "Besides, Franny, even if I could reach it, what would happen if I grabbed it? How would you pull me up?"

I'm holding on to a tree root, but it's not like I've got my leg wrapped around my desk chair for ballast. Even if she could reach the rope, if she yanked on it, I would be catapulted right down into the pit with her, and we would both be gone.

I killed him.

So I make a decision. I don't care if she doesn't like it. I don't care if she has to wait here alone. "I'm getting your dad!" I shout.

And as I say it, Margie screams. A piece of her ledge breaks off and tumbles into the pit. Like an avalanche, rocks and dirt roar into the void.

"Don't leave me, Franny! Please!"

I pull my scarved hand back to me and shove myself backward on my stomach to a safe place. I have ruined Jo Ellen's skirt; it mangles itself every which way underneath me. I drop my forehead to the cool of the hard earth and close my eyes. I don't know what to do. Margie begins to cry.

The cold and damp wrap themselves around me like a blanket. Out of the darkness, in the most sincere voice I've ever heard her use, Margie says, "I'm sorry for everything, Franny."

I am so tired of talking.

"I'm sorry, Franny. Really, I am."

I lie there, the smell of the earth taking up all the room in my nose, the sounds of the night taking up all the room in my ears, until I hear a jingle on my right. I turn my head and peer through my bangs to see Jack — Jack! — skirting the broken limb that the older boys pulled down an eternity ago, and trotting toward me, all smiles, all happy to have found me.

"Jack!" I wrap myself around the solidness of his sturdy body and the sureness of his presence. He wags his tail like there's no one else in this world but me.

"Is it Jack?" calls Margie from down below.

"Yes!" I shout. "Go home, Jack," I order my dog. "Go home and get Drew. Get Jo Ellen. Send them here. Send help, Jack!"

Jack wags his tail. He looks like Lassie, but that's where the resemblance ends. Lassie would go get help and save the day. Jack doesn't leave, ever. Jack's whole purpose in life is to stay. He scampers to the fallen tree limb and stares at me, as if to say, *Come on! Don't you want to play?* Then he runs back to me.

"Home!" I say in my sternest voice. Jack scampers to the tree limb again. And this time, he rummages in the fallen leaves and brings me a present, like he always does — something to throw, something to play with.

I see it trailing behind him and I know exactly what it is: It's a rope. It's the rope those boys were using to lasso that limb when we came into the woods after school on Friday. *It's a rope.*

I scramble to my feet and run toward Jack. "Here, Jack! Bring it to me, boy!" I call, and he does, dutiful dog that he is. I clap my hands as I run up the slope to Jack, I reach for him, and then — *smack!* I run right into the seat of the rope swing. I can't see it hanging there in the dark, but I feel it smart my shin.

"Oomph!" I drop to one knee, pop up, then fall right across the wooden seat. I can't help it. But I keep going — I need that rope! The wooden seat plasters itself to my belly and I have a wild thought: *This is how I used to swing, before I was big enough to sit on the swing by myself!*

My momentum takes me two more steps uphill, to where Jack is waiting. I reach out both hands and take the rope from him. He barks and turns in a happy, tight circle. And then, before I realize what's happening, before I can stop myself, the swing sways from side to side underneath me, picks me up, and begins its long, slow sail down the slope, on its way to the gravel pit.

All I can do is hang on for dear life.

36

Dear life! I am so stunned I can't even scream. I cling to Jack's rope with both hands. I cling to the swing seat with my elbows, and soon I am flying *backward! backward! faster! faster!* and my hair billows around my face as I look down, down, down at the earth, racing like a rocket beneath me, now disappearing as I am hoisted *higher — higher — higher —* until I have left the earth —

You are leaving the American sector.

I am the rocket, shooting into space. I am trailing two comets beneath me — the gypsy scarf-rope and the real rope — the rope that just might rescue Margie.

I find my voice. "Margieeeeeeeee!" I scream at the top of my lungs. "Rope!"

Jack barks wildly and Margie — who must see me — screams back at me. "Frannyyyyyyyyyyy!" Her voice bounces and echoes off the walls of the gravel pit.

Way, way out, over the middle of the gravel pit I glide. I can only look down, down into its belly, as the wind rushes past me, and everything — my mind, the swing, my very existence — snaps into slow motion.

Under me are the sparkling stars, the alabaster moon, and the frosty night clouds. I blink at the sight and realize it's a reflection. The night sky is reflected in the rainwater at the bottom of the gravel pit. It is so black down there, so shiny, so wide, so beautiful. So quiet. I hear nothing but the creak of the knots against the wooden swing as it strains against my weight as I arc over the pit.

This must be what it feels like to be weightless. This must be what it's like to fly. It's so rare, this feeling. No wonder Drew loves it so.

The moon turns the deep, dark sides of the gravel pit into sandy crags of shadow and light rising out of the Milky Way at its bottom. I am a speck above this crater, an invisible atom among the giants of rock and water and trees. But at the same time, I realize I am a part of everything I see.

*The earth is the Lord's
and the fullness thereof;
the world,
and they that dwell therein.*

Every atom in my body is alive and tingling with a delicious feeling I can't describe. It's beyond fear. It is, in this moment . . . bliss. And knowledge, because I know something, in this moment, that I may never know again: In this moment, I am afraid of nothing.

In the next moment, the swing suspends itself in the brilliant night at its highest point. For a second or two, it hovers in the air but does not move. It's as if the swing and the rope have to take a breath, have to get ready for the ride back to earth. And in

343

that next moment, as the swing begins its swoop back across the pit, the fear I had abandoned comes rushing back to me a hundred times stronger — I am about to swoop across this pit and crash-land on the other side.

I will land blind as well — I cannot lift my head up, or I might fall off. I cannot twist myself sideways or I *will* fall off. I have to ride the swing back to earth and crash-land with no astronaut's helmet, smack on my head. And I cannot let go of the rope for Margie, the rope that trails behind me like a comet. If my momentum will allow the rope to swing close enough to her, she can grab it, and we can figure out the rest.

"Grab the rope!" I scream as the swing swoops to its lowest place.

"I got it!" Margie screams as I whiz past her, my elbows locking the swing to my belly and both hands clutching the rope that Jack brought me.

The earth comes back to me, racing underneath me, and I know my time is at hand. I squeeze my eyes shut and try to hunch over the swing as best I can to break my fall. I hear a heavy *craaaack!* — pain! — as my shoulders slam into the earth. The swing disgorges me — I tumble off and flip over onto my back.

"Are you okay?" shouts Margie, but I can't answer. "Franny, I got it! I got the rope!" I close my eyes. *Is this what it feels like to die?* "Do you still have your end of the rope?" shouts Margie, but I can't answer her. I think I dropped it. I know I did. I know I dropped the rope.

I open my eyes and see a bright light — so bright it blinds me.

There is a bright flash, brighter than the sun, brighter than anything you've ever seen!

But it's not the atomic flash, not the bomb. It's heaven, it must be heaven. And Drew's face is above me in the light. *I did it,* I telegraph him. *I know what it feels like.* Drew begins to cry.

Then there's Uncle Otts above me in the light. I can see every whisker poking out of every pore on his face. He cradles me in his arms and buries his old face next to mine. *Nicky! Nicky!* he sobs.

Terrible to burn like that.

The bright, burning light is everywhere. It bounces from me, to the trees, and to Jack, who is hovering by me and Uncle Otts. *Good dog,* I telegraph him.

Now I see Mr. Gardener's face, too — *What a strange death this is,* I say to myself. Mouths open, tears flow, hands touch me — I feel and hear nothing. *I must be dying soon,* I think. *Where is Jo Ellen? Where are Mom and Dad?*

Chris appears, still in his Superman costume. *I brought help,* his lips say, but I don't hear him. I telegraph him the question: *Is this what happens when you die?* He doesn't answer me.

I close my eyes and drift over the gravel pit again, over the entire world, over Russia, over Cuba, over my house on Coolridge Drive, over my school on Allentown Road, over all the teachers and all the words, over Andrews Air Force Base, over the pilots, the pilots' wives at their bridge games, and the kids, all the kids in all the countries, the baseball games in back lots, and the dogs who bring things for the kids to play with.

I finish my letter to Chairman Khrushchev. I write it to President Kennedy, too.

345

Dear Chairman Khrushchev and President Kennedy,

My name is Frances Chapman, and I live in America, which is part of the world, which is part of the universe. If you could see the world from outer space, the way my brother, Drew, sees it, you would know that we are all made of the same things: atoms and air and water and skin and bones and blood, and lots of the same hopes and fears.

Chairman Khrushchev, we are scared of you because we don't know you and we think you want to hurt us. If you knew us, you wouldn't want to hurt us — you would love us because we are just like you. We have shaggy dogs and families and schools and friends and meat loaf for supper.

President Kennedy, the Russian children must be just as scared of us as we are of them. We don't know them. I'll bet they play jacks and read books and love their moms and dads and brothers and sisters.

The secret to not being afraid is to understand what scares you.

We should get to know one another.

Sincerely,
Frances Chapman

37

"She's alive!"

It's Uncle Otts's voice. He sounds completely different. He's in charge.

"Drew, get over here!" he orders.

"Yessir!"

"Don't let her sleep! Keep her awake!"

Drew slaps my cheeks. "Franny! Wake up!"

I try to swat him away with both hands, like he's a fly, but it hurts too much to move my arms.

"Don't smack her, boy!" says Uncle Otts. "Just talk to her. She's had a bad tumble — she's probably got a concussion. Just talk to her."

I can hear all of this — my hearing has returned. The burning light is the emergency lamp Uncle Otts bought for the bomb shelter — it must put out a million lumens of light. Lumens. I love that word. Thank you, *Word Wealth Junior*. I hear clanking and rustling and I manage a whisper: "What's happening?"

"Uncle Otts brought stuff," says Drew. "When Chris and I told him about the gravel pit, he brought rope and flares and all kinds of stuff from the bunker."

"Margie," I whisper.

"I know!" spouts Drew. "Uncle Otts is saving her!"

Soon the entire gravel pit area is alive with a yellow-red glow. Flares. Uncle Otts has lighted the flares.

"Murga —" I whisper. That's all I can get out.

"— troyd," finishes Drew. He looks at me anxiously.

Uncle Otts is back. "Good! You're awake! Let me see that hand, little lady." He takes my right hand into his hands and comes at it with an enormous pocketknife.

Instinctively, I pull my hand back to me. "No!" I say, but nothing comes out.

"I need your scarves, Franny, honey," says Uncle Otts, and I remember — I tied them on to my hand.

"I dropped the rope," I whisper.

"No, you didn't," says Uncle Otts. "It's right here, tangled up in all these scarves. They grabbed it for you. It's a miracle you didn't kill yourself." He speaks quickly and moves swiftly, like he's a young man again.

And he has called me Franny.

"You shoulda seen yourself, Franny!" Drew's voice is full of awe.

"It was amazing," says Chris. More awe.

"Got that rope, Mr. Chapman?" calls Mr. Gardener.

"Coming!" says Uncle Otts. He pats my knee with his big hand. "Don't go anywhere."

"He's like John Wayne," says Drew, admiration spilling everywhere.

"What's he doing?" I whisper. I have no spit — my teeth are stuck to the inside of my lips.

"He's making a rope pulley and sending it down to Margie on the rope you gave her."

"Come here and help, Drew!" commands Uncle Otts.

"Be right back!" says Drew and he is gone.

I open my eyes to the stars and moon above me. *Hello again,* I telegraph them. *I feel like we know one another so well now.* I hear the jingle of Jack's collar, and then I feel him. He sidles up next to me and lies down against my side, silent and affirming, as if to say, *I'm here. I'll stay with you.*

My head feels like it has cracked open. I can't think. My eyes are hot. Swallowing is such an effort. Chris stands next to me, watches me, anxious.

"I'm sorry I didn't stay with you, Franny," he says.

I want to thank him for bringing help, but I can't say that much. "Superman," I whisper. I try a smile. Every atom of my body hurts. Every heartbeat hurts.

"Pull!" Uncle Otts shouts. Margie screams. The ledge crumbles into the abyss. I hear everything suddenly, every little thing.

"We got her!" shouts Mr. Gardener. I hear the relief in his voice.

I close my eyes, and the tears slip from the outside corners, down into my ears.

"Franny!" Margie stands over me, crying and calling my name, over and over, but now I can't hear her.

I'm sorry, she says. What a strange thing, that I can read her lips.

It's okay, I telegraph her.

Margie wipes her eyes with the heels of her hands. *You're a good friend, Franny,* she says to me. *The best.*

Fading. Fading. Fade to black.

Sunday, October 28, 1962

The crisis is over. In a speech aired on Radio Moscow, Khrushchev announces the dismantling of Soviet missiles in Cuba.

"Tell it to me again." I want to get the story straight. My addled brain will need to hear it over and over.

"Okay." Drew, very serious, clears his throat. "Jo Ellen waited for Mom and Dad and tried to get a phone call through to them. . . ."

Mom and Dad have left the room to talk with the doctor. Just outside my room, the radio at the nurse's station crackles with the latest news. The crisis is over. The Russians have backed down. The bombs will leave Cuba. The whole world breathes again.

Mom stayed with me all night, holding my hand, brushing little wisps of hair out of my face, reading me an old Nancy Drew that Jo Ellen brought to the hospital for me. I drifted in and out, hearing and not hearing, conscious and not conscious, and she was always there. I didn't once say, *You can't be my mom! You must be an alien. What have you done with my mom?*

I am wearing a special sling contraption to keep my shoulders still. I hurt. My head pounds like someone is taking a sledgehammer to it, and my neck is so stiff, it's hard to move at all.

"I dropped the rope," I say. "I know I did." I search my memory, but it won't come to me. "Didn't I?"

"Yes and no," says Drew. "We had to cut the scarves off your hand because they were tied so tight, we couldn't get them off. They were wrapped around and tangled in the end of the rope, and that's how you didn't drop it. Uncle Otts said it was a miracle you didn't drop your end, and a miracle that Margie was able to grab hers. A miracle!"

Drew is more animated than I've seen him for days.

"Are you eating?" I ask him.

"I ate three bowls of Rice Krispies and two pieces of toast this morning!" he crows. "And a big glass of orange juice! And guess what else?"

"What?"

"I threw up after that, right in the front yard!"

I roll my eyes. "You're not so perfect, you know."

"I don't want to be perfect," Drew says.

We sit in soft silence and gaze out the window of my Malcolm Grow hospital room. I wonder if I might be in the very same room that Uncle Otts was in just a week ago. The chapel parking lot is full. Sunday school is going on without me. I am missing my great moment with Psalm Twenty-four.

Lift up your heads, O ye gates.

Mom and Dad are back, smiling at me. "Just another day or two for observation," says Dad, relief filling his face. "We want to make sure those collarbones are set and healing."

"Will I be home for Halloween?"

Mom gives me her stick-to-what's-important! look but then softens. "When is Halloween?" She's forgotten.

"Wednesday!" spouts Drew. Of course he remembers. And for once he doesn't say, *And I'm going to be an astronaut!*

So I say it for him. "And you're going to be an astronaut."

Drew grins. "John Glenn."

"You should be home by then," says Daddy, "but you won't be able to go trick-or-treating. You've had a serious concussion. The only walking you're going to be doing this week is to the bathroom and back."

Mom looks at me with the strangest look — I expect her to chew me out for all my wrongdoing, but instead she says, her voice cracking, "You are out of danger," and she bursts into tears. Daddy wraps her in his arms, and my heart melts all over my chest.

Daddy is wearing his flight suit — he must be going on a trip. Mom still wears her evening dress — she hasn't even been home to change. Jo Ellen comes through the doorway, smiling widely, carrying her record player.

"You'll need some music," she says.

"I ruined Miss Mattie's scarves," I say immediately as if she might not know this, and I need to make sure I tell her about it.

"Shhhh . . ." says Jo Ellen. "Thank goodness you had them! Miss Mattie says so, too. We called her last night. She's coming for Thanksgiving, to check on you herself — and she's bringing Annie Mae."

You'll do good work, I telegraph Jo Ellen, and she kisses me on the forehead like she's heard me.

Uncle Otts lumbers through the doorway, his face full of John Wayne strength. He has shaved and he is wearing every one of his medals. They make his sweater droop terribly, and that makes me smile. He is a hero, and finally he knows it.

353

He does a strange thing, though. He walks right to my bed-side and says, "Private!"

"Yessir?"

Uncle Otts fumbles with his medals. He removes the biggest one and pins it to the pillow behind my head. "For bravery in battle," he says. He salutes me.

Tears sting the inside of my nose and crowd at my eyes as I look at them all looking at me.

"I wasn't brave," I say. "I wasn't brave at all."

I start to cry and my nose drips like a faucet. Mom wipes it with Daddy's handkerchief. "There's plenty of time to talk about all this later," she says.

I shake my head — just a tiny shake, because it hurts so much. "It was an accident, my . . . riding the swing. And the rope. And the rope tied on to the scarves, and all of it. It was an accident." Tears stream down my face. "I'm not brave. I'm . . . a yellow-bellied coward."

What a time to tell the truth. Here I could be lauded as the hero — no one would know any different — and I choose to tell the truth.

"I won't hear this," says Uncle Otts. "Private, look at me."

I do.

"It wasn't an accident that you stayed with your friend."

"She's not my friend."

"That's for you two to figure out," says Uncle Otts. "What I know is that it's an act of courage to stay with someone who needs you. It's a sign of character." His voice cracks as he says, "A hero can be afraid, but a hero never runs away."

Now Mom and Dad have tears in their eyes.

"So, Private," says Uncle Otts. He stands as straight as a

statue and draws his hand to his forehead. He stares straight ahead and, with great grace, he salutes me.

I salute him back with my good arm.

Then Uncle Otts turns to everyone else in the room, his hand still at his forehead, straight and true and good. And everyone else salutes him back.

Even Mom.

No one says a word. The moment is like a prayer that brings us all together. And then Jo Ellen starts to giggle. Mom smiles — and she giggles, too — Mom giggles! Which sets the whole room to laughing, even Uncle Otts.

A jet roars overhead, then another. I watch my laughing family, gathered around my bed in this tiny hospital room, love oozing from every face.

What brave hearts.

I love every one of them more than I can say.

HERBLOCK'S CARTOON

"Let's Get A Lock For This Thing"

WHAT A WONDERFUL WORLD

We're eyeball-to-eyeball and I think the other fellow just blinked.
Dean Rusk, U.S. Secretary of State, October 24, 1962

DON'T KNOW MUCH ABOUT HISTORY,

DON'T KNOW M
BIOLOGY.

In response to the Soviet Union agreeing to remove its missiles from Cuba, President Kennedy has ended the quarantine of this Caribbean archipelago nation. U.S. troops are coming home. *December 1962*

I thought I might never live to see anot
Robert S. McNamara, U.S. Secretary of Defe

16,300 American advisors are in Vietnam by November 1963, up from 800 when John Kennedy took office in January 1961.

Cuba releases 1,113 prisoners of the 1961 Bay of Pigs invasion attempt. The U.S. government agreed to pay $53 million in food and medical supplies, to Castro's Cuba, donated by companies all over the USA, as a condition for their release. The deal was worked out by Attorney General Robert Kennedy.

December 1962

Telstar 1, the first active communications satellite, launched successfully and is already bringing in a new, benevolent age of technology. It will relay the first television pictures and telephone calls through space, and provide the first live transatlantic television feed.

DON'T KNOW MUCH ABOUT A SCIENCE BOOK, DON'T KNOW MUCH ABOUT THE FRENCH I TOOK.

The "Memorandum of Understanding Between the United States of America and the Union of Soviet Socialist Republics Regarding the Establishment of a Direct Communications Link" was signed by President Kennedy and Chairman Khrushchev today, linking the White House and the Kremlin with a direct telecommunications line. No longer will they have to rely on hand-delivered encoded telegrams to communicate.

June 1963

Richard Nixon loses the California governor's race and speaks to the nation, on television, saying that this is his last press conference, and "you won't have Nixon to kick around any more."

June 1963

There he stands, and
who can believe him?
Black corduroy cap,
green corduroy shirt,
blue corduroy pants.
Hard-lick guitar,
whooping harmonica,
skinny little voice.
Beardless chin, shaggy
sideburns, porcelain
pussy-cat eyes.

Time Magazine on Bob Dylan 1962

AND I KNOW THAT IF YOU LOVE ME, TOO,

WHAT A WONDERFUL

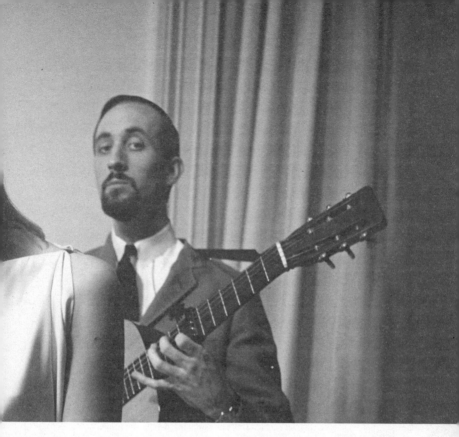

WORLD THIS WOULD BE.

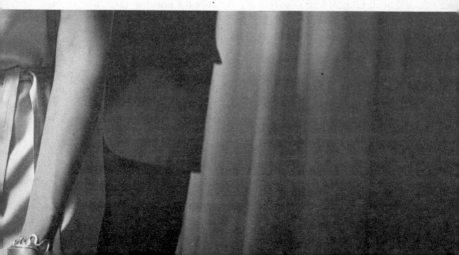

October 31, 1962.

I am wearing a special sling for my broken clavicle, I am recovering from a concussion, and I am grounded.

Never mind that I can't go to school until next week (and maybe not then). Never mind that Drew brings my homework home every day and I do it. Never mind that I am missing glee club and French and reading out loud in social studies. I am also, on top of everything else (including having almost died) — grounded.

"You know the rules," says Mom as she brings me home from the hospital.

"But —"

"No buts," she says as I slowly and carefully slip under the covers of my own good bed and sigh with relief. "You and Jo Ellen both knew better." She plumps my pillow, kisses me on the forehead, and lights a cigarette.

Jo Ellen has moved into the dorm with Lannie. She called me just as I got home from the hospital. "I'll be back on the weekends. You can call me anytime," she said. "If the number I gave you doesn't work, call the one for Ebenezer." So. She knows I have the letter. She figured it out. Maybe one day I'll tell her all about it. Maybe not.

"I heard you was grounded again," says Uncle Otts at dinner-time. *Agin*. We are sitting around the table, all of us but Jo Ellen and Daddy, who is on his trip. We're eating meat loaf TV dinners, my favorite.

"Yessir," I sigh.

"For how long?"

"I don't know," I tell him. "Maybe for life."

"It won't be that long," says Uncle Otts. "I put in a good word for you." He looks across the table at Mom, who drinks her iced tea and says nothing. "Come on and help me and the corporal." *Come own.*

Evidently, Drew got a promotion while I was in the hospital.

"I have to work on my science fair project," I say. "It's due on Monday."

I hazard a glance at Mom. She's returning Uncle Otts's look. She stubs out her cigarette and says to me, "Mrs. Rodriguez gave you a week's reprieve on your project. Besides . . . I don't have the slightest idea where those paints and brushes are."

I don't tell her it's going to take more than paints and brushes to save my science fair project.

As Uncle Otts heads outside, Mom takes off my headband, carves her fingers through my hair to straighten it, then slips my headband neatly back onto my head. "You're not to over-exert yourself right now, Franny," she says. "We just got you home."

"Yes, ma'am," I say.

Uncle Otts and Drew have set up the card table on the drive-way. This is something new — nobody ever sits outside on Halloween night. People wait inside for their doorbells to ring.

"Who carved the pumpkins?" I ask Mom.

"Drew and I did them together yesterday," she says. "Do you like them?"

"They're nice," I say. "Should I help clear the table?"

"Not tonight," says Mom. "I want you to rest."

"Can I just sit outside and watch for a little while? Please?"

Mom gives me a long look, walks to the hall closet, and comes back with a blanket. "Bundle up," she says. "And only for a little while."

She wraps the blanket lightly around my aching shoulders. It's not cold outside. It's the warmest Halloween I can remember. But I wear my blanket outside and sit on a lawn chair. I also wear my medal.

I take Jack with me. And, as night falls, here they come. I can hear them from way down the street, on the other side of Napoli Drive, gaggles of trick-or-treaters carrying their paper sacks, shuffling through the crackling brown leaves, running from house to house, calling, "Trick or treat!" and laughing.

Drew bursts out the front door. "Ready!" he yells. I can't turn my head to see him, but when he runs in front of me to show off, I see he's wearing a football helmet and a silver space suit.

"You're an astronaut!" I say, proud.

"I'm hot!" he replies.

"Well, I guess so," I say, "with all that tape. Can you bend your arms?" The space suit is actually duct tape, a new tape that Daddy brought home from Pyles Lumber Company. He's been using it on everything. Uncle Otts must have spent hours taping up Drew's old dungarees and a sweatshirt. I can picture Drew standing there, arms and legs outstretched like the scarecrow in *The Wizard of Oz*.

372

Drew flexes his arms. Pretty good.

"Too bad Daddy's on a trip and we don't own a convertible," I say.

"I got Bobby!" says Drew. "He's an astronaut, too! See ya!" and he staggers across the street to pick up his friend. Uncle Otts and I are left sitting alone with Jack, at the card table as the kids down the street approach our house.

I don't know why I say it. Maybe it's because the dark makes you say things you wouldn't say in the light of day.

"I'm sorry about your brother Nicky, Uncle Otts."

Uncle Otts looks at me with the sweetest face I've ever seen. "Me, too, honey-girl," he says softly, and he pats my hand. "Me, too."

And with that, the first trick-or-treaters are upon us. They scramble up the driveway, then stop cold when they see Uncle Otts and me sitting outside, waiting for them.

"Hey, Franny!" Judy James calls in a voice that says, *You're alive!* She's got Tom West with her, and Chris and Gale.

"Hey." I can tell they want to ask me questions, but they're shy about it, and they're shy around Uncle Otts, too.

"Hey, Mr. Chapman," says Chris. *Good for you*, I telegraph him.

"Son," says Uncle Otts. "Candy?"

Nervous but game, everybody opens their bags, and Uncle Otts fills them with enormous fistfuls of Tootsie Rolls.

"Thanks!" they all chime.

Jack is so beside himself with happiness — *You're all here! And it's nighttime!* — he steals candy from the basket in Uncle Ott's arms and offers it, slobbering wet, to everyone, which makes everyone laugh and relax.

Gale gives me Jo Ellen's shawl. "Thanks," I say.

"You're welcome," she says.

"Sorry if I wrecked your party."

"You didn't wreck it. My mom's going to call your mom and invite her over when you're better. You come, too."

"Okay," I say. I'm already thinking of how to describe Gale's very normal house and very normal mother to Mom.

Chris and I don't look at each other. We don't know what to say yet. Tom West, however, spouts off like he's been waiting to say something to me for years.

"Pretty cool what you did, Franny," he offers.

I smile and decide Tom West has nice teeth.

"All right, troops!" says Uncle Otts, standing tall and waving the back of his hand in their direction. "Time to fall out! Time to move on!"

Chris clears his throat. "Sir?"

"Private?" says Uncle Otts.

And then, as if he has been rehearsing it for days, Chris stands at attention and salutes Uncle Otts. Uncle Otts, a look of surprise on his face, salutes Chris. Then Tom salutes. Then Judy. Then Gale.

"Dis-missed!" barks Uncle Otts. As everyone scatters, Chris yells over his shoulder, "See ya, Franny!" and I note that my heart still does a tiny pitty-pat for Superman.

But it starts to beat hard when Margie walks across the grass, from her house to mine.

More kids appear. Uncle Otts is in his glory. "Fine-lookin' soldier!" he says to each ghost and ghoul, each ballerina and cowboy.

I walk across the yard and meet Margie halfway. It's so strange to see her here, in my front yard, looking just like Margie, just like she never spent a crazy, terrifying time in the gravel pit at the end of the woods road, like I never spent a crazy, terrifying time there with her.

"Hi, Dixie," she says softly, shyly, like she never said a mean word to me in her life.

I don't answer her.

In the awkward silence between us, she finally says, "They cut down the rope swing."

"I heard."

"They're going to fill in the gravel pit."

"I heard."

"You grounded?"

"Yeah."

"Me, too. I have to take the twins out trick-or-treating."

Serves you right, I telegraph her.

"I'm having nightmares," she says.

I change the subject. "What are you doing here?"

She hesitates and then says, "I've got something for you." From behind her back she pulls the rope I made from the scarves Jo Ellen gave me.

"I don't have any use for that," I tell her, but I notice my heart does a pitty-pat for the scarves as well. I want them back.

"I . . . I thought it would make a good sling."

"I've already got a sling, as you can see." She can't see. It's under my blanket.

"I'll just leave it on your porch, then," says Margie in a little voice. She steps between the low bushes and puts the scarf-rope

375

on my porch — the same porch that Drew sailed across with the couch cushion for Uncle Otts eons ago — and says, "I wish I could do everything over."

"Well, you can't," I say. "What's done is done." I sound like Mom.

Margie blinks as if she's been slapped. "I guess it is." She takes a deep breath and tries to smile, sees my face looking as cold as stone, and stops.

Jack, who has been busy with trick-or-treaters, comes bounding across the yard, so happy to see Margie. It takes two seconds for him to find the scarves, pick them up, and bring them to her. She buries her face in his shaggy body. "Good dog, Jack. Thank you."

My hard heart begins to melt and I hate that. I have every right to hate Margie Gardener forever.

Margie sniffs and says, "Well, I've got to get dressed for trick-or-treat. The girls are both Tweety Bird." She looks at me one last time, as if she thinks I might respond. When I don't, she turns slowly and walks away.

My gut begins to churn.

"Hey!" I call after her.

She spins around to face me, hope washing all over her face. I hate that, too. But there's something about it that helps me find some words.

I take a deep breath. "Maybe."

"What?"

"Maybe . . . I'll see you tomorrow."

Margie nods. "Tomorrow."

I watch her until she's out of sight, then I take the rope from Jack and walk back to the card table in the soft October dark.

"Could you tie this around my sling, Uncle Otts?"

"Let me see," he says.

And, while Uncle Otts ties a snug knot, it comes to me that I will go on to grow up now — I feel it. I will grow old, like Uncle Otts, with all kinds of stories to tell, all kinds of days to remember, all kinds of moments I will live, and choices I will make.

> **There are always scary things happening in the world.**
> **There are always wonderful things happening.**
> **And it's up to you to decide how you're going**
> **to approach the world . . .**
> **how you're going to live in it, and**
> **what you're going to do.**
> **— Jo Ellen Chapman**

Now I get it. Now I see what Jo Ellen was talking about. Now I understand what Margie wants, what Uncle Otts was searching for, why Chairman Khrushchev and President Kennedy finally listened, how no one wants the world to blow up, and why my family and my friends are mine to love, no matter what calamity befalls us.

It's not the calamity that's the hard part. It's figuring out how to love one another through it — that's the hard part. Or maybe that's the easy part. I don't know yet.

I've got a lifetime to figure it out.

It's good to be alive.

So, let us not be blind to our differences — but let us also direct attention to our common interests and to the means by which those differences can be resolved. And if we cannot end now our differences, at least we can help make the world safe for diversity. For, in the final analysis, our most basic common link is that we all inhabit this small planet. We all breathe the same air. We all cherish our children's future. And we are all mortal.

John F. Kennedy, June 10, 1963

A NOTE
ABOUT THE
CUBAN MISSILE CRISIS

On October 14, 1962, an American U-2 pilot flying over Cuba took reconnaissance photos that clearly showed there were Russian missiles on Cuban soil, missiles armed with nuclear warheads — bombs — and easily aimed at the United States, which lay ninety miles off the northern tip of Cuba. Thus began what we now call the Cuban Missile Crisis, thirteen days of negotiations between the Soviet Union (U.S.S.R.) and the United States, when the world came as close as it ever has come to nuclear annihilation.

The entire world lived in fear for those thirteen days, wondering if the United States would make a preemptive strike against the missiles in Cuba, wondering if the Soviets would retaliate — or would they strike first? Would this be World War III, fought with nuclear weapons? Relations between Cuba and the United States had worsened since the Bay of Pigs invasion in 1961, when President Kennedy sent forces into Cuba to liberate the Cuban people from Fidel Castro's rule and set up a government more friendly to the interests of the United States. The invasion failed and Castro aligned himself staunchly with Nikita Khrushchev, First Secretary of the Communist Party in the U.S.S.R. The missiles of October, as they came to be called, were installed in Cuba, and a potentially deadly game began.

The Cuban Missile Crisis was the height of the Cold War — a conflict mainly between the Soviet Union and its satellite states against the United States and its Western allies, a conflict full of threats and the constant American fear of the takeover of the "free world" by the forces of Communism. As Fidel Castro sided with the Communists, and President John F. Kennedy came before the American people on television on October 22, 1962, to say that Soviet Russia's missiles were discovered on Cuban soil, Americans quietly panicked.

I was nine years old during the Cuban Missile Crisis. I didn't understand Communism or know what a Communist was, but I knew fear when I saw it. We lived just outside Washington, D.C., the seat of the U.S. government and a prime target for Soviet missiles carrying nuclear bombs. My mother stocked the basement closet with water and canned goods, in case we had to live inside, in our makeshift basement shelter, for an extended time after the bombs incinerated our country and saturated the outside air with radiation. In school, we ducked and covered under our desks during air-raid drills designed to keep us orderly and to contain panic if there was a real attack. These drills had been going on for several years before the Russians put missiles in Cuba, but now there was a real sense of urgency and impending doom.

After two weeks of intense, secret negotiations between the United States and the U.S.S.R., the Soviets agreed to remove their missiles from Cuba in exchange for a promise from the United States not to invade Cuba. In addition, and in secret, the United States agreed to remove their long-standing missiles from an American air-base in Turkey so that U.S. missiles weren't so close to the Soviet Union and its satellite states.

As the missiles were dismantled, the world began to breathe again. It would take another twenty-seven years of Cold War negotiations and nuclear disarmament before the Berlin Wall, dividing East (Communist) and West Germany, began to come down and the Cold War officially ended. Two years after that (in 1991), the Soviet Union would be officially dissolved. Russia became Russia again, and the satellite states gained their independence, which gave rise to the many struggles that surrounded the birth of new nations that changed the maps of Eastern Europe.

The issue of nuclear warheads and who holds the power to blow up humankind is one that governments and their peoples still struggle with today.

A fine Web site for reading more about the Cuban Missile Crisis is ThinkQuest:

http://library.thinkquest.org/11046/index.html

ACKNOWLEDGMENTS

. I didn't anticipate the intensity of the time warp I would enter when I began writing this documentary novel, book one of three companion novels about the 1960s. So, first of all, I want to acknowledge my parents, the late T.P. and Marie Edwards; my brother, Mike, and my sister, Cathy; the neighborhood we inhabited in Camp Springs, Maryland, just outside Washington, D.C., from 1961 to 1968; and all the kids I played with, fought with, made up with, avoided, admired, and longed to know. I used some of their names in the book — Margie Gardener, Judy James, Gale Morris, Eddie Owens, Chris Cavas, Jeannie Martin, Tom West, Lynn Treakle, Larry Stoffle, Denise Dubose, Ann Jones — but their characters are completely fictional. I wanted to honor them, however, and to mention them in a way that would preserve, like a capsule, our richly textured days in that time and place.

These were pivotal years, not only in our country's history but in my personal history as well. I was eight years old when we moved to Camp Springs and fifteen when we left — a lifetime for an Air Force kid who got used to moving every year or two. I consider the years I lived in Camp Springs a gift from the United States Air Force, so I'll acknowledge the USAF here, too, and the privileged childhood I led under its sheltering wing.

The house on Coolridge Road was home base. There really was a cavernous gravel pit (and a rope swing) at the end of the road in the woods. Camp Springs Elementary School on Allentown Road was an intensely felt life laboratory. I set my fictional characters onto this landscape and allowed the real horror of the Cuban Missile Crisis to shape their actions.

Many thanks to Mr. Robert Spiers, historian of the 89th Airlift Wing, for touring me around my old haunts at Andrews Air Force Base so I could revisit the places that meant the most to young Franny in this book, and for giving me a glimpse of my father's life as chief of safety for the 89th in the sixties. Thanks also to Col. (ret.) Bill Ramsey and his wife, Betty, for remembrances of air force life at Andrews in the early sixties.

Camp Springs Elementary School is a senior citizen center now, but the folks who work there were kind enough to allow me the run of the place so I could take photos and remember. Because they shape this book particularly, I want to acknowledge my elementary school teachers, many of whom are named here, but whose characters are completely fictional. In particular I want to mention Miss Bourdon, who taught me to spell in third grade; Mrs. Wingfield, a long-term substitute teacher who read out loud to our fourth-grade class; Mme. Martin, who taught me her native language; Mr. Adler, who told me in sixth grade that I was a good writer; and my fifth-grade teacher, the real Mrs. Rodriguez, who loved history and taught me how to take notes, a skill that thrills me to this day. Then there was Mary Farrell, who was (I now know) a mere twenty-two years old when she appeared in my fourth-grade classroom, wearing a dozen tinkling bracelets, heady perfume, and high heels, who married the P.E. teacher and became Mary Cassidy. She taught me about the transformative power of music. This book is infused with her influence.

Kristil Fossett, principal at Thurgood Marshall Middle School on Brinkley Road (which was named Roger B. Taney Junior High when I attended), allowed me to roam the school at will one summer day and photograph to my heart's content.

I started this story as a picture book in 1996. It took a long time to grow into a novel, just as it took me a long time to grow into a novelist. I am still learning. I am ever grateful for the help of the editors who shepherded this story: the inimitable Liz Van Doren, who saw the possibilities before I did and handed them to me; Kate Harrison, who championed Franny's story and me; Kara LaReau, who helped me craft the beginning; and David Levithan, who grabbed hold of the whole unwieldy she-bang and championed this book, proffered key questions, invited me to rise to the occasion, and helped me steer the course. I salute you, sir.

Thanks to readers Nancy Werlin, Joanne Stanbridge, Dian Curtis Regan, Jane Kurtz, Deborah Hopkinson, Hannah Wiles, Allison Adams, and the fount of profundity, Jim Pearce, without whom there would be no novel. Poet and friend Norma Chapman lent me her last name, and James Walker introduced me to Uncle Otts.

A mighty countdown of thanks to everyone at Scholastic, who understood what I was trying to create and then embraced this idea enthusiastically and without reservation. Every working writer needs a publisher to believe so powerfully in her vision. Thanks particularly to those who were mired in gargantuan permissions work (I bow to you, Erin Black and Els Rijper) and design (thank you ever and ever, the amazing Phil Falco), and thanks to production editor Joy Simpkins and copy editor Susan Casel, who elevated this manuscript while teaching me the difference between "each other" and "one another." Now I have no excuse.

Heaps of thanks to Scholastic Book Fairs for being such a crucial and enthusiastic supporter of my body of work, and in particular thanks to Robin Hoffman for . . . just about everything.

I have talked about this book in schools for years, so I want to thank the many, many students, teachers, and librarians I've worked with who have been so enthusiastic about and patient in waiting for *Countdown*. I've blogged about the writing of the book, the idea of a documentary novel, and the many convoluted pathways to publication, so I want to thank loyal reader-friends who have sent me literally thousands of messages of support and have kept me going when the going got tough, which it often did. Writing is a solitary occupation, but I was never completely alone. I always felt your reassuring presence.

During the Cuban Missile Crisis, Attorney General Robert F. Kennedy was his brother's unquestioned confidante and closest advisor. Steven Malk is my RFK, and deserves his own paragraph. Here it is.

I have taken to saying that family is a circle of friends who love you. My family is broad and deep and varied and fine, and I appreciate every one of you more than I can adequately say. I know how lucky I am.

A BEGINNING BIBLIOGRAPHY

There are many good sources available that document the Cuban Missile Crisis and the Cold War, as well as the opinionated biographies included in this book, which include stories about World Wars I and II; the Civil Rights Movement; blacklisting and the Red Scare of the fifties; the Kennedy family; the trajectory of music, movies, and culture; and many other topics that directly influenced the 1960s. This list is a good beginning and is also where I started.

Anderson, Terry H. *The Movement and the Sixties*. New York: Oxford University Press, 1995.

Branch, Taylor. *Parting the Waters: America in the King Years 1954–63*. New York: Simon & Schuster Touchstone, 1988.

Branch, Taylor. *Pillar of Fire: America in the King Years 1963–65*. New York: Simon & Schuster, 1998.

Dalleck, Robert, et.al. *The Kennedy Mystique: Creating Camelot*. New York: National Geographic, 2006.

Dorr, Robert F. "A History of Presidential Air Travel" from *The Sam Fox Story: 89th Airlift Wing*, Andrews AFB, Maryland. Tampa, FL: Faircount LLC, 2005.

Dunaway, David King. *How Can I Keep from Singing? The Ballad of Pete Seeger*. New York: McGraw-Hill, 1981.

Fursenko, Aleksandr, and Timothy Naftali. *One Hell of a Gamble: Khrushchev, Castro, and Kennedy, 1958–1964: The Secret History of the Cuban Missile Crisis*. New York: W. W. Norton & Co., 1997.

Haber, Heinz. *Our Friend the Atom*. New York: Simon & Schuster Books for Young Readers, 1956.

Kennedy, Robert F. *Thirteen Days: A Memoir of the Cuban Missile Crisis.* New York: W. W. Norton & Co., 1999 (reissue).

Lansing, Chase, and Nivins. *Makers of America.* New York: D. C. Heath and Company, 1947.

McCullough, David. *Truman.* New York: Simon & Schuster, 1992.

Miller, Ward S. *Word Wealth Junior.* New York: Holt, Rinehart and Winston, 1952.

Olson, Lynne. *Freedom's Daughters: The Unsung Heroines of the Civil Rights Movement from 1830 to 1970.* New York: Scribner, 2002.

WEB SITES

The John F. Kennedy Presidential Library and Museum
http://www.jfklibrary.org/

The Harry S Truman Library and Museum
This is where the letters from Harry to Bess can be found.
http://www.trumanlibrary.org/

The Cuban Missile Crisis at ThinkQuest
http://library.thinkquest.org/11046/index.html

Civil Rights history
http://www.pbs.org/wgbh/amex/eyesontheprize/

PHOTOS

DUST JACKET

Front flap: *Soviet ship*, AP Photo; Back jacket, clockwise from top left: *U.K. protest*, Keystone, Hulton Archive/Getty Images, *air raid drill*, Bettmann/Corbis, *John F. Kennedy and Robert F. Kennedy*, Hank Walker, Time & Life Pictures/Getty Images, *Family in bomb shelter*, Library of Congress/The Art Archive, *mushroom cloud*, US Airforce; background: *map*, Bettmann/Corbis; Back flap: *Air Force plane*, Courtesy of Lockheed Martin Aeronautics Company;

YOU'LL NEVER WALK ALONE

Page vi: *Mushroom cloud*, U.S. Airforce; 2-3: *John F. Kennedy and Nikita Krushchev*, John Fitzgerald Kennedy Library, Boston; 4: *Fallout shelter sign*, iStockphoto; 6-7,8: *Duck and Cover comic*, Courtesy of the University of Nebraska-Lincoln; 10-11: *James Meredith*, Marion S. Trikosko, U.S. News & World Report Magazine/Library of Congress; 12: *Moon photo*, NASA-JSC; 13, 14-15: *Sandy Koufax, air-raid drill*, Bettmann/Corbis;

22: *Mushroom cloud*, U.S. Airforce; 28: *Harry S Truman*, AP Photo; 41: *Civil defense poster*, Swim Ink/Corbis; 46: *WWI soldiers*, Hulton Archive/Getty Images;

QUE SERÁ SERÁ

52: *Mary Ann Mobley*, AP Photo; 53: *1960s hostess*, Everett Collection; 54-55: *SNCC poster*, Danny Lyon/Magnum Photos; 56-57: *1960s family*, Petrified Collection/The Image Bank/Getty Images; 58-59: *Freedom Ride bus*, Bettmann/Corbis; 60 top: *SNCC button*, David J. & Janice L. Frent Collection/Corbis, bottom: *Air Force plane*, Courtesy of Lockheed Martin Aeronautics Company;

65: *Pete Seeger*, Walter Albertin, N.Y. World Telegram & Sun Newspaper/Library of Congress; 79: *The Clue in the Diary*, Courtesy of Penguin Group (USA) Inc.;

THE WORLD IS A CAROUSEL OF COLOR

100: *"Book Cover,"* copyright ©1962 by Fawcett Books, from *Fallout Shelter Handbook* by Chuck West. Used by permission of Fawcett Books, a division of Random House, Inc.; 102: *Family in bomb shelter*, Library of Congress/The Art Archive; 103: *Cassius Clay, a.k.a. Muhammad Ali*, Harold P. Matosian/AP Photo; 104-105: *James Bond*, United Artists/The Kobal Collection; 106: *Family in bomb shelter*, Dmitri Kessel/Time & Life Pictures/Getty Images;

158: *The Kennedys: Jacqueline, John Jr., Caroline, John Sr.*, AP Photo; 192: *Our Friend the Atom*, Courtesy of Random House Inc.; 193: *Duck and Cover comic*, Courtesy of the University of Nebraska-Lincoln;

GOOD EVENING, MY FELLOW CITIZENS

202: *John F. Kennedy*, Robert Knudsen, White House/John Fitzgerald Kennedy Library, Boston; 204-205: *Cuban Missile site*, Bettmann/Corbis; 207-209: *Cuban launch site*, U.S. Airforce; 210-211: *Map*, Bettmann/Corbis; 213: *Missile crisis protest rally*, Phil Stanziola, N.Y. World Telegram & Sun Newspaper/Library of Congress; 215: *October 23, 1962, front page*, New York Daily News;

227: *Map of Cuba*, MAPS.com/Corbis;

A SUMMER PLACE

230: *Cuban stamp*, Brendan Howard/Shutterstock; 232-233/4: *Cuban palm trees*, Alfredo Maiquez/Lonely Planet Images; 235: *Desi Arnaz and Lucille Ball*, Hulton Archive/Getty Images; 236-237: *Havana Cathedral*, AP Photo; 238-239: *Fidel Castro and Nikita Kruschev*, TASS/AP Photo; 240-241: *U.S. patrol plane over Soviet freighter*, Getty Images; 242-243: *U.K. protest*, Keystone, Hulton Archive/Getty Images;

251: *Duck and Cover comic*, Courtesy of the University of Nebraska-Lincoln; 256: *Photo of LeRoy Mendenhall Perkins*, Courtesy of JoLyn Day;

DO THE LOCOMOTION WITH ME!

259-261: *Soviet ship*, AP Photo; 262: *Duck and Cover comic*, Courtesy of the University of Nebraska-Lincoln; 264-265: *Lunchroom counter*, Bruce Davidson/Magnum Photos; 266: *John F. and Jacqueline Kennedy*, Abbie Rowe, National Park Service/John Fitzgerald Kennedy Library, Boston; 268-269: *Segregated water fountains*, Danny Lyon/Magnum Photos;

278: *Fannie Lou Townsend Hamer*, Warren K. Leffler, U.S. News & World Report Magazine/Library of Congress;

MOON RIVER AND ME

300-301: *Trick-or-treating*, Superstock; 302: *Personal Preparedness Pamphlet*, Courtesy of Curt Lundgren; 303: *Dr. Martin Luther King, Jr., Coretta Scott King, and children*, Donald Uhrbrock, Time & Life Pictures/Getty Images; 304-305: *John F. Kennedy and Robert F. Kennedy*, Hank Walker, Time & Life Pictures/Getty Images; 306: *SNCC button*, David J. & Janice L. Frent Collection/Corbis; 307: *John Glenn and Friendship 7*, NASA; 308: *Witch sketch*, Thecla Coesel;

WHAT A WONDERFUL WORLD

356: *November 1, 1962 political cartoon*, The Herb Block Foundation; 358-359: *WWI poster*, Hulton Archive/Getty Images; 360-361: *John F. and Jacqueline Kennedy greet members of the 2506 Cuban Invasion Brigade*, Cecil Stoughton, White House/John Fitzgerald Kennedy Library, Boston; 362: *Telstar 1*, Courtesy of AT&T; 364: *Rocky and Bullwinkle*, Photofest; 366-367: *Bob Dylan*, Frank Driggs Collection/Getty Images; 368-369: *Peter, Paul, and Mary*, Michael Ochs Archives/Getty Images.

LYRICS

This book was edited by David Levithan and designed by Phil Falco. Its documentary features were coordinated by Erin Black and Els Rijper. The text was set in Futura, a typeface designed by Paul Renner between 1924 and 1926. The display type was set in FF Identification 04S, designed by Rian Hughes in 1993. The book was typeset at NK Graphics and printed and bound at R. R. Donnelley in Crawfordsville, Indiana. The production was supervised by Joy Simpkins. The manufacturing was supervised by Jess White.